PRAISE FOR T.R. RAGAN

Don't Make a Sound

"Those who like to see evil men get their just desserts will look forward to Sawyer's further exploits."

—*Publishers Weekly*

"Overall, a great crime read."

—*Manhattan Book Review*

"A dizzying flurry of twists and turns in a plot as intricate as a Swiss watch . . . Ragan's warrior women are on fire, fueled by howling levels of personal pain."

—*Sactown Magazine*

"A heart-stopping read. Ragan's compelling blend of strained family ties and small-town secrets will keep you racing to the end!"

—Lisa Gardner, *New York Times* bestselling author of *When You See Me*

"An exciting start to a new series with a feisty and unforgettable heroine in Sawyer Brooks. Just when you think you've figured out the dark secrets of River Rock, T.R. Ragan hits you with another sucker punch."

—Lisa Gray, bestselling author of *Thin Air*

"Fans of Lizzy Gardner, Faith McMann, and Jessie Cole are in for a real treat with T.R. Ragan's *Don't Make a Sound*, the start of a brand-new series that features tenacious crime reporter Sawyer Brooks, whose own past could be her biggest story yet. Ragan once more delivers on her trademark action, pacing, and twists."

—Loreth Anne White, bestselling author of *In the Dark*

"T.R. Ragan takes the revenge thriller to the next level in the gritty and chillingly realistic *Don't Make a Sound*. Ragan masterfully crafts one unexpected twist after another until the shocking finale."

—Steven Konkoly, bestselling author of *The Rescue*

"T.R. Ragan delivers in her new thrilling series. *Don't Make a Sound* introduces crime reporter Sawyer Brooks, a complex and compelling heroine determined to stop a killer as murders in her past and present collide."

—Melinda Leigh, #1 *Wall Street Journal* bestselling author

Her Last Day

"Intricately plotted . . . The tense plot builds to a startling and satisfying resolution."

—*Publishers Weekly* (starred review)

"Ragan's newest novel is exciting and intriguing from the very beginning . . . Readers will race to finish the book, wanting to know the outcome and see justice served."

—RT Book Reviews

"*Her Last Day* is a fast-moving thriller about a woman seeking answers and the man determined to help her find them."

—New York Journal of Books

COUNT TO THREE

Other Titles by T.R. Ragan

Sawyer Brooks Series

Don't Make a Sound
Out of Her Mind
No Going Back

Jessie Cole Series

Her Last Day
Deadly Recall
Deranged
Buried Deep

Faith McMann Trilogy

Furious
Outrage
Wrath

Lizzy Gardner Series

Abducted
Dead Weight
A Dark Mind
Obsessed
Almost Dead
Evil Never Dies

Writing as Theresa Ragan

Return of the Rose
A Knight in Central Park
Taming Mad Max

COUNT TO THREE

A **SAWYER BROOKS**
THRILLER

T.R. RAGAN

THOMAS & MERCER

Published by Thomas & Mercer, Seattle

www.apub.com

Amazon, the Amazon logo, and Thomas & Mercer are trademarks of Amazon.com, Inc., or its affiliates.

ISBN-13: 9781542093941
ISBN-10: 1542093945

Cover design by Damon Freeman

Printed in the United States of America

For Joe

PROLOGUE

Dani Callahan pulled out the last tray of chocolate chip cookies, shut off the oven, and then quickly removed her apron. It was time to pick up Tinsley from her first day of kindergarten.

Although her five-year-old daughter had spent two days a week last year in preschool, and despite all the preparation of school clothes and snacks and the endless talks with Tinsley about what to expect, dropping her off this morning had been incredibly emotional.

Dani's good friend and neighbor, Sally, had five children. She'd warned Dani the first day of kindergarten would feel different from preschool and playdates. Kindergarten was a big change for both child and parent. Letting go was hard.

Dani had been convinced she would be perfectly fine, but after saying goodbye to Tinsley, she had walked back to her car, buckled her seat belt, and then sobbed for five minutes straight.

She blamed the high emotions on the difficulty she and her husband, Matthew, had conceiving. After five years of trying to get pregnant, they'd ended up at a fertility doctor's office. Blood tests, sperm-level checks, yoga, and meditation then led them to IVF, where two eggs were successfully fertilized. After they implanted the first embryo, Dani miscarried. But the second embryo took hold, and despite heavy bleeding, Tinsley was born premature but healthy.

Their little miracle.

Dani had wanted a sibling for Tinsley, but Matthew had been done. "No more," he'd said. "We have a beautiful child. Leave the rest to fate."

Knowing Tinsley might be her only child, Dani had quit her job as a fashion and editorial photographer for a clothing store because she'd wanted to be there for Tinsley's first step, her first word, her first everything.

Dani glanced at her watch. If she left now, she would get to the school a few minutes early. She grabbed her purse and headed out the door. As she approached her car parked in the driveway, she noticed the back tire was flat.

Damn. She pulled her cell phone from her purse and called her husband. No answer. Next, she tried his assistant, Mimi Foster, who answered on the second ring.

"Hi, Mimi. It's Dani."

"Hi, Dani! How are you?"

"A little flustered at the moment. I'm supposed to pick up Tinsley from school, but I have a flat tire. Is Matthew in his office?"

"Afraid not. He took a late lunch and hasn't returned."

"He's not answering his phone," Dani told her. "Any idea where, or who he's having lunch with?"

"No. Sorry. Would you like me to leave a note on his desk?"

"Sure. That would be great. Just have him call me. Thanks."

After hanging up, she began to scroll through her contacts for the school's number when she heard a familiar voice—Sally, from across the street.

"Car trouble?" Sally asked.

"Yes. I have a flat."

"I'm going to the school right now. Want a ride?"

"Are you sure? Will we all fit?"

Sally held up a brown paper bag. "Plenty of room. It'll just be me, you, and Tinsley," she said. "Joey forgot his lunch."

Relief flooded through Dani as she rushed across the street.

"Get in," Sally said. "I think kindergarten gets out when the lunch bell rings."

Dani climbed into Sally's car and buckled her seat belt. Her insides quivered when she glanced at her watch. She was going to be late.

For such a short ride to the school, the drive felt interminably long. Dani jumped out of the SUV as soon as Sally pulled into a parking space. The buses had left, and the parking lot was half-empty.

"After I drop off Joey's lunch, I'll wait for you in the car," Sally called out as Dani rushed off.

Dani and Tinsley had met her teacher, Ms. Helm, last week at orientation. She was a twenty-two-year-old, newly minted graduate. What she lacked in experience, she made up in enthusiasm and passion for being a teacher, like three generations of Helms before her.

Dani spotted Ms. Helm just outside her classroom door. The kindergarten teachers each held two classes per day, and she was in the process of greeting the children in her second class.

"Sorry I'm late," Dani said, out of breath as she approached. "I had a flat tire of all things."

Ms. Helm held up a finger to stop her for one quick moment while she greeted two students. A darling boy named Liam and a little girl with pigtails. Ms. Helm then looked up at Dani and said in a cheerful voice, "How can I help you?"

"I'm here to pick up my daughter, Tinsley." Dani stretched her neck so she could see over Ms. Helm's shoulder into the classroom. Just like this morning, some children had already found their desks, while others took great care in putting their belongings into their cubicle. There was no little girl in a flowery dress with a braid and a gold ribbon with red hearts.

Where is Tinsley? Dani's mind swirled with speculation. Maybe Tinsley had gone to the front office. If that were the case, she would be with Sally about now. Her shoulders relaxed at the thought.

"I'm sorry," Ms. Helm said, her brow furrowing. "But I think there has been a mix-up." She looked Dani over, starting at her feet and working up to the crown of her head.

Dani didn't like the worry lining the young woman's face.

"Did you send your sister to pick up Tinsley from school?"

Dani's chest tightened. "What? No. I don't have a sister."

One of the mothers assigned to help in the classroom appeared and asked Ms. Helm if she should get the kids seated and ready for class.

Ms. Helm grabbed the woman's arm. "Would you mind watching over the class while I take care of Mrs.—?"

Relief swept over Dani. Ms. Helm didn't know who she was, which meant she clearly had Tinsley mixed up with someone else. "I'm Mrs. Callahan," Dani offered as her gaze swept over the parking lot and beyond. She pivoted, looking toward the noise coming from the playground, where she could hear kids playing.

"Yes, of course," Ms. Helm said before telling the other woman she'd be right back.

The main office sat directly in front of the loop-around parking lot. Kindergarten and preschool classrooms were to the right, and first through sixth were to the left. Dani did her best to keep up with Ms. Helm, who walked at a clipped pace toward the front office, her heels clicking hard against the concrete path. "Is Tinsley in the nurse's office?" Dani asked.

Ms. Helm said nothing. Not one word. She held her head high, her chin jutted forward, and walked stiff-legged, as if she were in a marching band.

Dani could see Sally talking to another woman near the office. "Have you seen Tinsley?" Dani asked.

"No. Why? What's going on?"

"Not sure," Dani said. "I'm trying to find out. I'm going to check the nurse's office. Would you mind looking for Tinsley on the playground?"

Ms. Helm held open the office door for Dani.

"I'll look around," Sally said, waving her off.

The moment Dani stepped inside the front office and saw no sign of her daughter, tension rippled through her body. Tinsley was either injured or missing. That had to be why Ms. Helm had been acting so strange. Dani's gaze fixated on a door with an engraved metal sign that read NURSE'S OFFICE. She headed that way and opened the door to an empty, sterile room. When she returned to the front area, one of the ladies behind the counter told her Ms. Helm was talking to Principal Sprague and would be right out.

"My daughter, Tinsley Callahan, is missing. Have any of you seen her?"

"I haven't," one of the women said.

Dani's heart skipped a beat. A river of sweat worked its way down her spine as she headed for the principal's office.

"Mrs. Callahan," one of the women called out.

Dani ignored her and kept walking. When she opened the door, both women—Principal Sprague and Ms. Helm—stopped talking and looked her way.

Principal Sprague sprang to her feet. She was five foot two and had thick brown hair cut bluntly a few inches above her shoulders. Her blue eyes looked beseechingly into Dani's as she gestured at the chair next to Ms. Helm. "Please have a seat."

Dani remained standing. Her phone vibrated. She picked up the call when she saw that it was Matthew. "I'm at the school," she told her husband. "You need to come right away. Tinsley is missing." Her hands were shaking, her body trembling as panic began to take hold. She hung up. "He'll be here in twenty minutes," Dani said. "Have you called the police?"

"We need to follow protocol," Principal Sprague said. "Did you ask anyone to pick up your daughter for you?"

"No," Dani said, reining in her frustration.

5

"We have security cameras in place, and I've pulled up a video that shows a woman picking up Tinsley approximately ten minutes before you arrived."

Dani tried to breathe. "A woman?"

Principal Sprague nodded. "Ms. Helm tells me she thought the woman was you."

Ridiculous. Strangled laughter escaped. "I'm right here. I dropped off my daughter this morning, and now I'm here to pick her up."

Ms. Helm visibly swallowed before speaking. "She was the first person in line at the door when the bell rang. She smiled broadly and waved at Tinsley, who seemed happy to see her." Ms. Helm shook her head. "The big floppy hat and sunglasses might have thrown me off." She met Dani's gaze. "I'm so sorry."

Dani stared at Ms. Helm for a long second before looking at Principal Sprague, praying for this nightmare to stop.

Principal Sprague swiveled her computer on its stand so Dani could see the video on the screen.

Dani stepped closer and leaned forward as Principal Sprague hit "Play." Her pulse raced as she tried to make sense of what she was seeing. A woman stood at the front of the line outside the door to Ms. Helm's classroom. She wore a straw hat with a wide brim. Her hair, wavy and sandy colored, swept down two inches past her shoulders. Whenever the woman looked to the left or right, Dani would catch a glimpse of her chin and neck.

Dani took in the woman's clothes—a blue sundress and a light-beige sweater with three-quarter-length sleeves. It was an outfit Dani recognized because she'd worn the same dress, sweater, and hat many times.

Same outfit. Same hair color. An impostor.

The woman stood at the door for a full minute before the bell rang. Not once did she look at the women conversing behind her. When the door opened, she waved at someone inside the classroom. Tinsley, no doubt.

Dani's stomach roiled. *Who is this impostor?* "You've met me twice," Dani said to Ms. Helm, trying her best to stay calm. "Did you see her face?" she asked in a shaky voice. "Did you talk to her? Couldn't you tell that she wasn't me?"

Ms. Helm drew in a shaky breath. "She could have been your twin."

Dani rubbed her arms. The room began to spin. "Tinsley," she cried. "Where are you?"

CHAPTER ONE

Five years later . . .

Private investigator Dani Callahan carried her mug to her desk and took a seat. As she sipped her coffee, her gaze fell on the bronze-framed picture of Tinsley on her desk. Tomorrow her daughter would have been missing for five years—five unbearably long years. Long enough that Dani was beginning to forget some of the heart's most precious gifts—memories. The sound of her laugh, her facial expressions, the little things.

The picture had been taken a few days before she'd disappeared. Five years old and dressed as a princess, she'd been ripped from Dani's life at the time when playing pretend had become more complex and her favorite three words seemed to be "Look at me!"

The door opened and her assistant, Quinn Sullivan, walked in, carrying a bankers box.

"Hey," she said as she strolled across the room, set the box on her desk, and went about removing her backpack.

At five foot seven inches, twenty-two-year-old Quinn was a good three inches taller than Dani. Her long dark-brown hair was parted down the middle. She never wore makeup. Her teeth were straight and white, her brows naturally thick. The jeans she wore were ripped so that when she sat down, her knee jutted out like a sun-bleached bone in the Sahara Desert.

"Good morning," Dani said. "What's in the box?"

"Grandma decided to take up watercolor, which meant cleaning out the extra bedroom. I wasn't happy about it, but then I remembered the unused basement here at the office and figured you wouldn't mind if I set up shop down there." She gestured toward the door that led downstairs to a damp, windowless room.

Dani raised an eyebrow. "'Set up shop'?"

"Yeah. I like to spread out all the information I've collected over the years on Tinsley's case and others, like the teenage girl who disappeared recently. Seeing everything together helps me focus on what I'm trying to accomplish."

"I had no idea you've been gathering information all this time."

"Really? Even before you took me on my first stakeout, I would spend hours on the internet. If I wasn't at the library, I was usually sitting in front of Detective Whitton's desk, picking his brain about one case or another. In fact, that's where I was when I first heard about Tinsley."

James Lee Whitton, a detective with the Sacramento Police Department, was the lead investigator for Tinsley's case. He'd always been there for Dani, listening when she called him with a new lead. No matter how many times the information went nowhere, he took what she had to say seriously. She trusted him.

"How did you meet Detective Whitton?" Dani asked. "I always assumed it was through his wife, Teresa, since she worked at the high school you attended."

Quinn shook her head. "I've never met his wife. After Mom took off and Dad got sick, I called a taxi and was dropped off at the police station. I sat in the front lobby all morning until Detective Whitton took pity on me and brought me into his office. I was sixteen and more determined than ever to find my mom, refusing to believe she would just up and leave us without a word said or even a note." Quinn looked to the ceiling as if in thought. "I believe I had just turned seventeen when I was sitting in his office and he got the call about a little girl who'd gone missing on her first day of kindergarten. Detective Whitton wouldn't tell me what was going on. After he jumped up and left, I noticed he'd scribbled the name Tinsley Callahan on his desk calendar."

Dani's chest tightened.

"Months later," Quinn went on, "you moved onto our street, and I remember thinking it was fate. We both had someone we needed to find, and two heads are always better than one."

Quinn scooped up the box again and looked at Dani. "The five-year anniversary of Tinsley's abduction is coming up. I have a great picture of her that I think I'll print and distribute to keep her in people's minds."

Quinn headed off before Dani had a chance to respond.

Again she looked at the picture and exhaled. *Tinsley.*

Three months ago, a man by the name of Kyle Harmon, doing time in the high-security lockup at Corcoran, had confessed to Tinsley's abduction. His face had been plastered on every news channel for weeks. Dani didn't believe his story about how he'd gotten the help of a random woman whose name he didn't recall. He said he'd buried Tinsley in a greenbelt off Bond Road in Elk Grove. So far, though, no body had been located.

Whitton's superiors. The prosecutors. The judge. And even Matthew, her ex-husband, had been quick to believe him, certain that Kyle Harmon, a drug user with violent tendencies, was their man and justice was being served since he was already behind bars. Harmon had confessed from his prison cell, where he was doing time for killing a man during a bar fight. Dani thought his confession had appeared forced—a plea-bargaining ploy to escape a life sentence.

Everyone wanted closure.

They wanted the case closed.

But Dani wanted more than that. She wanted to find her daughter. It was exactly the reason she'd become a PI. As it turned out, she was a decent investigator. Although she had yet to find Tinsley, she'd had the good fortune of finding other people's children.

Despite Kyle Harmon's confession, her daughter's case was still open. The number of officers working the case had long ago been scaled down from twelve to one, leaving Detective Whitton as the last man standing.

The sound of Quinn trudging back up the stairs caught her attention. She looked up in time to see a Channel 10 News van pull to the curb across the street.

After all the brouhaha with Kyle Harmon's confession, Dani had thought the media would have forgotten about Tinsley. But the fifth anniversary of her daughter's abduction was tomorrow. Having the media show up was a surprise—a good surprise—and yet talking to reporters, trying to stay optimistic year after year, was beginning to take its toll on her psyche.

Quinn stood at the window, looking out. "They're here to talk about Tinsley, aren't they?"

"I think so," Dani said, swallowing the knot lodged in her throat. As lucky as she was to have the media show up, especially since most missing children were never publicized at all, she was suddenly flooded with emotions.

"I'll take care of them," Quinn said, as if she sensed Dani's reluctance to talk to reporters.

Quinn took long, brisk strides toward the door.

Dani considered stopping her, and yet she didn't budge. Another year had passed, and she still had no idea who might have taken her little girl. Nothing had changed in all these years. The first question asked when a young child went missing usually had to do with custody violation and visitation rights—but she and Matthew had been happily married at the time. Next came other relatives who might have a bone to pick—but Dani was an only child, and Matthew's sister lived back East and they rarely talked. That left a stranger abduction, which was extremely rare.

And if that were the case, why Tinsley? That was the second question authorities and Dani asked themselves over and over again. Someone went out of their way to dress up like Dani and walk right onto the school premises—a high-risk scenario with lots of people and security cameras. Who would do such a thing?

The third question was about Dani and whether she had enemies. People who would want to cause her pain or make her suffer. How many nights had she spent over the past five years, staring into the dark while trying to recall if she'd upset a friend, coworker, acquaintance, or complete stranger?

No one ever came to mind.

Dani wasn't one to make enemies.

She wasn't perfect. Not even close. Like most people, she had bad days. When she used to get frustrated, she would sometimes cry. But she'd never been one to shout or curse. She'd never understood road rage, and never once had she thrown an object in anger. It wasn't who she was.

At least it didn't use to be.

These days, she often felt restless and jittery, irritated and hostile. Sometimes her hands would involuntarily curl into fists at the slightest upset. The changes had happened slowly. In the beginning, a perceived offense made her heart race. As time went on, frustration turned to anger.

Anger had become her friend.

Not always a good friend, but a friend all the same. Hovering and protective. She felt it most days—the physical and mental changes in her body as adrenaline soared through her veins, affecting her organs, digestion, and mood. Her heart rate would elevate and get her blood pumping fast until she felt an incredible heat. Her breathing became shallow, and her abdomen would tighten. Sweaty and shaky, she wondered sometimes if she were morphing into the Hulk.

And she was glad for it because feeling angry was so much better than feeling pain.

Outside she could see the camera crew setting up equipment on the sidewalk. Quinn approached a woman in a suit who was holding a microphone and barking orders at those around her.

Quinn started talking to the woman, and when she finished speaking, the reporter signaled to her crew, prompting the cameraman to rush over.

Dani found the remote in her desk drawer and clicked on the television mounted on the wall. She scrolled to Channel 10 News. After a commercial break, the camera zoomed in on an anchorwoman sitting behind a desk. She talked about Tinsley's abduction, updating viewers about what had happened five years earlier. Then she turned it over to reporter Abby Moretti, who was on the scene for a live update.

"Good morning," Abby Moretti said, the microphone held close to her chin. "I'm standing outside Dani Callahan's office in Sacramento. After five-year-old Tinsley Callahan went missing, Dani Callahan spent every waking hour searching for her only child. Month after grueling month, without an answer to what happened, led to Dani Callahan's decision to become a private investigator. Although she now spends her time helping others find missing loved ones, she has yet to find Tinsley."

The cameraman panned outward so viewers could see Quinn.

"I've been talking to Dani Callahan's assistant, Quinn Sullivan, about the disappearance of young Tinsley Callahan. Five years ago, Tinsley's abduction held the world's attention. Quinn, what can you tell us about Dani Callahan? How is she holding up?"

"She is just as heartbroken today as she was the day Tinsley was taken." Dani watched with surprise as Quinn held up a five-by-seven-inch picture of Tinsley on her first day of school. "She will never give up hope of finding Tinsley alive."

"What about Kyle Harmon's confession?"

Quinn snorted. "Kyle Harmon is serving time for murder, and we believe he made a plea deal to avoid additional prison time."

Dani groaned. Not because that wasn't the truth, but because she had no way of proving it.

Abby Moretti perked up. "Are you saying you believe Kyle Harmon is not responsible for the disappearance of Tinsley Callahan?"

"That's exactly what I'm saying."

"Do you have evidence?"

"Not at this time," Quinn said. "But I think it's important we ask ourselves why he chose to confess now. And where's the body?"

"If Harmon didn't take Tinsley," the reporter asked, "then who did?"

"The woman seen on the security camera at the school," Quinn said with confidence. "We are tracking her down and getting closer every day."

The reporter pursed her lips, seemingly thrown off her game by the unexpected. "Can you tell us more?"

"Afraid not," Quinn said. "I've said too much already."

Dani's cell phone buzzed just as Quinn held up Tinsley's picture again so the viewers could get a good look at her. Dani's ex-husband, Matthew, was calling. Dani turned down the volume on the TV and picked up the call.

"Why the hell are you letting Quinn speak to reporters on our behalf?"

"She's not speaking on anyone's behalf," Dani said.

"You need to put a stop to it right now."

A few seconds ago, Dani had been caught off guard by Quinn's falsehood about being closer to tracking down the woman who took Tinsley, but as she listened to her ex-husband's complaints, she realized there was a reason Quinn was showing Tinsley's picture and stirring the pot—she wanted to get people talking about the case again. Kyle

Harmon's confession a few weeks ago had brought Tinsley's abduction back to the forefront of national news, but when a body wasn't found and seventeen-year-old Ali Cross went missing, Tinsley had been quickly forgotten again.

Dani's heartbeat kicked up a notch. Quinn was onto something. She could feel it in her bones. "I'm not going to stop her," Dani said, interrupting Matthew midsentence as he rambled on. "Until we find Tinsley this case is still open."

A low grumbling came over the line. "Not again, Dani. We need to move forward, not backward. Kyle Harmon confessed to the crime. It's time to take down the website."

"Don't you dare."

"Dani," he said with a sigh. "It's over."

Her pulse accelerated. Other than setting up the website and keeping it updated, which took no time at all, Matthew had rarely talked about their daughter after she went missing. The second their divorce was finalized, Matthew had begun dating. Two years ago, he had married a woman named Carole. Their first child was due next month. Dani couldn't help but feel envious.

"I never believed Kyle Harmon was the culprit," Dani said. "Doesn't it bother you that they haven't found her remains, that there is zero proof he's our guy?"

"He confessed. They will find her."

"You don't know that," Dani said, fighting to stay calm. "Until Tinsley is found, nothing has changed."

"You're obsessed."

"She's my daughter."

"Did you stop taking your medication?"

She didn't need this. Her life was no longer his business. She disconnected their call. After their divorce, her obsession with finding Tinsley had become a major source of contention between them. He'd begged her to go to therapy, pushed her to take whatever medication the therapist—his therapist—suggested. He hadn't stopped bugging her about it until she'd told him she had a prescription for Prozac. That much was true. But she'd never taken a pill. Not because she didn't believe in taking medication, but because she wanted to feel every emotion that came with losing her daughter. She wasn't a sadist. She was an optimist—at least when it came to finding her daughter. It would happen. She would find her.

The door opened. It was Quinn. Her face appeared flushed, invigorated. She glanced at the television on her way to her desk, took a seat, and got to work as if nothing unusual had just happened.

"You lied to the reporter about being on the trail of the woman who took Tinsley."

Without looking up, Quinn shrugged. "It wasn't a lie. We will find that woman *and* Tinsley. It's only a matter of time."

CHAPTER TWO

Ali Cross woke with a start, her heart pounding against her ribs. The cold seeped up from the cement floor through the paper-thin mattress, reminding her that this wasn't a nightmare—it was real. She'd been taken by a madman, thrown into his van, and then dumped in a cold, dark room in a garage or warehouse, she wasn't sure. Her throat was raw and sore from screaming and calling out for help for too many days and nights. She pushed herself to her feet, her legs weak and knees wobbly as she blindly made her way across the room. She walked slowly with her arms held out straight in front of her, careful not to run into a wall.

It was pitch dark—nighttime. During the day, light seeped in through cracks and crevices. There were no windows in the room. Just a mattress, a couple of cases of bottled water, and a small plastic portable potty for her to relieve herself.

Today would be day nine, maybe ten—she was no longer certain. Until a few days ago, a tray of food had been left near the door, but it stopped coming after she was awakened by a man in the middle of the night.

She hadn't been able to see him clearly, but he was sitting or kneeling on the floor, his face inches from hers, his hand sweeping the hair from her forehead. She'd hoped he was there to save her. She'd cried and begged for help, but he just kept talking, telling her she was special and that he'd been watching her for months. All hope drained from her when she realized he was her captor. He said they were destined to be together and she was his girlfriend. Anger set in and she lowered her head and bit his hand, ground her teeth, and wouldn't let go. She'd made him bleed—felt the blood on her lips, tasted it.

His cry sounded like a wounded animal.

She hadn't seen him since. And now she wondered if he'd ever come back. Her stomach growled. Her tongue felt dry, her lips parched.

The tips of her fingers finally brushed against the door. She felt around for the doorknob. Locked. She got down on her knees and crawled around on all fours, hoping he'd left something to eat while she was sleeping. But there was nothing.

A horrible thought sprang to life. What if he was dead—killed in a car accident on his way to the store or work or whatever? She never should have bitten him. She should have stayed calm and asked him questions. Sitting now, her back against the wall, her legs pulled up close to her chest, she tried to think of how she might escape. If only she had a weapon, a stick, anything at all, she could bash him over the head when, or if, he opened the door.

Things like this didn't happen in real life, she thought. Child abductions and serial killers only happened in the movies. And yet here she was, shivering and scared, wondering if she was going to die.

She thought of her mom and her sister and hoped they were looking for her. The last time she'd seen her mother was early morning before she left for school. They had fought, like they often did. It was finally summer and school would be out soon. All her friends were going to the water park to celebrate early. Ali had been excited until Mom told her about the promotion she'd received at the bank where she worked, which meant Ali would have to watch her little sister, Gracie, every day.

Guilt crept through her. The last text she'd received before she was taken was from Gracie: Will you be home soon? Mom left for work and I think someone is in our backyard. At the time Ali had been annoyed. Ever since Dad left them and ran off with his secretary, Gracie had

19

become extra needy, always hovering as if she were afraid Ali and Mom would disappear if she looked away for too long.

Ali had texted her sister back that day, told her she was only a few minutes away and would be home soon. When she looked up from her phone, she nearly rammed into a man who was opening the back of his cargo van. "Sorry," she muttered.

He smiled, his dimple catching her attention. She'd seen him somewhere before but couldn't remember where. Twenty-nine, maybe thirty. His body was lean. He wasn't too tall or too short. He had kind eyes, a strong jaw, and nicely toned biceps. She had blushed, her cheeks burning hot.

"Nice day we're having, don't you think?" he asked.

"Don't talk to strangers," one of her mother's favorite sayings, had been beaten into her skull. So she smiled but didn't respond. Just kept walking. That's when she spotted a boy riding his bike. He did a wheelie off the curb just as a car whizzed by. She squeezed her eyes shut, waiting for the screech of tires and squealing brakes. But the kid made it to the other side of the road safely, and the car disappeared out of sight.

Two seconds later, a hand holding a damp rag reached over her head and covered her nose and mouth. The odor was horrifying. She couldn't breathe and panic set in fast. Eyes wide open, all she'd seen was a crazed look in the man's eyes as he dragged her back toward the van.

Her first thought had been, *Where is the man with the dimples and friendly smile?*

She'd struggled to free herself, slapped and kicked, dug her fingernails into flesh, but it was no use. He was strong. She was weak.

Her screams for help were muffled by the smelly cloth. In her attempt to escape, she'd planted her foot on the bottom frame of the cargo door.

She pushed.

He grunted.

Dizziness overcame her.

Out of the corner of her eye, just before all was lost and she was tossed into the dark abyss, she saw the boy on the bike across the street, half-hidden beneath the shade of a leafy tree. Their gazes met, his expression grim, worried.

Or maybe her imagination had been playing tricks on her, giving her hope where there was none.

Chapter Three

It was Saturday morning, the air still cool and crisp, when Dani slipped the key into the door of her agency's office and stepped inside. Quinn's sweater and backpack were hanging on the coat hook near her desk, but her car was nowhere to be seen, which was odd.

The door leading downstairs was open and the light was on, so Dani shut the main door and headed that way. In the basement she found Quinn on a stepladder, using tape to hang pictures.

"Hey there," Dani said. "I didn't realize you were coming in today."

"I was bored. Grandma took the car to go see her friends at Eskaton Village in Carmichael and dropped me off on her way."

The new LED bulb made a huge difference in brightening the room. Two dusty bins were on the floor near the wall where Quinn was working. After signing a rental agreement when she'd opened her agency, Dani had cleared out part of her garage at home and brought the bins here, thinking she would go through them when she had time, and had forgotten all about them.

One wall, Dani noticed as she moved closer, was already half covered with pictures and articles about people who had gone missing, mostly teenagers. Some had disappeared five or more years ago.

"It's sad, isn't it?" Quinn asked. "How many missing persons cases do you think are most likely due to a homicide?"

Dani didn't like to think about those sorts of things since it always seemed counterproductive, so she said nothing.

"There's a backlog of more than two hundred fifty thousand unsolved murders nationwide," Quinn went on. "The National Institute of Justice has called it a 'cold-case crisis.' The backlog grows every time a homicide isn't solved. Police departments all across the country are lucky if they can clear sixty percent of their cases."

"Not a good trend," Dani said.

"Not at all," Quinn said.

Dani began to read aloud one of the articles Quinn had taped to the wall. "Eight hundred thousand children are reported missing in America. Some are lost, injured, have run away from home, or are abducted. More than ninety-nine percent of children reported missing in America in recent years have come home alive. But of the estimated one hundred fifteen children abducted by strangers, only fifty-seven percent of them come home alive, forty percent are killed, and the rest remain open cases."

"It seems like I'm always reading about how rare stranger abductions are because they are only one percent of the total number of cases," Quinn said. "But one percent equals hundreds of children. That's way too many."

Dani nodded as she made her way to the wall opposite where she'd been standing and came to a picture with the name ALI CROSS written with a red marker in all caps. Underneath the picture were articles and newspaper clippings. The teenager had been missing for over a week. Dani's heart went out to the girl's friends and relatives, and especially to her parents.

"I put her on that wall because she hasn't been missing very long," Quinn explained. "The police investigated but decided there wasn't evidence to indicate foul play. She falls under the header 'Runaway Or Foul Play?'"

Dani nodded. She knew that if she did a quick search on the internet, she would find a similar header in every state, if not every city. In fact, Quinn's mom, Jeannie Sullivan, fell into that same category. One sunny day, eight years ago, Jeannie had been home folding laundry, and the next day, she was gone. So was her car, an orange Volkswagen Bug, along with her purse. Quinn's father, years older than his wife, told police Jeannie had not been happy for a while; he was convinced she'd run off to find a better life. Quinn's grandma had never been close with Jeannie and agreed with her son's assessment. But Quinn thought otherwise. She loved her mom and was convinced she would never have left Quinn without talking to her first. The event changed her life, setting her on a path to find Jeannie Sullivan and prove everyone wrong.

Dani had known Quinn for nearly five years now. Their relationship was complicated. Dani had a tendency to want to mother her, protect her, and give her advice, even when she hadn't asked for it. Quinn, on the other hand, would share only so much with Dani. There were times when Dani sensed she wanted to vent or talk but held back, like an abandoned and starving dog who won't eat until its rescuer walks away. For the most part, their relationship was defined by loss and hope.

Dani's chest tightened when her attention fell on multiple pictures of Tinsley. Her little girl was always so sweet—kind and gentle, curious and happy. Dani missed her, ached to hold her in her arms.

Quinn looked over her shoulder at Dani. "Have you thought more about when you're going to make me partner?"

"I have," Dani said. "I'm not sure if you're ready."

Quinn climbed down the ladder and plunked her hands on her hips. "What? You promised."

"I don't make promises. You know that."

"Well, you hinted strongly that the idea was viable."

"I don't think I said that." Dani hoped she would let it go, but chances of that happening were slim. Quinn was stubborn. She was also a conundrum—sweet and sour. Bossy but friendly. Controlling sometimes, and yet also strangely submissive.

Quinn's gaze bored into her. "Why don't you think I'm ready?"

"Because you're young and inexperienced, and you get too emotionally attached."

"What! That's not true."

"You spent four weeks looking for the neighbor's missing dog," Dani reminded her.

"And I found him, didn't I? Dexter is adorable, and he would have starved to death in that guy's barn if I hadn't been persistent."

That much was true. The only reason the dog had survived so long was because it had rained and the barn roof had more than one leak. "It's not just Dexter," Dani said. "What about the workers' comp case you helped me with?"

Quinn's eyebrows squished together.

She was trying to play dumb, Dani thought, but it wasn't working. "You know exactly what I'm talking about. The woman—Claire—turned out to be the real deal. She wasn't faking her injuries, and you felt so badly about anyone having doubted her that you took it upon yourself to take care of her."

"That's not fair," Quinn said. "She was elderly—"

"She was sixty."

"Okay, fine. She wasn't old, but she was definitely in pain. She could barely get to her mailbox, so I helped her out a little. I don't see the problem."

"The problem is you spent the next month doing everything for her. You took her to the grocery store, cooked and baked for her, and mowed her lawn."

"I still got all my work done. And besides, I meet all the requirements. All I need is a criminal background check, and I'm good to go."

Saved by the bell, Dani thought when she heard the tinkling sound of the door being opened upstairs. "We'll talk about this later. I better go see who it is."

Quinn followed close behind.

When Dani reached the landing, she saw a young male standing inside the office near the door. He was bony, just under five feet tall. Dani guessed his age to be hovering around twelve, but he had a street-smart look to him that made her think he could be older. His dirty-blond hair was on the long side and hung over his eyes and just past his chin. His denim pants were worn and ripped, but not in a stylish way kids considered cool these days. He wore a gray, short-sleeved T-shirt with a faded American flag on the front.

"Hello," Dani said. "Can I help you?"

"Um, are you a private eye?"

"Yes," Quinn blurted. "She's an investigator. And I am her assistant, at least for now."

He flipped his head to one side in what looked like a practiced motion that made his hair follow suit, making it possible to see his eyes, which were sort of squinty and very blue. He reminded Dani of a young Leonardo DiCaprio.

Dani didn't know what to make of the boy. He looked harmless enough, and yet there was something unsettling about him, as if he'd somehow squeezed a hundred hard-lived years into twelve.

Dani gestured toward the chair in front of her desk. "Would you like to have a seat?"

He looked from the chair to Quinn, then back to Dani before finally walking toward her and taking a seat. He slouched, his back pressed up against the wooden slats, his knees spread wide.

"So why don't you tell us what's on your mind," Dani said.

"That girl who's missing—the one—"

"Ali Cross?" Quinn asked from across the room.

He looked at Quinn. "Yeah. Her."

"What about her?" Quinn wanted to know.

"I saw it happen," the boy said. "I saw him take her."

"Who took her?" Quinn asked, her voice high-pitched and anxious.

Dani's instinct was to tell Quinn to settle down, to relax, but she knew it probably wouldn't help matters, so she said nothing.

"Some guy," the boy said. "I couldn't see much of his face, but I don't think I've ever seen him around town before. He was a little taller than you," he told Quinn. "And he was wearing a dark-blue shirt with the sleeves rolled up. His hair was dark brown, shorter than mine."

"Was he in a car?" Quinn asked next.

"No. It was a van. White. With double doors in the back. That's where he was . . . at the back of the van when the girl walked by. I was across the street on my bike, kind of hidden in the shade of a tree. Something seemed off. And then I saw him drag her to the back of his van, his hand clamped over her mouth. She was struggling, but all I really saw were her eyes and the look of desperation before she went limp and he tossed her inside." The boy looked at his feet. "I should have yelled something or rushed to help her, but I froze." He looked up and met Dani's gaze. "Instead of helping, I stood there and watched the guy jump in behind the wheel and take off."

"Did you go to the police?" Dani asked, her heart pumping faster.

"Yeah. I filled out a form—a report—or whatever they call those things. I was there for a few hours while they asked me the same questions over and over, as if they were trying to confuse me and throw me off. They made me feel as if I'd done something wrong." He shrugged. "After I left, I thought maybe they would call me with updates, let me know if they found any leads at the site, but nothing happened. Nobody ever contacted me again. So a few days ago, I called the police department, told them who I was, and asked them if they found the girl yet. They said it was an open investigation and they couldn't tell me nothing."

"You don't think they took you seriously?" Quinn asked.

"Nope."

Dani frowned. "Are you sure Ali Cross was the girl you saw?"

"Positive."

"Do you mind if I call the station to ask them about your report?"

He stiffened. "You don't believe me?"

"I don't know you, and I certainly don't know enough about what happened between you and the investigators to have an opinion either way. I am having a difficult time imagining the police not following up with an eyewitness to an abduction."

"Go ahead and call," he said. He stood, flicked his hair. "I'm going to go outside and have a smoke."

Dani had to stop herself from lecturing him about smoking. She picked up her phone as she watched him head outside. She waited a minute to see if he took off, but he didn't. He sat on the bench outside the window, pulled a cigarette and a lighter out of his pants pocket, and lit up.

Quinn looked at Dani. "Why don't you believe him?"

"I never said that. I just want to know why the police didn't follow up." Dani pulled up Detective Whitton's number on her cell and hit the call button.

"Detective Whitton here. What can I do for my favorite PI?"

She smiled. "Hi, James. How are things?"

"My hips have seen better days. It doesn't help that I've packed on a few pounds since I saw you last, but overall things are good. I know you're not one for small talk, so what is it you'd like to know?"

"I've got a young boy here who says he witnessed Ali Cross's abduction and filled out a police report but nobody followed up."

"Ethan Grant," he said, reminding her that she'd never asked for the kid's name. "Hold on a minute. I'll grab the file."

"It's Saturday. What are you doing at the office?" she asked.

"I could ask the same of you."

She chuckled.

"I'll get the file."

"Sure." So it was true, Dani thought. The kid had gone to the police, just like he said.

A few minutes later, James Whitton was back on the phone. "Ethan Grant. Twelve. Lives in the trailer park off Westacre Road with his alcoholic mother. He has a tendency to lie and steal, and he is not as socially advanced as his peers."

Dani said nothing as she waited to see if he had more to say, which he did.

"Despite the kid's story having a lot of holes in it, it appears they followed up and went to the spot where Ethan Grant said he'd witnessed the girl's abduction, but there were no tire marks, no footprints or drag marks. Nothing to back up his story."

"What about other witnesses?" she asked.

"They posted a couple of flyers in the area, asking for information, and talked to a few shop owners, but nothing came of it. I recall the lead investigator saying he thought the kid's story was just an attempt to get attention."

"Hmm. Ethan Grant seems genuinely concerned for the girl," Dani said.

Dani could hear papers rustling on the other end of the line before James said, "They certainly did their homework. Investigators talked to Ethan's teachers, neighbors, and a couple of kids at his school." James whistled through his teeth. "I'm looking at a list of grievances a mile long."

Through the front window Dani watched Ethan blow perfect smoke rings into the air. "What sort of grievances?"

"Let's see. He started a fire when he was ten, but someone caught him and was able to put it out before things got out of hand. His neighbor came home from work and found him in her kitchen making a snack. The boy took off his shirt in the middle of class because he was hot, called the principal a few choice words, got caught stealing cigarettes from a corner market. Shall I go on?"

"No need." She scratched her head. "It just doesn't make sense, though, does it? That the boy wouldn't just give up after he'd already talked to the police and filled out a report?"

"Who knows what goes through a kid's head at that age. I do know that his description of the van and the driver changed over the course of a few hours. First the man who took her was forty and then he was twenty-five. His hair color was dark, and then it was dirty blond. Same with the vehicle he was driving. It went from being a truck, to a mini-van, to a cargo van."

"Trying to remember details can be a stressful experience, especially for a twelve-year-old kid talking to the police," Dani said in the boy's defense.

"True. You know as well as I do that most eyewitness accounts are shockingly inaccurate and cannot be relied upon." James sighed. "Not much we can do without a license plate number and no concrete description of the driver."

"Okay," Dani said. "So that's it, huh?"

"Afraid so."

"Forget about Ethan Grant," Dani said. "Are there any suspects in the Ali Cross case?"

"None."

"I read somewhere that detectives are now leaning toward her being a runaway. Is that right?"

"Ali Cross and her mother did get in a fight the morning she went missing," James answered. "So yes, it's safe to say she isn't a top priority at the moment."

"Then I guess I'll just thank you for your time and let you get on with your weekend."

"Before you go," James said, "any thoughts as to why the kid might have picked you to talk to?"

"No idea," Dani said. "Maybe he heard I have 'sucker' written across my forehead."

James laughed. "Don't be so hard on yourself. You're one of the good ones, and don't you forget it."

Dani said goodbye and got off the phone. She wasn't at all surprised to see Quinn outside, sitting on the bench next to Ethan. Knowing Quinn, she saw the boy as an underdog who needed her help. When Dani stepped outside, they both looked at her with identical blank stares.

"What did they say?" Quinn asked.

Ethan flicked the butt of his cigarette onto the strip of lawn next to the sidewalk. "They probably told her I was a liar and a thief and my mom drinks too much," he said.

Dani crossed her arms. "That about sums it up."

Ethan stood, his gaze locked on hers as he said, "If nobody wants to believe I saw what I saw, then fine. My mom would be pissed, anyway, if she knew I hadn't let the whole thing go like I promised. But whatever happens to that girl now is on you and the police. I tried."

Dani cocked her head. "Why would your mom be upset by you talking about what you saw?"

"Because she has enough problems. The last thing she needs or wants are newspeople with cameras coming around the trailer park and causing her grief."

"Is she in trouble?"

"None of your business." His blue eyes darkened. "This isn't about my mom. I came here today because I can't get what I saw out of my head. The terrified look on that girl's face right before the man pushed her inside the back of the van makes me wish I'd cut school altogether that day."

"Do you do that often?" Dani asked. "Cut school?"

Ethan shoved his hands deep into his pants pockets. "What's it to you?"

Before Dani could answer, Quinn jumped to her feet and said, "I want to help him. I want to take on his case."

Dani sighed. "It's not a case, per se. Ethan isn't here to hire us to find the girl."

"Yeah, I am."

Dani lifted an eyebrow. "Do you know Ali Cross personally?"

"No."

"But you want to hire us to help find her?"

He nodded. "I've got a few hundred dollars saved up, hidden in a jar at home. I figured that would be a good start."

"There are dozens of other investigators in the area," Dani said matter-of-factly, not bothering to tell him that amount wouldn't cover more than a day's work. "Why me?"

"Because your daughter was taken and I thought maybe you might care more than most, but I guess I was wrong."

Dani's chest tightened.

"I know this girl ain't my sister or cousin or even my friend," Ethan went on. "But the look she gave me made me feel like she was pleading for help." He shifted his weight from one foot to the other. "In that moment, a split second in time, it was just me and her." He looked to the ground, shrugged, then raised his head and caught Dani's gaze again. "She only went missing a little over a week ago, and yet the news-people aren't even talking about her anymore. I've heard people saying they think she's just another runaway, but I know that's not true. I saw what happened with my own eyes, and I guess I've just been feeling like it was up to me to help her . . . like I might be all she's got, you know?"

Chills crawled up Dani's spine. She did know. A lot of what he'd just said summed up how she felt about Tinsley—that she was her only hope and if she ever stopped looking for her daughter, it would be over because nobody else would bother.

Ethan started walking toward the beat-up bike he'd left on its side on the grass.

"I think we should help him," Quinn said as soon as he walked away. "Please."

What if Ali Cross had been tossed into the van and taken, just as Ethan said? If what Whitton had said about Ali Cross was true and she was no longer a priority, then her chances of being found alive were growing slimmer every day. How could Dani live with herself if she didn't at least try to help? She hadn't liked the way Ethan Grant had made her feel—guilty, as if she didn't care. She met Quinn's gaze. "If I say yes, we work together. That means we keep each other informed before rummaging through trash cans or knocking on doors. No running off to see Detective Whitton to pick his brain without me by your side. In fact, don't tell anyone what we're working on. Not yet."

Quinn smiled, then looked over her shoulder at Ethan, who had stopped at the street corner to light up another cigarette.

"And one last thing," Dani said.

Quinn waited.

"I don't want you to be upset if this goes nowhere. Investigators talked to Ethan Grant for hours, and from what Detective Whitton told me, they did their due diligence where Ethan is concerned, followed up accordingly, and came up empty."

Quinn started walking away.

"Tell Ethan no more smoking around the agency. He's underage and it's not good for him."

"Anything else?"

"Yes. You have some filing to do. Tell him to come back Monday morning at eight. You can get started then."

She took off before Dani finished her sentence, calling out to Ethan and stopping him before he reached the other side of the street.

CHAPTER FOUR

Ali Cross awoke when the door opened and flooded the space with light. A man stood there, unmoving. At first she thought she might be hallucinating, but then she realized it was him—her own personal monster.

Her legs wobbled as she pushed herself to her feet. She was famished and she wanted out of there. False bravado prompted her to raise her chin. But hunger and fear made her tremble.

His hair was damp, his jeans and T-shirt clean. "I made you some breakfast if you're hungry."

The sunlight pouring in revealed cracked gray walls that were covered with dust and mildew.

He pulled a collar and leash from his back pocket and held it in the air for her to see. "I'm going to have to put this on you, and you have to promise not to scream or bite."

This couldn't be happening. Locked away for days, starved, and now he wanted to put a dog collar on her. She wanted to run, fight, escape. And yet she was too weak to do any of those things. She had no choice but to do as he said. Her nightmare would not end in this room.

"Use your words," he said, holding up the collar. "Either this goes around your neck or I leave. You have until the count of three to make up your mind."

"Okay," she said, refusing to cry, unable to bear the thought of spending another day, let alone another minute, inside this place. "I want out of here."

He smiled as he walked over to her.

The hand she'd bitten was wrapped in gauze. "If you ever do anything like this again," he said, holding up his bandaged hand, "I'll have to punish you." He brought the thick leather collar to her throat and very slowly slid the strap around her neck, making her skin crawl. She closed her eyes, willing herself not to cry, hating herself for allowing him to put the collar on her without a fight. He took his time fastening the buckle, making it snug, but not so tight she couldn't breathe. After clipping the leash to the metal ring, he gave it a tug to make sure it was secure.

He sniffed. "It sure smells bad in here."

Never in her life had she felt so demeaned, demoralized. It didn't matter that she didn't know anything about him. She hated him. Wanted him dead.

He walked to the door, tugging the leash even though she was at his side, seeming to take pleasure in having her in his control as he pulled her outside behind him and into the blinding light.

She lifted her face to the sky and sucked in a breath of fresh air.

"If you're good," he said, glancing her way, "maybe I'll bring you outside again sometime."

Despite his hold on her, she wanted to kick him and run screaming. But she was weak and wobbly and wasn't ready to risk being thrown back into that cold, dark room. She glanced over her shoulder, back at the place where she'd been cooped up for too long. It wasn't a garage or a warehouse. It was a small shed, detached from the house.

Chills crawled up her spine. No. She couldn't risk it. She was hungry and weak. She needed to stay calm and think things through.

He tugged on the leash, forcing her to turn back his way. Saplings, giant oaks, and trees she couldn't name surrounded the house they were walking toward. It was at least two stories and had what looked like an attic with dormer windows. On the first floor there was a wrap-around porch. Under any other circumstances she might have thought the house was charming instead of frightening. The ground beneath her feet was covered in layers of fallen leaves, branches, and bark. The windows on the bottom floor, she noticed, were covered with iron bars. To her right, far off in the distance, she saw the tip of a rooftop peeking out above the trees. Another home? It gave her hope to think someone, anyone, might be close by.

He led her up two wooden stairs to a deck, opened the back door, and waited for her to step inside before he began securing more than one lock to make sure she didn't escape. Out of the corner of her eye she watched to see which key he used before shoving a ring of keys into his pants pocket.

He led her to a rectangular table in the kitchen. There were four chairs; she sat in the one facing the kitchen. He tossed the leash over the back of her chair.

She could run. But what if this was a test to see if that's exactly what she would do? Instead, she took in her surroundings. The smell of bacon made her stomach grumble and her mouth salivate. The kitchen was narrow and long with veiny stone countertops on both sides. Old wood cabinets contrasted with the shiny new appliances. The wood floors looked clean and dust-free. She could see him from where she was sitting. He opened a drawer, pulled out a flowery place mat, then walked over and set it in front of her, along with a small glass of orange juice. "Drink it slowly so you don't get an upset stomach."

She took a sip, swirling bits of pulp around her tongue. It tasted like heaven.

A minute later, he brought her a simple white plate with a tall stack of golden-brown pancakes, served with crisp bacon and a side of warm syrup.

By the time he sat down across from her, they both had a plate, along with a fork and a napkin. She poured on the syrup and took a bite, trying to hide her pleasure since pancakes were her favorite food of all time. She could eat them for breakfast, lunch, and dinner.

"I know how much you love pancakes. How do they taste?"

How did he know she loved pancakes?

He laughed. "I know everything about you, Ali Cross."

The thought irked her. "What's my favorite color?" she asked after she swallowed.

"Green."

"What's the name of my best friend?"

"Kristin Wright."

She took another bite and another, refusing to look at him. Her orange juice was gone. She wanted to ask him for a glass of water but didn't want to talk to him, let alone ask him for anything. He must be following her on social media. Her mother had warned her not to share too much, but she hadn't listened.

As if he'd read her mind, he pushed back his chair and went and got them both a glass of water. She gulped hers down, her thirst finally quenched, then took another bite of pancakes, eating fast, afraid he might take her plate away.

"I like watching you eat."

The notion made her want to spit out her mouthful of pancake, but she pretended not to hear him and simply chewed and swallowed and took another bite instead.

"Gracie is worried about you," he said.

Ali's head snapped up. She looked him directly in the eyes for the first time. Dark-blue eyes. Evil eyes. "You talked to my sister?"

"I did," he said. "She's angry with your mother because she thinks your mother is the reason why you haven't come home."

"You're lying."

37

He shook his head. "She told me you got into a pretty big fight with your mother before you left for school on the day I found you and brought you home. Now everyone thinks you ran away. Nobody's looking for you, Ali."

His eyes glimmered with mischief, as if he were excited to tell her the bad news. "I will admit to being surprised to see your mother on a local news channel, pleading for your return," he went on. "I suppose it might have taken her a few days for the truth to settle in."

"But that's not the truth. I would never run away."

"But you ran away before." He wagged a finger at her and said, "Never lie to me."

She wanted to take her fork and stab his eyes out. She gritted her teeth. "I love my family."

"Even your dad?"

"What do you know about my dad?"

"Everything. You could even say I know too much!" He laughed. "I never met *my* dad, but if he was anything like yours, I guess I should consider myself lucky. Have you met your dad's new girlfriend?"

"No." She hadn't meant to lie, but it still angered her to think of her dad and his secretary making a new life together. It was one of the reasons she and her mom fought so much. She blamed her mom because she was there at home and Dad wasn't.

"That's two lies. Man, oh, man. One more and you're going to be so sorry."

He was a certified sicko. Her stomach churned. How did he know so much about her? The truth was she *had* run away before, and it made sense the police might stop looking for her. Her inability to do anything about her situation filled her with despair.

"Look at me and tell me you understand."

Her pulse elevated. "I understand." She might be quick to anger when it came to her mom, but she'd never been a violent person.

And yet, if she had a gun, she wouldn't hesitate to shoot him squarely between the eyes.

"Let me ask again. Have you met your dad's new girlfriend?"

Ali nodded.

"Tell me about her."

Ali hated this game he was playing. She didn't want to tell him anything. "Are you ever going to let me go?"

"Tell me about your dad's mistress."

Ali imagined she wasn't looking at him but through him. She envisioned his brain morphing from a hard, rubbery substance into runny goo as she talked. "She used to come to Sunday barbecues at the house. She also spent a few days with us during our vacation in Lake Tahoe. I hardly talked to her."

"She vacationed with you. Wow. That must have been a tough pill to swallow. Do you think your dad and his secretary were making love in the pontoon when they took it to the middle of the lake?"

Ali swallowed. He had seen the picture of her dad and his girlfriend on social media. She knew this because she'd seen it too. She wanted to tell him to fuck off. "I don't know what they did or didn't do."

"Someday the two of us will take a leisurely ride on a boat across the lake. Would you like that?"

He was a psycho. How could he not be, after what he'd done? But his sickening fantasy of the two of them taking a boat ride was too much. "You kidnapped me. I didn't ask to be brought to your house and locked in your shed. So what do you think my answer to that question might be?"

His eyes hardened. In one swift motion, he reached for the leash and yanked hard. She gagged and coughed. He didn't care. He just kept pulling on the leash until she was bent so far over the table he was able to lean forward until they were nose to nose. "Talk to me," he said, blue eyes twinkling. "Tell me something I might not know."

"Okay," she said. He let go of the leash, and she fell back into her seat and slipped the fork into her waistband. "Did you know that your mom was very popular and everyone knew her as the Whore of Midtown?"

His eyes blazed.

"The men liked her because she was big-chested and easy—"

He bolted upward. His hand shot out, and he slapped her hard against the cheek.

The shock of it took her breath away. The left side of her face stung, but she refused to cry. Her mom always told Ali she was stubborn and too easily provoked. She was right, and Ali had regretted the words the moment she opened her mouth.

"Say you're sorry, or else."

Heat spread through her body as she sucked in air until she was able to calm herself. "I'm sorry. I've never met your mom. I'm sure she's as lovely as you."

"That's better."

He was either too dumb to realize it wasn't a compliment or he didn't care. He collected their plates and took them to the kitchen sink. When he returned, he looked around and said in a parental tone, "I'm going to count to three. If your fork isn't on the table by the time I'm done counting, it's back to the shed. One." Long pause. "Two."

She reached under her shirt and pulled the fork out from the top of her jeans. Her hand hidden beneath the table, she held the utensil in a tight grip. It was a good solid piece of metal, not the kind of fork that could be easily bent.

She was about to place it on the table when something stopped her.

"Three," he said.

This could be her last chance to escape. Maybe her only chance.

Jumping to her feet, she lunged, jabbing the fork prongs into his face, hitting her mark and stabbing one of his big blue eyes.

His scream sounded like the high-pitched wail of a siren.

Her adrenaline spiked and she took off running, through the living room to the front door. She plucked off the chain at the top, then slid another bolt open before turning the knob and tugging at the door. It wouldn't open. Her hands were shaking. She looked everywhere until finally she noticed a third latch near the floor. She bent down and pushed the metal piece to the side before springing to her feet and opening the door just before it was slammed shut from behind her.

She pivoted around, brought her knee up fast and hard, connecting with his groin and giving herself enough space to take off down the hallway. She could hear the latches being pushed back into place. The first room down the hallway was locked. The room to the left was small and jam-packed with boxes and sheet-covered furniture. The next room to the left was a bathroom, but the window was barred so she kept going. At the end of the hallway was a large bedroom with a queen-size bed, two side tables, and a tall dresser. Like the rest of the house, everything was neat and tidy. She knew the windows facing the backyard had iron bars, so she rushed over to the window facing the front and pulled the curtain to the side. No bars. She unlocked the latch, then pulled on the wood frame, but the window had been painted shut.

Her breathing was erratic as she glanced around the room. Unfastening the collar from around her neck, she tossed it along with the leash to the ground. *What now?*

She needed something heavy enough to break glass. Her gaze settled on a set of leather-bound books centered between marble bookends on top of the high dresser. She ran to the dresser, grabbed a heavy bookend, then rushed back to the window and threw the marble at the glass like it was a baseball and she was throwing it to home plate. Glass shattered.

Heavy footfalls sounded in the hallway. He was coming this way. *No. No. No.*

She needed more time, just a moment longer.

She ran to the door, hoping to lock him out, but she was too late. He rushed for the door like a defensive linebacker, sending her tumbling

41

backward to the floor. Blood oozed down his face, making it hard to tell how much damage she'd done earlier.

He stood over her, his chest heaving.

"They're going to find you," Ali growled. "There was a boy on a bike who saw everything."

"You're a liar."

"You'll see."

He gestured toward his injured face. "I should kill you for this."

"Go ahead," she said. "We both know you're going to kill me sooner or later. Do it!"

He let out a low growl as he scooped up the collar from the floor. She scooted backward and was about to roll herself under the bed when he jumped on top of her, straddling her middle before she could make a move. He fastened the collar around her neck and pulled it tight. She grasped at the collar, trying to loosen it. She couldn't breathe.

A drop of blood fell from his face and hit her forehead. The veins in his forehead bulged as he pulled the collar tighter. "I've worked hard to find the perfect woman. You're the one, Ali. The one I chose. The one I love. Someday you'll love me too."

Light-headed, she felt herself being pulled into a dark tunnel. She welcomed death—anything but this—and that's when he loosened the collar a notch before pushing himself to his feet.

She rolled to her side, coughing and gasping for breath, her head pounding.

He reached down, grabbed hold of her arm, and pulled her to her feet. "Come on. Off we go," he said, ushering her out of the room and down the hallway. He stopped at the locked door and pulled out his keys.

Too weak to fight him, she sagged against the wall, praying it would all be over soon.

Her neck was sore. Her throat felt raw.

It was over. He had won.

He dragged her inside a room she hadn't seen before. In the middle of the room was a type of dental chair with steel plates and straps for the arms and legs.

Suddenly she shot back to life. "No! Please! I'm sorry. I won't run again. I promise."

"It's too late. I warned you." He scooped her up, carried her to the chair, and plopped her down. By the time her fight-or-flight response hit her fully, he'd strapped her arms to the metal plates. She kicked her legs, screaming, doing whatever she could to stop him from buckling the straps around her thighs and calves.

"Please. No."

"There's no getting away, Ali. You were warned, but now you must be taught a lesson."

Placing his palm on her forehead, he buckled the final strap across her head.

She couldn't move.

He disappeared from sight. She heard wheels rattle as he rolled a metal tray like the ones she'd seen at the dentist's office across the floor. It was covered with shiny utensils: pliers and scissors, a dental drill, and an assortment of scalpels.

He picked up the drill. "Now be a good girl and open your mouth."

She clamped her lips together.

He set the drill back on the tray and crossed his arms over his chest. "You are a tough nut to crack. Set to graduate high school at the age of seventeen, highly intelligent, accepted into some of the best schools in the country, and loyal to those you love. Your little sister adores you and looks up to you. But there is one thing about you I failed to recognize: you, Ali Cross, are stubborn to a fault. No wonder you and your mother fight like cats and dogs." He shook his head. "You can relax," he said. "I'm not going to yank out a tooth or anything. I have another idea."

He pushed the tray back to the corner of the room. When he returned, he held up a cylindrical club made of wood. "This is a truncheon, also known as a baton. Police use them as a compliance tool and defensive weapon." He swung it through the air a few times, even managed a couple of practiced twirls, and before it registered that he might use it on her, he swung downward, hard and fast, making contact with her ankle and foot.

The sound of bones cracking competed only with her scream as a white, sparkling light filled her head, the pain so mind-numbingly intense she felt her body drifting far, far away, the monster's words the last thing she heard before white light faded to black.

"I warned you, Ali. I did, but it had to be done. You won't be running away again."

Chapter Five

When Dani arrived at the office on Monday morning, Ethan Grant was sitting on the bench in front of her agency. She was glad to see he wasn't smoking and there weren't any cigarette butts lying around.

"Did you have a good weekend?" she asked as she unlocked the door.

"It was okay." He reached into his pocket and pulled out a wad of cash. "Here," he said, trying to hand her the money. "I should have more in a few weeks."

"Keep it," she said. She looked him over, noticed the wrinkled shirt and the holes in his shoes. "Come on inside. Quinn should be here soon."

He stood and followed her into the office.

She flicked on the lights and shut the door behind him. "Why don't you have a seat while I get the coffee going?"

"I can make it," he said. "I make coffee for my mom every morning."

"Okay. Great." She gestured to the small room to the right where, even from here, she could see the Formica countertop, refrigerator, and sink. The counter had a few cracks and was yellowing from age, but the office and the kitchen served their purpose.

While Ethan set about making coffee, Dani put her sweater on the hook behind her chair. She always wore layers. The mornings tended to be chilly, but the temperature would most likely hit the high eighties by noon. After taking a seat at her desk, she went through the mail, which was mostly junk. Although business tended to be slow overall, she always had enough workers' comp claims to keep her busy. Corporations didn't like to pay benefits if they didn't have to. If a claimant followed their doctor's orders and restrictions, there usually weren't any problems. But it always surprised Dani how many claims were fraudulent and how easy it was to keep track of the claimants on social media.

She picked up her landline phone and listened to the messages. She only gave her cell phone number to clients. New business came through the office.

The first message was a telemarketer. Delete. The second message was from Cameron Bennington, a thirty-five-year-old lawyer who was convinced someone was entering her house at least once a week, rearranging pictures, sometimes taking personal items, and even eating leftovers in her refrigerator.

This wasn't the first time Cameron had contacted her. After going to the police and being told they couldn't help her without some sort of proof, she had paid Dani a visit. Dani suggested she have digital cameras installed in and around her house. This was the first time Dani had heard from her since. Apparently Cameron's living room furniture had been rearranged and yet nothing showed up on the video.

Dani returned her call. It turned out Cameron had installed only one camera at the front of the house. They arranged to meet at six tonight after Cameron returned from work.

Just as Dani finished with her call, the door opened. Expecting to see Quinn, she was surprised to see her ex-husband, Matthew, instead. He lived with his new wife in the house he and Dani had bought together in Poverty Ridge, a nice quiet area with some of the stateliest historic homes in Midtown. When they divorced, he paid her half of the principal they had invested in their home, which she used to put a down payment on a two-bedroom, one bath in East Sacramento.

Matthew's face was flushed, making her wonder if something was wrong.

Of course something was wrong. He rarely stopped by just to say hello. "Hello, Matthew."

He looked from left to right. "Where's that girl you work with?"

"She's twenty-two. An adult. And her name is Quinn." He knew all this, but obviously needed to be reminded. "She should be arriving soon."

A noise sounded in the kitchen, and he looked that way. "Who's in there?"

"Why all the questions? What's going on?"

Matthew had a newspaper tucked under his armpit. He tugged it free, unfolded the paper, and set it firmly on Dani's desk in front of her. The headline read Five Years Later, Still Hope of Finding Tinsley Callahan.

Below the headline was a picture of Tinsley and a smaller one of Quinn talking to the reporter with the agency's signage in the background.

"I hadn't seen this," Dani said. She clasped her hands together. "Are you angry about something?" Before he could answer she added, "You know as well as anyone that any and all attention brought to Tinsley's case is a blessing." She thought of the phone call and how adamant Matthew had been about taking down the website and moving on. "Why do I get the feeling you don't care to know what happened to our daughter?"

His shoulders sagged. "Of course I care. I loved Tinsley as much as you did. I would give my life to bring her back. But a known murderer confessed to her abduction, and yet you still can't let it go. She's not ever coming back, Dani."

She saw the tension visibly leave his body as he said, "I've got a little one on the way, and you know how much all of this upsets Carole. You said we would always be like family. You told me you cared about my happiness. If that's true, please just stop this nonsense. Tell Quinn to stop spreading false news, so we can all move on with our lives. It's not healthy to hang on to hope when there is none."

She'd had enough. He had no right to tell her what to do or how to live her life. She would never stop looking for Tinsley. Period. "Get out," Dani said, her voice trembling.

He looked confused. "What?"

"You heard me. If your wife is too frail to handle *my* loss, then maybe both of you should stop reading the paper and watching the news. Why don't you go home right now and tell her to bury her fucking head in the sand, and if and when I find proof that my only daughter is gone to me forever, I'll let you know. Until then, I'm tired of playing nice."

"What's wrong with you? In all the years I've known you, you've never sworn."

"I'm just getting warmed up."

Instead of leaving, he jabbed a finger at the newspaper still on her desk. "If any of this is true, then please fill me in. What new clues have you and your bossy, out-of-control assistant unburied? Tell me. I have a right to know."

She lifted her chin, surprised when the lie easily slipped out of her mouth. "It's too soon for me to share anything with you."

"Because you don't have anything new, do you?" His eyes widened. "I knew it. I can see the answer in your eyes. You have nothing, and yet you're spreading lies and giving false hope to my friends and family. Do you have any idea how many calls I've gotten about this already? This notion that you have a new lead has brought my mom to tears. She's eighty years old, Dani. She can't handle losing Tinsley twice." He let out a long sigh. "And neither can I."

Dani scooped up the newspaper as she stood. Crumpling it in one hand as she walked around her desk, she shoved the wad of paper into his chest. "Get out, Matthew. Go take care of your new little family and leave me to find our daughter. And for the record, I'll never stop looking."

"You're being unreasonable."

"And you're being an ass."

He grunted.

She pointed at the door.

It seemed like forever and a day before he was gone and she could take a breath.

When Dani sat at her desk again, Ethan appeared with a mug filled with hot coffee. "Cream or sugar?" he asked as if it were just another day and he hadn't overheard the whole thing, which would have been impossible.

She smiled. "I like it black. Thank you."

"You were married to that man?"

"I was," Dani said. "Almost seven years." She shook her head. "I used to think he was quite the catch."

Ethan pushed his hair to the side and said, "People change, I guess."

"Yes. I guess they do."

"Why doesn't he like Quinn?"

"Because he doesn't like himself," she said matter-of-factly.

Seconds later, Quinn walked in. "Was that Tinsley's dad I just saw leave?"

Dani nodded. There was something about the way Quinn always talked about Tinsley as if she was alive and well that warmed her heart.

"What did I miss?" Quinn asked when no one said anything.

"Nothing," Dani said, hoping to start her morning over fresh.

"It had to do with me, didn't it?" Quinn asked. "He was carrying a newspaper, and I bet it was today's paper." When Dani didn't respond, she looked at Ethan. "Am I right?"

He shrugged. "I was making coffee in the other room."

"You're right," Dani told Quinn before she worked herself into a tizzy. "He's convinced that Kyle Harmon is responsible for Tinsley's disappearance, and he thinks it's time to move on."

"Seriously?" Quinn raked her fingers over the shaved section of her head. "Tinsley is his daughter too."

"Yes. She was . . . is."

"I hope you told him we'll never stop looking for Tinsley."

"She pretty much told him to take a hike," Ethan said with delight.

Quinn looked at Ethan. "I thought you were in the other room?"

"I was, but I overheard the last bit."

Quinn's attention returned to Dani. "Did you really tell him off?"

"I did."

"Well, good. He's too bossy and always acts like he's in charge."

Ethan and Dani exchanged a quick glance.

Quinn plopped her hands on her hips. "What?"

Dani smiled. "He said the same thing about you."

Quinn rolled her eyes. "He doesn't like me because I tell it like it is."

"Okay," Dani said. "Let's forget about Matthew and get to work."

"Good idea," Quinn said. As she walked toward her desk, she told Ethan to pull up a chair.

Once Quinn had started making monthly updates to Tinsley's website, it seemed she and Matthew were always butting heads. Mostly because Quinn had a tendency to be blunt and say whatever was on her mind.

Dani stood, then took her mug to the kitchen, where she refilled her coffee.

In the other room she heard Quinn get right to business, explaining to Ethan how she wanted to start from the beginning, pretend he'd only just witnessed Ali Cross's abduction yesterday. Once Quinn began to ask him questions, it was clear she had spent a lot of time preparing. Her questions included "Tell me in detail what, exactly, you witnessed?"

"What was the date and time of the incident, and how long did it last?" "Where did it happen?" "Who was involved?" and so on.

Quinn wanted details, and Ethan did his best to oblige.

An hour later, Quinn asked Dani if she wanted to take a drive with her and Ethan to check out the spot where Ethan had seen Ali Cross abducted. Dani wanted to go along, but she had to testify in court for a workers' comp case at the end of the week and needed to get things in order.

"You can give me an update later," Dani told her. As she watched them go, she thought about what Detective Whitton's colleagues had said about Ethan Grant. She could tell the boy had a hardened edge to him, that much was clear, but he came across as genuinely concerned about Ali Cross's well-being—a person he'd never met. Despite meeting resistance with the police and his own mother, he hadn't given up on trying to find her.

Once they drove off, Dani set about organizing her desk space and noticed Quinn had never returned her tape dispenser. As she made her way downstairs, she found herself thinking of Ali Cross. What if everything Ethan had told Quinn was true? Had Ali Cross been harmed in any way? Killed? Dumped in the woods somewhere, or buried in someone's backyard? Or was the man driving the cargo van holding her captive?

The questions running through her mind were all too familiar. Questions she'd asked herself over and over after Tinsley disappeared. There were other queries that had taken hold too: If Dani hadn't had a flat tire, would she have made it to the school in time? Where had the roofing nail found lodged in her tire come from? What if Matthew had been home and she'd been able to take his car instead? What if, what if, what if? The questions came to her at night, hitting her like bullets, one after another, keeping her awake.

But the questions were better than the alternative, which would be to believe Tinsley was buried somewhere off Bond Road, as Kyle

Harmon had said. When Dani was a child, she'd had a bunny named Pee Wee who escaped from his cage and never returned. Her parents convinced her Pee Wee was alive and well, living with a loving family of bunnies in another county. She often imagined Tinsley in the same way . . . living with a nice family with other children, well fed, warm, and safe.

All thoughts were pushed aside the moment Dani's gaze fell on the wall covered with a giant collage of pictures—all of Tinsley. She walked over to get a closer view of a picture of Tinsley attempting to blow out the candles on her birthday cake. Her cheeks were round, her eyes bright with happiness and innocence.

God, how Dani missed the feel and smell of her, and talking to her, holding her, teaching her about the world.

Dani pulled down the picture, sank slowly to the ground, her back against the wall as she slid downward, and kissed the tip of Tinsley's paper nose. The tears came at once, flowing freely down her cheeks and off her chin.

It had been a long time since she'd had a good cry. She welcomed the release.

After a moment, she wiped away the tears and took a breath. Her gaze fell on a dusty bin to her left. The label, written in her own handwriting, read **PHOTO ALBUMS**. She flipped open the lid, hoping to find photos of her and Tinsley that she could frame. Instead of photo albums, though, she found an old jar filled to the brim with pennies and a scrapbook from Dani's childhood. Some of Matthew's stuff was inside the bin too. Like the track-and-field medals he'd won during high school. There were also a couple of yearbooks. At the very bottom of the bin was a pile of RAYTEX Annual Employee Reports.

RAYTEX was a tech company based in Sacramento that helped small businesses get connected, and where Matthew still worked. She pulled the reports from the box. What had started out as a simple trifold brochure had grown over the years into slim, saddle-stitched booklets with multiple pages and an eye-catching design.

She riffled through the booklets, stopping at the one dated a week before Tinsley went missing. The first page was a message from the CEO, talking about the new start-ups that had benefited from RAYTEX's help. Next came information about what was happening in their city, along with the best conferences and tech meetups to attend. She flipped the page, surprised to see a two-page layout that was basically a collage of pictures beneath the header RAYTEX EMPLOYEES ARE FAMILY.

Every year, RAYTEX held a picnic for its employees and their families. It made sense she wouldn't have seen the booklet, considering everything going on at the time.

The photo that grabbed her attention first was the one front and center. There were four people—Dani, Matthew, Becca, and Todd. She and Matthew used to hang out with Becca and her husband, Todd. The four of them had joined a bowling league and used to get together every few weeks to play mah-jongg.

A twinge of sadness swept over her. Dani and Becca used to talk every day, but since Tinsley's disappearance, they had talked only a handful of times. It wasn't anyone's fault. Dani had only one thing on her mind after Tinsley was gone. Conversation became awkward. They both had moved on, gracefully and without guilt.

There were truly no words to express what it felt like to lose a child.

Dani still held on to hope that Tinsley was alive. She often imagined the homecoming, a surreal moment when she would see her daughter again. She imagined Tinsley would appear as an apparition right up until the moment Dani wrapped her arms fully around her. Only then would an overwhelming peace settle within and blanket her with joy.

She sighed. For now, all she felt was loss—an empty black void.

All those hopeful expectations for the future, gone in a flash. It was still, after all this time, impossible to make sense of what had happened.

Dani's world had truly been turned upside down, her hopes and dreams broken, tossed away, destroyed.

Some of the pictures in the collage were so small and grainy it was hard to tell who was who. Her gaze settled on a group picture taken of everyone who had attended the picnic. She scanned the faces, looking for Matthew, finally spotting him in the background, talking to a woman. At first Dani thought it was herself he was chatting with, but the woman had on a summer dress, while Dani had been wearing a green blouse and white shorts.

The woman who picked up Tinsley could have been your twin.

That's what Tinsley's teacher had told Dani five years ago.

She looked at the picture again, staring for so long at the woman talking to Matthew her eyes began to water. Leaning her head back against the wall, she inwardly scolded herself for being so quick to assume the woman might have anything to do with Tinsley's disappearance.

This wasn't the first time she'd thought she spotted Tinsley's abductor. She saw the woman everywhere, pushing her cart through the produce section at the grocery store, in line at the post office, working the register at Macy's department store. All this time, and she still couldn't get the woman out of her head.

Maybe Matthew was right about her being so obsessed with finding Tinsley alive she would never be able to accept evidence to the contrary.

And yet . . .

She held tight to the booklet as she pushed herself to her feet and headed upstairs. Back at her desk, she opened the Annual Employee Report and used her magnifying glass to get a better look. She recognized the outfit Matthew was wearing, remembered picking it out for him. The woman, on the other hand, did not look familiar, which was strange considering Matthew's department at the time had consisted of about twenty people. Back then, she had known every single one of them. Maybe the woman was someone's wife or girlfriend whom she hadn't met.

The woman wasn't the only one Dani saw everywhere she went. She saw Tinsley too. Over the years, whenever someone spotted a girl who fit Tinsley's description and left a comment on the website Matthew had made to keep the community informed about Tinsley's case, she'd gotten her hopes up.

"Don't get too excited," Matthew would tell her. But she *always* got too excited. It didn't matter where some random person said Tinsley had been spotted, Dani would seek out the person who'd commented and question them personally. She'd made a trip to New York City once and staked out an apartment where the person said he'd seen Tinsley. Five days later, Dani saw the girl exit the apartment. The only resemblance to Tinsley was hair color and height.

Since that time, she'd become much more fastidious when it came to following a lead. It was one thing to be hopeful and quite another to spend thousands of dollars to follow a likely dead end.

Again, Dani stared at the picture of Matthew and the woman before finally moving the magnifying glass over the other pictures, hoping to find Tinsley. The memories brought her back to a time when she had been so sure she and Matthew would spend a lifetime together. Like most marriages, things weren't always perfect. But she'd been content. They'd had a beautiful daughter and a nice home. Matthew had loved his job.

After Tinsley was born, Matthew had worked more and more, and although Dani could remember feeling lonely at times, Tinsley had kept her busy. Dani and Matthew had hardly ever argued back then, and maybe that should have been a warning. They hadn't argued because they hardly saw one another. She had thought they were both happy. But then Tinsley had been taken, and their marriage had toppled like a house made of sticks.

Looking through the magnifying glass, Dani spotted the mystery woman in another picture. She was working a booth, sitting on a bench and painting a little girl's face—Tinsley's face.

A sudden coldness hit at Dani's core. She shivered.

Who was she?

She could ask Matthew, but he wasn't good with names and probably wouldn't remember. Even if he did recall, he would most likely get angry with Dani for obsessing over the case after Kyle Harmon's confession.

Mimi Foster.

Mimi had been at RAYTEX since Matthew was first hired. If this woman was still at RAYTEX, she would remember.

Breathless, Dani looked through her contacts and found a number for RAYTEX. She called the number and waited for someone to answer.

"RAYTEX. How can I help you?"

"Hello. This is Dani Callahan calling. I would like to talk to Mimi Foster, please."

"Thank you. Transferring your call now."

After a few rings, another voice came on the line and said hello. It was strange to hear Mimi's voice after all these years. "Hello, Mimi. It's Dani Callahan. I hope I'm not catching you at a bad time."

"Talk about a blast from the past," Mimi said. "It's always a good time to hear your voice. How are you?"

"I'm doing okay. How about you?"

"Henry and I are getting ready to head to the Bahamas next week for a much-needed break, so I am doing spectacular." She laughed.

"I'm glad," Dani said.

"You should come to the office sometime and say hello to everyone. We all miss you."

"I don't think Matthew and Carole would approve," Dani said.

"No comment."

That made Dani smile. She knew Carole tended to be pushy and opinionated, which got on people's nerves. "I have a favor to ask of you."

"Shoot."

"Well, I was looking through an old bin, and I found a pile of the Annual Employee Reports, including the one printed just before Tinsley disappeared. It looks like pictures were taken at the last RAYTEX picnic I attended at McKinley Park."

"Okay."

"Someone made a collage of the pictures, and there's a woman I don't recognize in two of the photos. In one of them she appears to be talking with Matthew. At first I thought the woman was me—same height, hair color, body shape—but it's clearly not. I don't remember meeting her at the picnic or at any other time, and I was hoping you might be able to put a name to the face."

"I'll be happy to take a look," Mimi said.

"If you give me your email address, I can scan the page in the booklet and email it to you. Will that work?"

"That would be fine," Mimi said before giving her an email. "Send it over."

"I'd like to keep this between you and me, if that's okay," Dani added, worried that Matthew might get upset if he knew what she was up to.

"I understand."

Once the call ended, Dani sat quietly for a moment. All she could hear was Matthew's voice. *It's over. Time to move on. Let it go.*

She would do no such thing, she thought as she came to her feet and took the booklet to the scanner.

Hope was all she had. Hope was what kept her going.

CHAPTER SIX

Ali Cross woke up in an unfamiliar bed, sitting upright, propped against a wall of pillows. Her eyelids felt heavy—so heavy it took a tremendous amount of effort to keep her eyes open. When she attempted to move, an excruciating jolt of agonizing pain zipped through her lower half. Eyes clamped shut, she gritted her teeth until the pain subsided.

How long had she been in this bed? An image of her captor hitting her with a baton flashed through her mind's eye. Lifting the blanket, she saw that her right foot had been wrapped with clean white cloth and secured with adhesive tape. Her left foot had some bruising, but she could move her toes and turn her ankle from one side to the other.

"You're awake!"

Her head snapped up at the sound of his voice. He stood beneath the doorframe, holding a tray of food and looking chipper despite the gauze and tape covering his bad eye. She hoped she had blinded him. She wanted to shout at him, tell him he was insane and needed help. Instead she said, "Please let me go."

"Never. The sooner you grasp that reality, the better off you'll be."

"What did you do to my leg? If I'm bleeding internally, I could die. You need to get me to the hospital as soon as possible."

"Don't worry. You're not bleeding internally. Your ankle is definitely fractured, maybe even broken. It might take a few months to heal, but you'll be fine." He smiled as he came into the room and set the tray on a long bench at the end of the bed. "It was your fault it came to this, not mine. I warned you, but you wouldn't listen. Anyway, the swelling and pain could worsen over time, but it won't kill you. What it will do," he said with raised brows, "is stop you from trying to escape. You're lucky I have enough pain pills to get you through the worst of it." He crossed his arms over his chest. "Are you hungry?"

She said nothing.

"I'm going to count to three. If you can't be reasonable and talk to me like a grown-up, I'll take the food back to the kitchen. One . . ."

She could smell the food from here. Her stomach grumbled. "Yes," she said. "I'm hungry."

He picked up the tray and brought it to the bed, making sure the wood legs rested on the mattress and not on her lap. Next, he picked up the neatly folded cloth napkin and laid it over her chest. She tried not to cringe when his knuckles brushed against her collarbone. He pulled a water bottle from his back pocket, unscrewed the plastic lid, and handed it to her. While she guzzled the water, he pulled the plastic wrap from around the top of the glass of orange juice. Straightening, he asked if she would like coffee.

She shook her head.

"I need words. One . . . two . . ."

"No, thank you," she said through gritted teeth. Coffee sounded good, but she wanted him to leave her alone. Unfortunately he grabbed the wooden chair with a leather padded seat from the corner of the room, dragged it over to the side of the bed, and sat down.

"You're going to watch me eat?" she asked.

"I have a few questions for you."

She did her best to ignore him, to pretend he wasn't there, as she picked up the fork and cut into the omelet. There were mushrooms and cheese inside. It tasted good. She wished he'd brought pancakes too.

"Do you have a boyfriend?"

She took her time chewing and swallowing, using it as an excuse not to answer right away. Then she said, "No."

He stared at her, his eyes narrowing slightly. "Don't lie to me. What about Dylan Rushdan?"

She *was* lying. But how could he possibly know about Dylan? Nobody knew about her and Dylan. Not even her mother. She and Dylan had known each other since grammar school. Until recently they were best friends, but everything changed after Dylan kissed her and confessed his love for her. In that moment, she realized she'd always loved him. It had been one of the happiest moments of her life. If she told him the truth, though, she worried he might go after Dylan. "Dylan is not my boyfriend."

His eyes narrowed. "Who is he, then?"

"One of my very best friends," she said, trying her best to sound natural. "I've known him since the second grade."

She noticed his shoulders relax. *Thank God.*

"I have to admit that makes me happy to hear."

She said nothing, wishing he would go away.

"I am sorry about your foot. It's true what I said before about it being your fault, but still, I never even considered you might break a window to get away. I'm not a monster."

You're the worst kind of monster, she wanted to say, but didn't.

"The window has been fixed. I had a security bar placed on the window too."

How could that be? She hadn't heard a thing. "When were they here?"

He shrugged. "I don't know . . . three days ago, I guess." He shook his head. "Time really does fly."

She swallowed hard, and for the first time, now that the grogginess was wearing off and she'd eaten something, it dawned on her that her clothes had been replaced with a cotton nightshirt. *Had she been knocked out for three days?*

"You were delirious at times," he said, seeming to take note of her sudden worry. "I admit, I started to grow concerned when all you did for the first twenty-four hours was moan and groan and cry out in pain, even in your sleep. Nothing quieted you until I finally doubled the number of pills I gave you."

She didn't remember any of it.

He raked his hands through his hair. "I crushed the pills and put them in your water, but it wasn't easy, getting you to drink it. Once I managed, though, you were out cold in a flash." He snapped his fingers for emphasis, startling her.

"I changed your clothes," he went on as if he'd done something heroic, "and cleaned you up every time you filled up the inflatable bedpan. There's a bathroom, of course," he said, gesturing over his shoulder to a closed door, "but every time I tried to move you, you howled like a coyote with its foot in a trap."

The thought of him stripping her clothes from her body, seeing her naked, touching her, washing her, made her feel nauseous. She set her fork on the tray. She couldn't look at him. Didn't dare.

"I'm not some sort of disgusting pervert," he said, again seeming to know exactly what she was thinking. "I would never take advantage of you in that way."

That's exactly what he had done!

"Of course," he went on, "after we've gotten to know each other better and you've met my mom, we can talk about taking our relationship to the next level."

Her stomach churned, but still, the prospect of someone coming to the house, someone she might be able to convince to let her go, made her feel a little better. "Is your mom coming here?"

"Of course. She's dying to meet you. It's all she talks about when I call her."

"When?" she blurted, trying to hide her excitement and failing miserably. "When is she coming?"

"Calm down," he said with a laugh. "She'll be here in two weeks. I had no idea you would react this way. My last girlfriend was very upset when I talked about my mom coming to visit."

"What happened to your girlfriend?"

"What do you mean?"

"How long did you date? Did she break up with you?"

"Of course not. I broke things off because she was too demanding. She was exhausting."

Ali wasn't sure she believed he'd ever had a girlfriend. And if he had, she couldn't imagine he was the one who'd broken things off. But she let it go because she wanted to know more about his mother so she could prepare for the visit. "What have you told your mom about me?"

His gaze settled on hers, his eyelids heavy, a look that spoke of intimacy. Chills crawled up her arms and legs.

"She knows that you have bright-green eyes, a smattering of freckles, and full lips. Most importantly, based on everything I told her, she is confident, as am I, that the two of us will make beautiful grandchildren to entertain her in her old age."

Bile threatened to come forth. "I've already decided I will never have children. There are too many things I want to do, places I want to see." Another lie. But one she would cling to.

"Of course you'll have children—*we* will have children."

Her stomach roiled as she let her body lean farther back into the pillows. "I'm not feeling well. I think I ate too fast. I need to rest."

"You must have a million more questions about what I told Mother, though."

The only thing she wanted to know was if there was anything, anything at all, she could say or do to convince him to let her go. She raised her eyes to his, saw the little-boy look in his eyes, the sulky pout, and the moody silence. He loved playing these games, asking her questions, knowing she had no choice but to play along. If she didn't, he might break her other foot . . . or worse. "How did we meet?" she asked, finally relenting, not the least bit curious.

"I told Mother the truth—that you were walking home from school and I gave you a ride home."

"But that's not the truth. This isn't my home. My home is with my mom and sister."

"That's your second home," he said in an expressive voice that a teacher might use on a struggling student. "This is your home, Ali."

"Why are you doing this?" she asked.

"I told you before. Fate brought us together. The first time I saw you, I knew you were the one. And now you're my girlfriend."

"But I'm not. I don't even know your name."

His head fell to the side. He held it there for what seemed like forever, then grinned and jumped to his feet, startling her. "I never told you my name?"

She shook her head.

He stepped closer to the bed. Too close. "My name is Carlin. Carlin Reed." He put out his hand, palm held up, for her to take hold of. When she placed her hand on his, he tightened his grip and said, "Nice to meet you, Ali Cross."

Carlin Reed. The name meant nothing to her. She didn't know anyone with that surname, which was disappointing since there would be no way for her mom and sister to connect her to him. "I'll be going to college soon, living in a dorm with two other girls," she said, unable to hide the panic she felt. "Maybe we could arrange to meet and I could give you a tour of the campus."

The deep furrow in his brow told her he wasn't happy about her talk of college, but he managed a tight smile regardless. "Your college plans will have to be delayed. Maybe down the road you could sign up for some online courses. I'll have to give you a new name, but it might work. We have plenty of time to think about that."

Her fingers curled into fists. "Most boys try to get to know a girl before they even think about living with her," she said. "They ask the girl to meet them for coffee or maybe take the girl to dinner." She frowned. "They don't drug the girl and then shove her into the back of their van."

She noticed his jaw clench. *Shit.* The words had just flown from her mouth without much thought. She'd pissed him off. Again.

The vein in his forehead was engorged, pulsing with fury. "You don't think I ever tried to get a girlfriend the so-called 'normal' way? I'm not stupid."

"I know you're not. I'm sorry." Judging by the way his eyes darkened and the crease in his brow deepened, he was working himself into a rage.

"I did everything right," he said, stabbing a finger into her arm, making her wince. "Gifts and endless compliments," he went on, his voice high-pitched and filled with resentment. "All those expensive meals, all my time spent asking about their lives, their families, their hobbies and interests. When my efforts failed, I did my homework and decided to work on myself—my appearance and confidence. I started exercising and learning new things to make myself more interesting."

Spittle collected at the corners of his mouth. "It got me nowhere," he said. "Do you have any idea how difficult it is to be rejected over and over? Women are cruel."

"Maybe you just haven't found the *right* woman," she stupidly tried again.

His face reddened. "*You* are the right woman!" His hands fisted at his sides. "I think you've had enough to eat." He took the tray from her lap and placed it back on the bench, then returned to the bed, grabbed a fistful of her covers, and whipped them from the bed, leaving her scrambling to pull down her nightshirt, wincing from the pain the sudden movement caused.

"Don't be a prude. I've seen it all before. Many times."

The pain, together with the thought of him looking at her, touching her while he washed her body, made her sick. She held back the urge to cry. *Why did I have to go and get him angry?* If she ever hoped to get out of here, she needed to earn his trust, which started with trying harder to be friendly. Maybe then he would take her outside to get some sun. Until that time she needed to find the strength and courage to figure a way out of this nightmare.

Carlin walked across the room to a tall dresser, where he used one of his many keys on the metal ring he kept in his pocket to unlock the top drawer. He returned to her side with scissors and neatly folded strips of cloth.

"What are you doing?" she asked.

"I'm going to change the bandages." He sounded calmer, but his movements as he cut the bandages from her leg were rough and jerky. "You don't want to get an infection, do you?"

"No," she said, gritting her teeth. Her ankle and foot throbbed as he hastily unwrapped layers of cloth and gauze. The moment her wounds were exposed, bile crept up her throat. Bruised and swollen, she could hardly tell where her ankle ended and her foot began.

She laid her head back on the pillows and sucked in a breath. How would she ever get away if she couldn't even walk?

As he lightly massaged gobs of greasy ointment over her ankle and foot, she hardly took a breath until he began the process of wrapping her foot with clean bandages. She looked around the room for the first time since he'd brought her the tray of food, and realized she was in a room she hadn't seen before. Sunlight poured in through a window— one of the dormer windows she'd seen from outside the shed when he first led her to the house.

Her shoulders sagged.

She was in the attic.

With her foot shattered to bits, how would she ever escape Carlin Reed? His mother might be her only hope. Until then, she had to find a way to convince him she cared about him. *Pretend he's your friend,* she thought. As distasteful as the idea was, she had no choice.

"There," he said when he finished wrapping her foot. "You'll be as good as new in no time."

"Thank you," she said.

He looked at her, his expression a mixture of suspicion and surprise. He then gently replaced the covers, told her he would be up to check on her later. She didn't take another breath until he left the room, locking the door behind him.

CHAPTER SEVEN

Quinn Sullivan swatted away a fly and then sighed when it landed on her ankle, making her skin tingle. For the third day in a row, she and Ethan sat on a cracked and crumbling sidewalk beneath the partial shade of a maple tree, the exact spot where Ethan swore he saw Ali Cross disappear. Ethan wasn't happy about her insisting they come to the same place, but it had worked yesterday when he remembered almost being hit by a car after doing a wheelie off the curb and onto the street, so it was worth another shot. She'd read once that a witness to a crime was capable of seeing things more clearly hours or even days after observing a traumatic event. In any case, they had nothing to lose.

Across the street, Quinn took in the now familiar stucco walls, some covered with colorful graffiti, some newly painted. The stucco walls were actually the back side of a strip mall, which included a sandwich shop, a florist, and a hair salon. There were other stores too, but Quinn was only interested in the shops she could see from where they sat. Unfortunately, there weren't any security cameras. Just a couple of dumpsters secured with padlocks to keep animals and people out.

To the far right she saw a quarter acre of land, consisting of dry dirt and a few determined weeds, surrounded by chain-link fence. To the left—the direction in which Ethan said Ali Cross had been walking the day she was abducted—was a sidewalk that went on for a while before disappearing around a bend. On the first day they'd both walked that way, following the path Ali would have gone to get home. The journey had taken them past a row of older homes running parallel with the freeway.

"What was the weather like that day?" Quinn asked now.

Ethan expelled a breath. "I already told you. The sun was bright and it was hot."

"What was Ali wearing?"

"Blue jeans. That's all I know."

"What were you wearing?"

"Seriously?"

"Yes," Quinn said. "I need to know how much you can remember about that day."

"I was wearing these pants," he said, pinching a bit of worn denim between his fingers. "And . . ." He paused and thought for a minute before shaking his head. "I have no idea what shirt, though. I have a bunch of T-shirts, and I never pay attention to what I wear."

"Seriously?" Quinn asked in the same tone he'd used a few seconds ago.

"Yeah." He let his gaze roam over her gray T-shirt and jeans. "I don't think you're one to judge, do you?"

She let it go because they had work to do. This case was her chance to prove to Dani that she had what it took to become an investigator. "We need to stay focused," she said. "Tell me what you saw."

He groaned.

"Close your eyes," she told him. "Let your mind run free." She nudged him with her elbow to get him going.

He closed his eyes.

After a few minutes passed, she asked, "What do you see?"

"I was riding my bike on the sidewalk, moving toward someone. Up close, I saw that it was a girl. I thought she was cute and wondered if I'd seen her before—you know, maybe at school or the ice cream store. I jumped off the sidewalk and did a wheelie. Like I told you yesterday, I nearly got hit by a car, but I made it safely across the street to this spot. I was on my bike, one leg on solid ground, when I looked back the way I had just come, hoping she might be watching me. That's when I saw the driver of the white-paneled cargo van.

"I can see him now," Ethan said excitedly, his eyes still clamped shut. "He was wearing one of those jumper things with the zipper down the front. A uniform, like a mechanic wears. His sleeves were rolled up just like I said before. His van was white with two doors at the back that opened away from each other. I can see a logo on one of the open doors. It's small. Mostly squiggly lines. Maybe an initial or two, twisted together."

Quinn's heart raced. She forced herself to contain her excitement, not wanting to throw him off, and pulled a paper and pen from her pocket and handed it to him. "Could you draw the squiggly lines you saw?"

He sighed as he took his time drawing what looked like a blur of fanciful lettering that overlapped:

$$\mathcal{STL}$$

He handed her the paper and she stared at it. "Any idea what letters these might be?"

He shook his head.

"Did you look at the license plate?"

"I tried, but the sun's rays were bouncing off whatever was inside the van, blinding me."

Quinn grabbed hold of his arm and squeezed.

Ethan's eyes widened. "What?"

"This is the first time you've mentioned seeing something inside the van."

"But I didn't see anything because of the sun's reflection."

"But that means whatever the sun was reflecting off had to be metallic, right?"

Ethan shrugged. "Sure. I guess."

"What could it be?" Quinn asked. "Bicycles, tire rims, portable heaters—"

"Pots and pans," Ethan added without enthusiasm.

"Medical equipment."

"Forks, spoons, knives." Ethan sighed. "Appliances, pipes, pretty much anything."

Quinn scratched the side of her head. "True. Never mind. Stupid idea. Let's go back to the coveralls the driver was wearing. Do you remember what color they were?"

"Uh, dark blue, I think."

"Okay. What about the car that nearly hit you? Any idea what kind of car it was?"

He looked at her, his brows slanted. "Why would that matter?"

Quinn's shoulders sank. "Every single thing you saw that day matters, Ethan. It's all in the details. Maybe someone in the car saw you or recognized the van or the driver. You never know. That's why it's important we turn over every stone."

He shut his eyes again. Seconds later he opened them and said, "I have no idea what kind of car it was."

"You're not even trying."

"Are you kidding me?" He sprang to his feet. "This is dumb. I never would have come to see Dani Callahan if I knew she was going to stick me with some lame wannabe investigator who has no idea what she's doing." He plodded toward his bike propped against the tree, hopped onto the cracked seat, and pedaled away.

Stupid little boy, Quinn thought as she pushed herself to her feet. She might not have a lot of hands-on experience, but she knew what she was doing. The only reason she'd brought Ethan to the same spot each day was because every time she did, he remembered something new. The driver wore blue coveralls and drove a cargo van filled with something made of metal. Maybe the man had a bike in the back of his van and it had nothing to do with his occupation. But she couldn't think like that. Every clue meant something until it was ruled out. There might be a lot of trades that had to do with metal, but how many of those carried their wares around with them? It was just a matter of elimination.

She put her face to the sun, soaking in its warmth before walking to the car she shared with her grandmother and climbing in behind the wheel.

She thought of her mom, something she'd been doing less often. After Mom had left her and Dad, their world had fallen apart. No more mom-and-daughter lunches or Sundays spent at the mall. Quinn had quit dance too. What was the point? Dad was working hard and didn't have time to take her to lessons. Even if he had, it wouldn't have been the same without Mom watching her.

Her mom was the reason she was here now, which was sort of weird, considering her mom was one of many missing persons who did not want to be found. Moms aren't supposed to leave their kids. It's sort of an unspoken societal rule. But that's exactly what she'd done. Up and left her and Dad and never looked back.

And yet something had niggled from the beginning. How could Dad or Grandma be so sure she left them? What if something bad had happened to Mom? An accident, or maybe a bad guy held her at gunpoint and took her.

That's when Dad would explain that her car hadn't been found.

But wouldn't Mom have left a note, telling them she was leaving? Quinn had asked him for the hundredth time.

Dad had been hurting as much as Quinn at the time, but he'd stuck to his guns, telling Quinn her mom had simply married too young. Mom, he'd told her, ached for something more, the freedom to choose a different path. He'd also assured Quinn he would never leave her.

71

Never. Two years later, he was diagnosed with cancer. After he passed away, the first thing Quinn would do when she awoke each morning was check to make sure Grandma was alive, sure she would leave her too, sooner rather than later. But her grandma was still going strong. She was tough and was fond of telling Quinn she didn't have time to be sad or dwell on the past.

After starting the engine, Quinn sat quietly for a moment longer, both hands clamped around the top of the steering wheel, and stared at the spot where Ethan had said the van had been parked that day.

Had the driver been following Ali Cross before pulling to the side of the road, or was he already parked there, perhaps delivering product to one of the stores when Ali happened by?

With those questions in mind, she merged onto the road, a back one with hardly any traffic. Only a handful of cars had driven past since she'd been there. Quinn took a right into the mall parking lot and kept driving until she was in front of Subway.

She parked and got out. She needed to critically assess the information in front of her. Ali Cross had been taken on a Wednesday. Was it possible the driver of the van was a delivery man? If so, Quinn needed to know whether or not any of the shops got weekly shipments of product or any type of service. The only way to find out was to talk to some people.

A couple of hours later, she returned to her car with a lot of information but nothing helpful, per se. The well-known franchises like Subway did receive weekly shipments, but not on Wednesday. The florist only scheduled deliveries on weekends, and the hair salon received packages on random days, usually delivered by UPS or FedEx.

Quinn left the shopping area, feeling slightly discouraged. For three days she'd been hanging out with Ethan and now this. She felt as if she was getting nowhere fast.

Chapter Eight

Dani had just returned to the office after doing surveillance work for Cameron Bennington, the woman who was sure someone was entering her house and messing with her things. At this point, Dani couldn't help but wonder if the woman was rearranging furniture in her sleep. Stress could lead people to sleepwalk and do things they might not remember in the morning. Until the problem was resolved, it was decided Dani would continue with her surveillance.

No sooner had she taken a seat at her desk than Quinn walked in, looking sullen. She let out a mumbled hello, dumped her bag onto the floor next to her desk, and plopped ungracefully into her chair.

"Where's Ethan?" Dani asked.

"I have no idea," she said. "He ran off right when things were getting interesting."

"Why would he leave? Was he upset?"

"He simply has no patience."

Dani frowned. "Did something happen to set him off?"

"I told him he wasn't trying hard enough, which he wasn't." Quinn blew out some hot air. "I guess that wasn't fair of me to say, considering he remembered there being some sort of company logo on the vehicle and that he was blinded by the sun's rays reflecting off something inside the back of the van."

Dani lifted a brow. "More than we had a few days ago. What was the driver wearing?"

"A blue jumpsuit, you know, like mechanics and painters wear."

"What did he say about the logo?"

"He said it was a bunch of squiggly lines and may have had an initial or two."

"Don't worry about Ethan," Dani said. "He'll come around. You're doing a good job."

"Thanks," Quinn said.

"You might be interested to know I did some research on Ethan and his mom. His dad took off when Ethan was two. His mom was doing drugs at the time, so after his father disappeared, Ethan was placed in foster care. For a couple of years he was passed around, but his mom cleaned up her act and Ethan got to go home."

"At least he has a mom," Quinn said.

"Nine months ago," Dani continued without responding to her comment, "Ethan's mom was arrested again. This time for selling drugs. Instead of serving time, maybe because it was cannabis she'd been selling, the judge went easy on her and ordered her to wear an ankle monitor. That might be why she didn't want Ethan to talk to the police. She's scared."

Quinn's shoulders sank. "I've been too hard on him, haven't I?" Before Dani could answer, she said, "It's easy to forget he's twelve instead of twenty."

"Agreed," Dani said. "His childhood has forced him to grow up fast." Ethan and Quinn had that in common. After being abandoned by her mother and losing her father soon after, Quinn had had to decide whether those events would break her or make her stronger. She'd chosen the latter.

As Quinn shuffled papers on her desk, she said, "This case has given me a new appreciation for what you do."

"Why is that?"

"Until now, I've done more paperwork than anything else. But these last few days have made me realize that searching for someone really is like looking for a needle in a haystack. Clichéd, but true. Ali Cross could be anywhere."

Dani nodded.

"I can't stop thinking about Ali, wondering what she might be going through," Quinn said. "If someone ever managed to get me in their car and hold me against my will, I would do anything to get away, even if it meant putting myself in harm's way."

"Thinking about being in a dangerous situation and actually being in one are two very different things," Dani said. "When we are threatened, our survival instincts are triggered. The will to live is strong."

"Yeah, I guess." After a quiet moment passed, Quinn told Dani one of her theories about how the person who took Ali Cross could have been delivering something to one of the stores near the area where Ethan said she was taken. She also mentioned how Ethan was almost hit by a car but couldn't recall the color, make, or model of the vehicle. "I'm starting to feel stuck," Quinn said. "What do you do when you run out of ideas on where to go next?"

"You find someone to talk to," Dani said.

"Who?"

"Why don't we start with Ali Cross's mother?"

"I thought you didn't want me knocking on anyone's doors."

"Not without me," Dani said, popping to her feet. "Come on. Let's go."

It was nearing two o'clock in the afternoon when Quinn and Dani arrived at the two-story home where Ali Cross lived with her mother and younger sister. When Mary Cross answered the door, Dani thought she looked like a clone of her seventeen-year-old daughter.

Mary was slender with shimmering red hair that fell to her shoulders in thick waves. Dark shadows circled her eyes, as if she hadn't slept since her daughter went missing.

Dani stood beside Quinn and introduced them as private investigators, then asked if it would be possible for them to have a chat about her daughter Ali.

Mary's brows shot upward. "Have you located my daughter?"

"Afraid not," Dani said. "But it has been brought to our attention that she may not be a runaway as reported."

"Why haven't the police informed me?" Mary asked. "If you're private investigators, who hired you?"

"A twelve-year-old boy named Ethan Grant," Dani said.

"I heard about the boy," Mary said. "Detective Hank Davine with the Sacramento Police Department told me they followed up and found no new leads."

"Ethan Grant is adamant about what he saw," Quinn said, "and upset because he believes authorities failed to take him seriously after reporting her as a runaway."

"Mom," a young girl said from inside the house. "Let them inside."

"This is my daughter Gracie," Mary Cross explained before reluctantly opening the door wide enough so they could enter. She led them to the living room and gestured for them to have a seat.

Mary sat on a cushioned chair while Quinn and Dani sat on the edge of the sofa. Gracie stood behind her mother.

"I've spent three days with Ethan," Quinn said. "He is very confident about what he saw."

Mary frowned. "I don't understand. If there is no evidence, how can he possibly help?"

"Every day," Quinn went on, "he recalls something new. For instance, he's certain the man responsible for your daughter's disappearance was wearing blue coveralls and driving a white cargo van."

Mary shifted in her seat. "The police convinced me she ran away. She's done it before."

"When?" Dani asked.

Mary appeared to be doing the math in her head.

"Eighteen months ago," Gracie answered for her mom.

"That's right," Mary agreed. "It was a difficult time. I contacted the police and filled out a report. I couldn't eat or sleep. Two days later, she came home. Apparently she had been at a friend's house whose parents were gone for the weekend."

Gracie rubbed her mom's back, then rested her hand on Mary's shoulder.

Mary released a shaky breath. "Ali and I don't always see eye to eye. I tend to be a little hard on her, but I love my daughter."

"Ali promised us she would never run away again," Gracie said. "And we believed her. I still don't think she ran away. She wouldn't do that to us after all the stress it caused the first time."

Mary blindly reached over her shoulder and covered Gracie's hand with hers. "This time, when Ali didn't return home after school, Gracie called me at work. I'm a nurse at Mercy General Hospital. She was crying and worried."

Gracie nodded. "Thirty minutes before calling Mom, I had texted Ali, and she said she would be home in a few minutes."

Dani looked at Mary. "What did you do?"

"I left work early, came home, and started calling Ali's friends. Nobody knew where she was. I went to the house of the same friend she had stayed with the first time she ran off. Her mom felt bad and invited Gracie and me inside, even took us into her daughter's room to have a look around. When we returned home, we made dinner, but neither of us could eat. After twenty-four hours had passed with no sign of Ali, I called the police. For the first few days, I would say investigators took Ali's disappearance seriously. But that all changed once they found out Ali and I had argued the morning she disappeared."

"Was that unusual?" Dani asked. "For the two of you?"

"Not really. On a scale of one to ten," Mary said, "this argument was definitely a ten, but—"

"She wouldn't have left us—not again," Gracie cut in, her chin jutting out as if she were angry at the thought of it.

"She's right." Mary straightened her spine. "Would it be possible for me to talk to the boy who saw Ali that day?"

"I'll text him and set up a meeting," Quinn said. "Does that sound good?"

Mary nodded. "Thank you."

"I have a few more questions, if you don't mind," Quinn said.

"That's fine."

"Does Ali have a boyfriend?"

"Dylan Rushdan," Gracie said.

"Well," Mary quickly countered, "I wouldn't call him a boyfriend."

Gracie made a Mom-doesn't-know-anything face. "I saw them kissing."

Mary looked over her shoulder at her daughter. "Ali told me they were friends and she wasn't interested in getting involved with anyone so soon before leaving for college."

Gracie didn't look convinced.

"Have you talked to Dylan?" Dani asked.

Mary nodded. "I called him the same day Ali didn't come home. He said he hadn't seen or talked to Ali in a few days."

"If you could write down his name and number, we could talk to him," Quinn said, pulling a notebook and pen from her shirt pocket and handing them to Mary.

Mary scrolled through her phone to find Dylan Rushdan's number and wrote it down, along with her own name and number so Quinn could call her to set up a meeting with Ethan.

"What about Ali's teachers?" Dani asked. "Have you talked to them?"

"Detective Davine assured me he talked to anyone who might have had contact with Ali at school, including her teachers. She attended all of her classes that day, which is not surprising since she's always been academically inclined. She's an A student."

"What about extracurricular activities?" Dani asked. "Sports, music, dance—that sort of thing?"

Mary shook her head. "None of that. Books and art. She loves to paint. Would you like to see her room where some of her work is displayed?"

Quinn stood. "I would like that."

Mary led the way and everyone followed her to Ali's bedroom. The room was neat and tidy with a double-size bed adorned with a fluffy white comforter and downy pillows. On the bedside table was a glass lamp with stacked crystal spheres. Across the way was a taller dresser and silver-framed mirror. White gauzy curtains covered a large window.

Everything was white except for Ali's artwork, displayed on the wall opposite the window. Canvases of all sizes. Abstract landscapes with bold and vibrant colors.

"These are beautiful," Dani said.

Quinn appeared to be mesmerized by the different lines and various colors that gave the illusion of plants and vines. One of the paintings had a moon as a centerpiece, so realistic it looked like Ali Cross had taken a photo instead of painted a picture.

When Dani turned back toward Mary Cross, she noticed she was crying. Instinctively, she put her arms around the woman and tried to comfort her. She knew firsthand the excruciating pain Mary must be feeling. Not even time would heal the hole in her heart. Not until the numbness wore off would guilt set in, because any mother who had lost their child, no matter the circumstances, knew that a parent's job was to protect their child and keep them safe.

Chapter Nine

The first thing Carlin Reed did upon awaking the next morning was head into the room downstairs that he used as his office. He locked the door behind him, a habit he couldn't seem to break, always afraid his mom would show up and barge right in like she used to do.

As he sat at his desk and waited for his computer to boot up, he thought about good old Mom. She'd been a loving and beautiful mom. When he was a young boy, she would give him a bath every night before bed, taking her time washing him, her soapy hands caressing every part of his young body. He didn't mind because it made her happy. On Sundays she bathed him early in the morning, dressed him in a suit and tie, rubbed gel in his hair, and combed it back just so. She loved showing off her son at church. When he was especially well behaved, she would say, *Close your eyes and count to three,* and when he opened his eyes, she would give him a treat, usually something sweet.

As he grew older, things changed between the two of them. Their relationship took a turn for the worse when he was ten and he told her he could wash himself. She wouldn't hear of it. In fact, she removed the locks from every door in the house, making sure he had no privacy. When she bathed him, she would yank and pull instead of caress. By the time he turned thirteen, she was climbing into the bathtub with him, doing things to his body that he knew weren't right. If he angered her, she would make him close his eyes as she counted to three. And when he opened his eyes, instead of sweets, she would show him some new crazy gadget. Kinky toys, she liked to call the objects she used on him, or sometimes the other way around.

His computer screen lit up before his mind took him too far down the scary, dark hole that was his childhood. He pushed his fingers through his hair, then stretched, trying to get the crick out of his neck. He hadn't slept well. All he could think about was the boy Ali said had witnessed her abduction.

Crazy talk. Nobody had been around; he was sure of it. If her story were true, he would have seen the kid.

He drummed his fingers impatiently on the top of his desk. The Wi-Fi in this place sucked. The clear quartz crystal sitting on the edge of his desk caught his attention and made him think of his last girlfriend. What he'd told Ali about his ex-girlfriend wasn't exactly true.

Gretchen Myles had turned out to be a whack job; that much was clear. But that's not how things started out. He'd met her when he got his hair cut at a salon. She was the new girl in town, and he came to find out she'd never cut hair before. And it showed. Not only had the hair on one side of his head ended up shorter than the other, but she'd also cut his ear. Snipped a sliver of his earlobe right off.

At the time, he'd figured it was the best thing that had ever happened to him because she'd quickly ushered him into the back room and tended to his wound. She kept touching his arm, her breasts pushing against him as she held a clean cloth to his ear to stop the bleeding. She kept telling him how sorry she was. She'd felt *so* bad that he'd been able to convince her to go out with him. On their first date he'd taken her to the movies. He'd been too nervous to put his arm around her, but they'd shared a big tub of popcorn and he'd made sure to reach for more popcorn every time she did so that his fingers would brush against hers. He'd tried to get her to go to dinner afterward, but she had said her parents would worry and insisted he take her home, which he had done.

After that first date, he could tell she was playing hard to get because for two weeks straight she kept coming up with excuses. As a last resort, he texted her and told her his ear had gotten infected and he hadn't been able to work because of the pain and he might have to talk to her boss about paying for his doctor's appointments and missed work unless she agreed to another date.

It had worked.

Instead of letting him pick her up at her house, though, she'd met him a few blocks from where she lived. She was a little strange that way. Whatever. This time he'd surprised her. Instead of taking her to Zócalo on Capitol Avenue as promised, he'd brought her to his house, where he'd cooked her fresh lobster and made a delicious salad with toasty croutons. She didn't relax until she finished the martini he made for her. Once she started talking, it was all about the house. She couldn't get over the fact that it was his, which wasn't the whole truth. The house belonged to his mother, who at the time happened to be traveling the world after finally retiring from her banking job.

Gretchen gobbled down her lobster in record time. Didn't touch the salad and declined a second drink. He didn't realize how nervous he was until he carried their plates from the table to the kitchen. While he cleaned up, she walked around the house, admiring the decor. He found her in the living room brushing her hand over one of his mother's favorite pieces, an antique bergère chair. That's when he spit it out, telling her what he'd been dying to all night, that the house would be hers too, if she agreed to marry him. Without hesitating, he pulled a black velvet ring box from his pocket, got down on bended knee, and recited a poem he'd written about all the reasons he loved her.

The moment was still ingrained in his head.

He'd never forget it.

She put a hand over her mouth so all he could see were her big round eyes looking down at him. A tiny noise escaped from beneath her dainty hand. At first he'd thought she was crying from happiness, but apparently she'd been laughing so hard her eyes watered because the second her hand dropped away from her mouth, she'd let out an unladylike, rip-roaring howl.

She was laughing at him, taking him straight back to grammar school, when girls and boys alike tripped him in the hallway, then pointed and laughed.

This time was different, though. He was older and wiser, and he did what he wished he'd done to those kids in school. He came to his feet and punched her in the mouth.

He'd never punched anyone in his life, but that didn't stop him from bending his knees slightly, tucking his thumb over his four other fingers, drawing back his elbow, and taking a jab, his fist hitting her squarely on the mouth.

Boom!

She staggered backward, collapsing to the floor, her buttocks hitting hard. He heard a crack and figured she might have fractured her tailbone. This time both of her hands went to her mouth, where blood streamed through her fingers. "My teeth," she said. "You knocked out my teeth."

She was right. Her front teeth were gone.

He stood there, waiting to see how the whole thing would play out, suddenly unsure about what he'd done. He remembered feeling a bit of regret mixed with pleasure. He knew he should've said he was sorry, but the words stuck in his throat. "You never should have laughed at me," he finally managed. "You're not going to tell your friends, are you?"

Her eyes widened. She pushed herself to her feet, holding on to the wall for support, the blood on her hands spreading across the paint. "My friends have no idea I'm here," she said over her shoulder, the pronunciation of her words thrown off due to her missing teeth, making her sound sort of silly.

"In fact," she went on, "my friends have no idea you exist. I only went to the movie with you because I felt bad about your ear. But then you threatened to get me fired, so I had no choice but to come tonight."

Blood was smeared across her jaw and neck. She looked at the floor near her feet, spotted a tooth, and picked it up. Holding it up so he could see, she said, "You're in big trouble. You will pay for this."

She walked with a limp to the chair where she'd left her coat.

He'd gone to a lot of trouble to make everything perfect tonight. She hadn't even looked at the ring, which had cost him a fortune.

Her friends didn't even know he existed?

Swallowing a giant lump in his throat, heart racing, he watched her collect her things. Panic seeped into his bones. He couldn't let her go, not after everything that had happened. He looked around until his gaze fell on the centerpiece on the table, a heavy glass vase filled with dozens of red roses. Two long strides brought him to the table. He grabbed hold of the vase and ran toward her.

Gretchen never saw it coming.

Carlin's computer screen came to life. Once he accessed the internet, he typed the words "boy witnesses the abduction of Ali Cross" into the search engine.

Quite a few links came up, many about Ali Cross being a runaway, some about a boy who had witnessed a bank robbery two years ago. His eyes scanned each header, then abruptly stopped at the one that read Twelve-Year-Old Says He Saw Ali Cross Tossed into a Van. Police Are Looking into It. He clicked on the link, swept past a picture of a mobile home park, and read through the entirety of the article, which included the boy's description of what he saw. Upon further investigation, detectives were unable to find any trace evidence. But the boy, the article went on to note . . . has no intention of leaving it at that. He's adamant about what he saw and refuses to stop looking for Ali Cross, a girl he's never met.

Carlin sucked in some air after realizing he'd been holding his breath.

Ali had been right! The kid had seen him toss her in the back of the van. How was that possible?

He might have shut down his computer at this point and let the whole thing go. But it was the last line that bothered him, niggled, made his eye twitch.

The kid refused to stop searching for Ali Cross.

There was no mention of the boy's name other than to say that he lived with his mother. Carlin scrolled back to the top of the article to take another look at the picture of the mobile home park where, according to the caption, the kid supposedly lived. There was no signage in the picture that would tell him which park it was, but that wasn't necessary, he realized, the moment he saw the palm trees at the front and the high-rise apartments in the foreground in West Sacramento, where he'd done some work recently. He did a quick search of "mobile home parks in West Sacramento." There it was: the Hawkeye Mobile Home Park. It was on an acre of land and held forty to fifty trailers.

Maybe he would pull the old Camry out of the garage and do a quick drive-by.

No. He would do better than that, he thought, as the phrase "keep your friends close and your enemies closer" crept through his mind.

He opened the top drawer of his desk and pulled out the lanyard attached to a badge holder. The one he'd been given when he attended a small business conference at Sacramento's community center in Midtown. He slipped the piece of paper with his name on it out from under the plastic badge holder, then used Microsoft Word to make a new badge with a new name and a new career as a journalist.

Once that was done, he shut off his computer and left the room. All he had left to do was find a nice pair of slacks and a button-down shirt, then he would be off to the races, ready to interview the kid himself and see if he had anything to worry about.

Chapter Ten

It was nearing ten o'clock when Quinn pulled her grandmother's blue 1988 Lincoln Town Car next to the curb just outside the Hawkeye Mobile Home Park in West Sacramento.

She hadn't slept well last night. After watching Dani comfort Ali's mother yesterday, she hadn't been able to stop thinking about her own mother. On one hand there was Dani and Mary, two grieving mothers who cared only about finding their missing daughters. And then there was Quinn's mother, who decided one day that she wasn't happy, that something was missing in her life. Of course, there had to be more to the story, but Quinn didn't care about why her mother left, just that she had. Maybe things would have been different if her mother ever thought to visit once in a while, or to write or call.

A few minutes later, Mary Cross appeared, parking her Toyota Corolla behind Quinn. They both climbed out. On an earlier phone call this morning, Quinn had explained that Ethan was upset with her after telling him he wasn't trying hard enough and she hadn't heard back from him.

Mary was insistent about meeting Ethan. She wanted to talk to him, decide for herself if he was to be believed.

And so here they were.

As they walked side by side, gravel crunching beneath their shoes, Quinn was sorry to see that the most neglected trailer on the lot was the one Ethan lived in with his mother. The wooden stairs leading to the front door of the trailer showed signs of dry rot.

Quinn knocked. Voices from a television sounded from inside as they waited. Quinn felt her chest tighten. She'd obviously hurt Ethan's feelings when she told him he wasn't trying hard enough. That wasn't fair. He was doing his best, and her words had been hurtful and unprofessional.

The thought of meeting his mom wasn't helping settle her nerves either, since she knew his mom had been through a lot and probably just needed a break.

Ethan's mom opened the door. She was short and rail thin with gray streaks running through her dark hair. She wore shorts and a tank top. The monitor around her ankle stood out. It looked like a giant iPhone.

"I'm Quinn Sullivan with the Callahan Agency and this is Mary Cross, the mother of Ali Cross, the teenager who went missing recently," Quinn said. "I've been working with Ethan—"

The woman put up a hand, stopping Quinn from going on. "Why can't you people just leave me alone? I clean houses six days a week, and on my one day off everyone suddenly needs to talk to me. I just sent a reporter packing. He wasn't happy about it. Something about the determined look in his eyes tells me he'll be back. So leave me be."

"Please," Mary said before the woman shut the door. "Your son might have seen something that could ultimately help me find my daughter. I'm begging you to let me talk to your son. Ethan could be my only hope."

Shaking her head, the woman said, "I'm sorry, but I don't want my son to get involved." The door shut swiftly before Quinn or Mary could do anything about it.

Quinn made her way down the stairs, then waited for Mary before heading toward the street. Mary's eyes glistened. Quinn worried she might cry. She wasn't like Dani when it came to comforting people. She wasn't a hugger, preferring to keep her distance. Being abandoned by your mother could do that to a person—harden them and make it difficult to trust. She'd been so angry after Mom left, she'd taken her anger out on Dad, blaming him for Mom's leaving. And then when Dad got sick, she blamed the only person left to blame. Herself. She couldn't look into a mirror without seeing the person deep within—ugly and selfish.

There was no hiding the truth.

She was the reason her mom had left. She knew that much was true because her dad was a kind man. Never raised his voice. Hundreds of people she'd never met before came to his funeral, and they all had a story about how Dad mowed his elderly neighbor's lawn every week for years, played his ukulele at the nursing home twice a month, and brought a rose for every lady in the place.

Out of the corner of her eye, she saw Mary use a tissue to wipe away tears. "Don't give up hope," Quinn said as they walked. "We'll find Ali."

They'd reached the end of the gravel road when someone called Quinn's name. She stopped and turned around. So did Mary.

Ethan was jogging toward them.

When he caught up, he stopped to catch his breath and shoved his hands deep into the front pockets of his dirty jeans. "Sorry about that. My mom is paranoid about people coming around, asking questions."

"That's okay." Mary introduced herself and offered her hand.

Ethan shook it, then pointed to a little grassy area with a picnic bench and swing set. "If you want to talk we could go over there."

Mary nodded.

Once they were all seated—Quinn and Mary on one side of the picnic table and Ethan on the other—Mary spoke directly to Ethan. "I understand you saw my daughter shoved into the back of a van."

"That's right."

"Are you sure it was her?"

"I didn't know who she was when I saw it happen, but a few days later when I saw her face on the local news station on TV, I knew. One hundred percent sure," he added.

"What was she doing before she was taken?" Mary asked. "I'm not questioning whether or not you saw her, I just need to know. Was she on the phone? Was she talking to the man? Did she look worried?"

"I was kind of far away when I first spotted her, but I do think she had her phone out. When I got close enough to get a really good look at her, she was walking past the back of the van where the driver was. I'm not sure if he said anything to her, but she did glance his way. I don't know if she said hello, but I would say she was minding her own business."

"The police didn't take you seriously, so why should I trust you?"

His body tensed and his jaw hardened. For a second there Quinn thought he might walk away. But he didn't.

"I can't say I'm proud of some of the things I've done, but I never harmed anyone. Some of the stories about me have been blown out of proportion." He kept his gaze on Mary Cross. "The thing is, I'm not a liar. From what I've heard, the police followed up on everything I told them. They just couldn't find any evidence—no security cameras, tire tracks, or signs of a struggle, so I can't really blame them for moving on." He folded his arms over his chest. "Don't mean no disrespect, but I'm not here because I want to earn your trust. I'm just trying to help."

"Fair enough," Mary said. "But when the police decided to move on, why didn't you?"

"Because less than a week after filling out a police report, I read in the paper that the police thought she was a runaway." He shook his head. "I just couldn't let it go."

"Why not?"

"Because I was there. I saw it happen. Ali looked right at me when that man was shoving her inside the back of the van. She looked scared, as if she were begging for help." He unfolded his arms and rested his hands on the table. "I should have done something, should have shouted at the man to stop, but I didn't. And now I can't get the look of panic in her eyes out of my mind. I don't care if nobody takes me seriously or anyone believes me because I know what I saw. That's why I went to see Dani Callahan."

"I believe you," Mary said.

Ethan's demeanor changed in an instant. He sat up a little taller, and his shoulders pulled back a tiny bit, as if those three words were exactly what he needed to hear. He tossed the bangs out of his eyes and looked directly at Quinn. "I *am* trying. I'm trying my hardest to remember everything, but it's not that easy. When I close my eyes, all I see is Ali looking at me. I don't see the van or the driver or feel the sun on my back. I see Ali looking at me."

Quinn hadn't realized how badly she'd hurt his feelings until that very moment. She'd pushed him too hard. She'd been working with Dani for years now. Her research skills were decent; she had the ability to get information from many sources, and her surveillance skills were instinctive. But getting out there and interviewing people, working closely with strangers, was a whole new world. Ethan might act like a tough guy who smoked cigarettes and cut school, aloof and sort of distant, but he was only twelve and he wanted to help. "I'm sorry about the other day," Quinn said. "I never should have pushed you so hard."

"Yeah," he said. "I'm sorry too."

A moment of reflective quiet hovered over them.

"So what now?" Ethan asked.

Quinn perked right up, ready to get back to work. "I have some ideas."

"I'm on leave of absence from work," Mary said. "What can I do to help?"

Quinn smiled, figuring Dani wouldn't mind a few extra helping hands. "That would be great, Mary. I need you to look up any and all companies in the area that might use a white cargo van. Construction crews usually tend to use trucks, but sometimes they call in painters or plumbers or electricians who may or may not use a cargo van. I know it might sound ridiculous and a bit overwhelming, but we have to start somewhere. Ethan thinks the logo on the van was some sort of squiggly or curly lettering. It might be initials, but we shouldn't limit ourselves. We need to keep an open mind."

Mary kept nodding her head as she took notes on her phone.

They talked about the driver and the blue coveralls and the way the sun bounced off something shiny, probably metal in the back of the van. Mary would keep that in mind too, when she did her research.

All three of them exchanged phone numbers, then Mary pulled out a hundred-dollar bill and slipped it across the table to Ethan.

He slid it back. "Keep it," he said. "I'm not doing this for money."

Mary tucked the bill back into her wallet. "I didn't mean any offense."

"None taken," he said. "In fact, when we find your daughter, I'll take the money."

"Deal," she said.

CHAPTER ELEVEN

Only minutes ago, Carlin Reed had walked through the Hawkeye Mobile Home Park with his head held high. Figuring he needed to start somewhere, he knocked on the first door he came to.

A shirtless man with so much hair on his chest it looked like shag carpet answered, and Carlin got right to it, explaining that he was a journalist and was looking for a twelve-year-old boy who had allegedly witnessed an abduction and who lived there with his mother.

The man dug his fingers through the mass of hair and scratched as if it might help him remember, but it didn't.

Carlin figured it might very well be his lucky day when the man's wife, who was apparently listening from another room, shouted, "Tell him he's looking for Ethan Grant. The boy lives with his mother on Lot 34."

Carlin thanked the man before heading off to Lot 34. Again, he rapped his knuckles on the door and waited. He wasn't worried about the boy recognizing him because even if the kid thought he saw something from wherever he might have been hiding out that day, Carlin had since cut his hair, shaved, and was wearing a fitted suit.

On his drive there he'd thought about turning around and forgetting about the boy, but he quickly changed his mind because he didn't like the idea that he might always be looking over his shoulder, suspecting every kid he passed on the street. Better to know your enemy and keep an eye on him, he decided.

When the door opened, a fragile-looking woman who seemed as if she hadn't slept in years greeted him. He plastered on his most charming smile, then introduced himself as journalist Mike Hinch.

Her gaze went straight to his badge. "He's not here."

"May I ask where I might find him?"

"No."

When she went to close the door, he put a hand to it and stopped her. "I'll pay you a hundred dollars."

"He's with his dad for the summer. He's not here. If you don't leave, I'll have to call the police." She looked at his hand, waiting for him to remove it.

His jaw quivered, but he managed to control his tone as he said, "Thank you for your time." The second his hand dropped to his side, she slammed the door shut.

She was lying. He hated liars. He needed to think.

He sucked in a breath as he walked down the stairs and headed back the way he came, gravel crunching beneath his nice shoes. This was the first time he'd worn them. Now they were sullied.

As he exited the mobile home park, two women entered.

His body tensed. *Keep walking. Do not make eye contact.*

The older woman was Mary Cross, his future mother-in-law. Despite her pale face and dark circles, Mary Cross was a pretty lady. If not for her, he never would have met Ali, the love of his life. The first time he'd met the Cross family was when Mary had called him on his business phone to do some work. She'd been so trusting! She left him completely alone inside her house while she ran off to pick up her youngest daughter. Since nobody was home, he hadn't been able to resist taking a look around. There were pictures of Mary and her two daughters all over the house. The older daughter instantly caught his eye. She was the most beautiful girl he'd ever seen, which was why he'd set out to find her bedroom. The walls had been covered with artwork signed by Ali. She was talented. On a whim, he'd gone through her drawers and had taken a pair of silky pink panties with a hint of lace around the edges. He wasn't a pervert. No way. He just wanted something of hers.

Thankfully, he'd gotten back to work a few minutes before Mary Cross came home with both daughters in tow. Ali had hardly glanced his way before heading up the stairs to her bedroom, no doubt. Her little sister, Gracie, though, was outgoing, friendly, and curious. It hadn't taken much to get her talking about her family. She talked while he worked. That's when he'd learned all about Mr. Cross and how he was living with his secretary across town. Despite the freckles and the braces, Gracie was cute.

Once he got to his car, he slipped behind the wheel and drew in a breath. That was a close call. What if Mary Cross had recognized him and then saw the badge around his neck? What then? *Calm down. Nobody saw you.*

Before he buckled up, he saw the women heading back his way. His insides flip-flopped when he saw a boy come out of the trailer on Lot 34 and run after them. *What the hell?*

The kid had been home, after all.

His hands clasped tightly around the steering column as he watched the boy catch up to the two women and usher them over to a picnic table where the three of them huddled together, everyone leaning in close.

The thing that bothered him most was seeing the younger woman. What was she doing here, and why was she chatting it up with Mary Cross and a twelve-year-old boy who claimed he'd witnessed Ali Cross's abduction?

Although he couldn't recall the younger woman's name, he was 100 percent sure she was the same woman he'd recently seen on a local news channel. She'd been holding up a picture of a little girl who had been abducted five years ago. The story had immediately captured his attention because it so happened that he'd abducted Ali a week or so before he saw her on TV. She worked for a private investigator, and she'd talked about having a new lead, confident they were closing in on the girl's abductor after all these years.

Dani Callahan. That was the name of the woman whose daughter had been taken. What were the odds that they would find her daughter alive? he'd wondered when he saw the younger woman talking to the reporter.

Watching the three of them sitting at a picnic table made him feel dizzy. His chest tightened. What was he going to do about the boy? If Ethan Grant was telling the truth, how much had he seen, and how good of a look had he gotten? It made him crazy to think someone had been watching him. How was that possible?

He cursed under his breath and then leaned forward and hit the dashboard with his fist.

A few minutes later, all three of them stood up. When the women started walking toward the street, Carlin started the engine and drove off, careful to stay at the speed limit and keep his eyes on the road.

He felt a stiffness in his neck and jaw. He didn't like feeling as if they were onto him. As if he were the one being watched instead of the other way around.

CHAPTER TWELVE

Dani spent the morning sitting in her Highlander, staking out Cameron Bennington's home in Sacramento near Land Park. It was a two-story house with wide stairs that led to an inviting porch and front entry. She made a point to come at different times of the day, hoping to catch the perpetrator making his way inside. Cameron had assured her she would install more cameras inside the house.

In the back seat of her car, she always kept a large canvas bag with lots of zippered pockets filled with binoculars, a telescope, a tape recorder, and two-way radios for team surveillance, as well as snacks and water.

As she sat there alone, the quiet seeping into her bones, she found herself thinking of her journey to this moment in time. After Tinsley had been taken, Dani had worked closely with James Whitton, the lead detective on the case. Noting her frustration and impatience, it wasn't long before he suggested she put some of her passion for finding Tinsley into helping other parents find their children. He happened to have a friend at the time, a private investigator named Hugo Cavin, who was interested in selling his business. To be a private investigator in California she needed to be eighteen, complete a criminal background check, and have at least three years, or six thousand hours, of compensated experience in investigative work. Hugo and Detective

Whitton became her mentors. The next three years had flown by in a blur. Hugo had never been the hovering type, which forced Dani to learn everything the hard way—from her mistakes. She enjoyed it too. Working closely with parents of missing children was deeply satisfying. She could relate to their pain and also feel incredible joy when a child was found safe.

Everything seemed to fall into place. Before Hugo moved to Australia, leaving her on her own, he told her she was a natural and that she had an instinctive mind for this sort of work. And yet she couldn't help thinking that it was all for naught if she couldn't find Tinsley.

She glanced at her phone. It was ten forty-five. She needed to get to the courthouse to testify for a workers' comp case she'd investigated over a year ago. Ninety-nine percent of the time, she wasn't required to go to court. But these things happened.

She checked her messages, hoping Quinn had sent a text updating her on how things had gone with Mary Cross and Ethan—assuming Quinn had been able to find the boy. Nothing there. Readying to go, she set her phone aside and reached for her seat belt.

There was a knock on her window.

Startled, she let go of the belt, heard it whirring back into place, her hand across her heart. It was a man with his dog, a white lab. She pushed the power button on her Highlander so that she could get the window to open a bit.

"Hello. My name is Frank Petri. This is my dog, Sadie."

She smiled but said nothing, unsure about what he wanted.

"I've seen you in the neighborhood a few times now, and I thought I would come introduce myself and see if there was something I could help you with."

She sighed. A good Samaritan, keeping an eye out for his neighbors. There was usually one on every street, which was why she tried to change up where she parked and at what time of day she came to observe.

But this guy was obviously onto her.

"I'm doing a speed study," she said, a line she'd rehearsed.

"Where's your equipment? Don't you need radar of some type?"

"That will come later. For now I keep track of the average number of cars that drive by." *A do-gooder or just a nosy man?* she wondered. Her car was still running. She reached for her belt buckle.

"Don't mean to run you off," he said. "I really was just curious. Any chance I can talk you into going to Starbucks for a coffee or tea?"

The buckle on her seat belt clicked into place as she peered up at the man, trying to glean whether or not he was serious. Tall and on the thin side, he looked to be in his midfifties. Under different circumstances she might have actually considered going. The notion caused her to inwardly question her sanity. He was a stranger, and she was here on business, conducting surveillance of all things. And yet there was no denying that she was flattered by the gesture. She couldn't remember the last time a man had asked her out for coffee or lunch or a movie. "I really should go," she said, looking from him to his dog.

"If you return to finish your study, maybe we'll run into each other again," he said, stepping back, still standing in the middle of the road as she drove off.

She didn't know whether to laugh or cry. That her life had come down to this. The truth was, his invitation had frightened her at first, but not in a dangerous way—she wasn't afraid of him. But in a nervous, jittery way. No one had shown interest in her in so long that the idea of it felt foreign and downright weird.

Who was Dani Callahan?

She had no friends. No family.

Quinn was her friend, of course, but there were twenty years between them. If anything, she was more of a mother figure to Quinn. And then there was Matthew. Since their divorce, she could count the number of times she'd had a friendly chat with him on one hand. They were different people now.

———

An hour and a half later, she was headed back to the office. Her day in court had ended early after the attorney's claimant decided to settle.

Her phone rang, and she hit "Talk" when she saw the name on the console. It was Mimi Foster from RAYTEX.

"Hi, Dani. It's Mimi. I have information about the woman you were asking about. Her name is Rebecca Carr. According to Cheryl Max, head of accounting, Rebecca was a temporary worker at the time, which is a convenient and cost-efficient way to recruit and test out new workers before hiring them full time. I was able to look at her file. She was at RAYTEX for four months, then let go after a complaint was filed."

Dani kept her eyes on the road. "A complaint?"

"Yes. It had to do with her excessive flirtatious behavior."

"Wow. Okay. If I remember correctly, there seemed to be a lot of in-house dating going on at the time," Dani said. "Who was she flirting with?"

"Matthew."

Dani's skin tingled. "My Matthew?"

"Yes."

Dani was at a loss. "He never mentioned any of this back then. I would have remembered."

Mimi released a long, drawn-out sigh. "Listen. As far as I can tell it's all conjecture, but apparently the woman somehow managed to get her claws into Matthew."

"Were they having an affair?"

"Looking back, I remember hearing a rumor about Matthew and Rebecca, but I didn't take it seriously because I knew Matthew was a good man. You and Tinsley were all he ever talked about. I do recall being relieved when she was let go. I thought she was toxic. But after she left, I didn't think of her again."

Dani didn't know what to think. It was sort of a cruel head trip to think that he might have cheated on her when she thought he was such a loyal man. It was as if her ego had taken a hit. Rationally, it didn't make sense to care one way or another, but she did, and she knew she would have to ask Matthew about the woman the next time she saw him.

"I'm sorry. I should not have said anything."

"No," Dani said. "Don't be sorry. I came to you about this. Thank you for being so honest."

"I should get going," Mimi said. "Take care of yourself."

Dani disconnected the call. Her stomach roiled. If Rebecca Carr had meant nothing to Matthew, he would have told her what was going on at work at the time. After Tinsley was taken, they both acknowledged that their marriage had been slowly disintegrating for a while. But she'd never once considered that Matthew had ever cheated on her. It wasn't in his DNA. Or so she thought.

Unsure as to what this all meant, she pulled to the curb outside her agency, walked up the path to the entry door, and had slipped the key halfway into the keyhole when the door opened.

Strange. Did I leave it unlocked?

The first things she noticed when she stepped inside were papers scattered across both desks and the floor. Drawers had been riffled through, and the closet door had been left open. Someone had been in a hurry. Worried about Quinn, especially since she hadn't heard from her, Dani walked toward the kitchen, calling her name, and didn't get a response. Next, she headed for the door to the basement.

Dani's heart rate intensified at the thought that Quinn might have been caught off guard in the middle of a burglary. She wrapped her hand around the knob and opened the door. A black-clad figure stood at the top of the landing holding a piece of wood—no, not wood, the base of a lamp—and took a good, hard swing at her, the solid heaviness of the lamp's base making contact with her left temple.

Dani fell backward, weightless, with nothing to stop her from hitting the floor, blinded by a kaleidoscope of colors as she went down, down, down.

Chapter Thirteen

Relief flooded Ali Cross the moment Carlin set her on the bed, adjusted her pillows, and then took a step back. She felt nauseous from all the movement. Her foot throbbed, her arms and legs trembled.

He brushed his hands together as if he'd just loaded a sack of fertilizer into a truck instead of carrying her one-hundred-twenty-pound frame from the bathroom ten feet away.

"I might have to find you some crutches," he said with a light chuckle. "I used a wheelbarrow to get you from the van to the shed when you first arrived. You're much heavier than I thought."

She thought of Dylan and how he often scooped her up into his arms as if she were as light as a feather. Mom had no idea she and Dylan were "a thing." It wasn't worth telling her and risking being bombarded with "You're too young," "You're leaving for college and won't be able to concentrate if you're always thinking of him," "Men aren't worth the stress," and so on.

Ali had known Dylan since the second grade, but they had only been together for six months. He was the first guy who'd made her think twice about settling down someday and starting a family—not now, but ten years down the road.

"Hey. Earth to Ali."

She looked at him, noticing for the first time since he'd entered the room that he no longer wore a bandage over his wounded eye. Without blood and bruising she got a good look and saw that she'd completely missed her target. The puncture marks, now scabs, were mostly on his nose.

"I'm talking to you," he said.

"What?"

"You looked miles away. What were you thinking about?"

"My mom and my sister," she said. Another lie. "I miss them."

He looked skeptical but shook it off easily enough. "It would be better if you just forgot about them. I'm your family now."

Ignore him, she told herself. She couldn't listen to his constant chatter about her being "the one" and how she would come around soon enough. She couldn't let his fantasy world eat away at her. If she did, she'd lose hope, and without hope she wouldn't have the courage to go on. "When are you going to take me downstairs? I'm bored. There's nothing to do—no TV, books, or painting supplies."

"We'll talk about that later. Right now, I have to go to work and you need to rest. But don't worry," he said. "I won't be gone long." He snapped his fingers and then walked jauntily to the dresser, pulled open the bottom drawer, and reached inside. "Here," he said, walking back her way and handing her a copy of the Bible. "Mom left it here when she moved. Praise the Lord!" He laughed.

He looked proud of himself, and she wasn't sure why. Maybe because he'd found her something to read. Or maybe he just thought he was a funny guy. He leaned down and kissed her forehead as if she belonged to him, which in a way she absolutely did. She made sure not to cringe or make any movement at all. She didn't want to anger him.

He stood tall afterward, anchored his hands on his hips, and took a last look around the room before finally leaving, locking the door behind him.

She set the book on the bedside table and listened to his retreating footfalls—across a hallway, she assumed, and then down a flight of narrow stairs? It was a guess, but she needed to keep track of every little detail for when the time came to attempt another escape.

A few minutes later, there was no mistaking the sound of a door being opened and closed. She hardly took a breath until she heard what sounded like a creaky garage door roll open, followed by the loud whir of an engine before it too disappeared, leaving her in silence.

The first thing she did was toss the covers to one side and then gingerly slide her legs over the edge of the bed, letting her good foot stand on solid ground. When he'd taken her to the bathroom earlier, he'd let her shut the door. There was no lock. After flushing the toilet, she'd stood on her good leg. Two hops had gotten her to the sink, where she had washed her hands and splashed cold water on her face. The pain caused by that movement alone had caused a tear to escape and slide down her cheek as she bit down on the washcloth to stop herself from crying out.

For that reason she grabbed two pillows and dropped them on the ground so she could put one knee on each pillow and crawl around. Once she was on the floor, pillows in place, she moved across the room like a baby on all fours toward the dresser, the downy pillow protecting her foot and ankle. She pulled open the drawer, disappointed to see that it was empty. She looked around before heading for the gabled window facing the street, hoping she might be able to see the other house, the one with the tall pitched roof she'd spotted through the trees when Carlin had brought her from the shed to the house.

It took some doing, but she was able to pull herself up so that she was standing on her good foot. Figuring she would see a long and winding dirt driveway lined by an endless forest of trees, maybe a grassy field dotted with cows, she was shocked to see something else entirely. Homes with yards and driveways. Although the houses were set apart and some were only half-finished, a few of the homes appeared to be lived in. The road leading to Carlin's house was paved. The driveway looked like a million other driveways.

There was shimmering water in the distance. It couldn't be!

She blinked, leaned closer to the window. Her heart pounded in earnest as she made out what was definitely the American River.

She wasn't too far from home.

Her *real* home. The one she shared with the two people she loved most.

Swallowing a laugh, she wanted to jump with joy. Knowing she was so close to home filled her with optimism and gave her fresh hope. All this time, she'd thought he'd taken her to a remote area, somewhere deep in the woods where no one would ever find her.

As she continued to stare out the window, she took in every detail, including the eight-foot chain-link fence covered with poison ivy that surrounded the property. She would know poison ivy anywhere. She was allergic and avoided the plant at all costs.

Her heart sank.

Even if she had gotten through the front door after stabbing him with a fork, she never would have had time to scale the fence. She wasn't athletic, couldn't climb a tree if her life depended on it. And now with a bum foot, her odds of escaping had grown even slimmer.

She grabbed hold of the window frame. It was old, the paint peeling from the wood. She pushed upward as hard as she could, but the window wouldn't budge. After closer examination she realized it had been nailed shut.

It seemed he'd thought of everything.

She thought of the metal brackets she'd seen on the floor near the table when he'd fed her pancakes. The brackets had been on the walls in the hallway and on the floor in the bedroom too.

And then she thought of the other girlfriend he'd mentioned, and now wished she'd asked more questions about her. Maybe Ali wasn't the first "girlfriend" he'd brought home to meet Mother. And maybe she wouldn't be the last.

CHAPTER FOURTEEN

Dani sat in a hospital bed, feeling antsy, wishing she could get up and walk out of the place. She was fine. Ready to go home. But her doctor wanted to keep her overnight for observation, and she'd given in. The top of her head was wrapped in thick gauze. Apparently she'd taken a blow to the temple and had been unable to communicate when she'd been brought in by ambulance, unable to follow simple instructions like "Squeeze my hand" or "Open your eyes."

It was seven o'clock at night. Quinn was asleep in a chair by the window.

The last thing Dani remembered was opening the door leading to the basement. After that, much of the day was a mystery except for flashbacks of Quinn hovering over her, pleading with her to wake up.

And yet, she remembered what came before she was bashed in the head, including her phone call with Mimi Foster at RAYTEX. The entirety of their conversation was hazy, except for the part about Matthew and his rumored involvement with the woman named Rebecca.

The idea of Matthew betraying her in that way didn't compute. He wasn't the type. She was no longer in love with Matthew, so that wasn't an issue. So what was the problem? she asked herself.

No answer came. Nothing about the conversation or what happened afterward made any sense. The pounding in her head wasn't helping matters. She couldn't think straight.

There was a quick three-rap knock on the door to her private room before Detective Whitton entered.

Quinn's eyes opened and she straightened in her seat.

He nodded at Quinn as he made his way to Dani's bedside. "What sort of trouble have you gotten yourself into now?"

Dani managed a smile, but even that hurt.

Quinn jumped up and went to stand by Detective Whitton. "Do you know who this is?" she asked Dani.

Dani frowned. "Of course I do."

Quinn wouldn't let it go. "What's his name?"

"Detective James Whitton."

"And you remember who I am?" Quinn asked.

"What's this all about?" Dani asked.

"Please, just humor me. What's my name?"

"Quinn Elizabeth Sullivan."

Quinn's eyes narrowed. "Where do I live?"

"You live with your grandmother in East Sacramento on the same block as me. You drive a blue 1988 Lincoln Town Car. You're twenty-two. Shall I go on?"

Dani was surprised by the emotion she saw on Quinn's face.

Quinn grabbed her leather bag from the chair where she'd fallen asleep and then headed for the door. "I'll give you two some time alone."

And then she was gone.

"Poor girl," Detective Whitton said. "After she found you passed out at the top of the stairs, she called 9-1-1 and then called me. There was blood everywhere, and she couldn't get you to respond to her voice. Maybe I should go after her?"

"No," Dani said. "I think she's the one who needed time alone. She'll be fine."

"Well, let's talk about you, then." He gestured to the gauze around her head. "You got knocked in the head pretty good."

"I'm fine. Really. I only agreed to stay overnight out of an abundance of caution and because the doctor insisted."

"Do you recall what you were hit in the head with?"

"I have no idea."

"We believe the weapon was the base of a lamp that may or may not have come from the basement. My team took pictures and checked for fingerprints. No luck there," he said, "which means the perpetrator was wearing gloves." He scratched his chin. "Are you up to answering a few questions?"

"I don't remember much, but I'll try." Dani gestured toward the chair where Quinn had been sitting. "Have a seat. I don't think she'll be back for a while."

He pulled out a tiny black book and a pen and took a seat. "Did you see your attacker's face?" he asked, getting right to it.

She closed her eyes in hopes that would help her remember, but drew a blank. "Afraid not."

"Height? Male or female? Anything at all?"

She shook her head.

He slid his notebook and pen back into his shirt pocket. "Why don't you go ahead and tell me what you do remember."

"I returned to the office before eleven. The door was unlocked. I should have known something was up, but I figured I must have turned the key in the wrong direction on my way out. When I stepped inside, I saw papers everywhere. My first thought was that Quinn might have interrupted a burglary and could be hurt. I remember feeling panicked as I checked the kitchen area before thinking she might be in the basement. I opened the door and wham!" She raised her hands and then let them flop down to the bed. "Next thing I knew, I was in the emergency room, dazed and confused."

"Okay, let's back up a bit. Before you entered your office, did you see anyone hanging around? Any cars you didn't recognize parked in the vicinity?"

"No. I was on the phone. I didn't see anything unusual, but I wasn't paying attention."

"Any idea who might want to do you harm?"

At the same moment he asked the question, Quinn reappeared.

"I can't think of anyone," Dani said in answer to his question.

Quinn walked to the window overlooking the parking lot and sat on the wide ledge. "Go ahead," Quinn said. "Pretend I'm a fly on the wall."

Detective Whitton looked at Dani, and she told him it was fine.

"We don't think it was a burglary," he said, "but when you get back to the office, I'll need you to look through your things, make sure nothing is missing."

Dani nodded.

"What sort of cases are you working on?" he asked next.

"I have a few ongoing workers' comp cases. Nothing that stands out," Dani said. "Quinn and I are working with Ethan Grant on the Ali Cross case. It did cross my mind that someone might not like the idea of there being a potential witness."

"But why attack you?" Quinn asked.

"I wondered the same thing. But I also don't think the intruder broke into the office intending to hurt anyone. Judging by the open drawers and papers scattered about, I think it's obvious they were looking for something. Whoever it was, I surprised them, and they used whatever they could find to knock me out and escape. If they had come with the intention of doing me harm, I would think they would have brought a weapon."

Once again Detective Whitton pulled out his notebook and pen. After making a few notes, he looked up. "Anything else?"

"When you were at the office," Dani said, "I assume you saw the pictures and articles on the walls in the basement."

Detective Whitton nodded. "I did wonder what all that was about."

"Quinn has been collecting information on missing persons for years," Dani said. "A few days ago, I was in the basement when I found some old employee booklets, reports that Matthew's company puts together every year. Anyway, there was one I hadn't seen before that included a collage of pictures taken at a RAYTEX company picnic held at McKinley Park a week before Tinsley disappeared."

Detective Whitton and Quinn stared at her, waiting to see where this was going.

"In the collage were two pictures that caught my attention. In both pictures was a woman whom I thought looked a lot like me. In one she was talking to Matthew, and in the other she was running the face-painting booth, and the little girl she was working on happened to be Tinsley."

"Interesting," Quinn said.

"I thought so, which is why I scanned the page and sent it to an old friend at RAYTEX."

"Did she recognize the woman in the pictures?" Quinn asked.

"Yes. Apparently the woman came through a temp agency and worked at RAYTEX for four months. I wrote down her name on a notepad at work."

"And you think she may have something to do with your being bashed over the head?" Detective Whitton asked.

Dani thought about it for a second. "Now that I think about it, it's highly unlikely since I only just found out her name minutes before the incident. I did learn something that's been niggling, though."

"Go ahead," Detective Whitton said.

"It seems there were rumors that Matthew and the woman in the picture were having a fling, and she was let go around that same time."

"We need to find this woman and talk to her," Quinn said. "She could hold the missing piece to the puzzle."

"We'll get back to that later," Detective Whitton told Quinn after he made additional notes. "Let's stick with one thing at a time. Any other cases you're working on?"

Quinn did not look pleased.

"Cameron Bennington. She's a lawyer," Dani said. "She lives near Land Park. Apparently someone has been finding a way to get inside her house while she's at work. Whoever it is moves furniture around and eats her food."

"So weird," Quinn said.

Dani nodded in agreement. "I told her to install digital cameras, and for a month or two that seemed to do the trick. But now the intruder is back." Dani sighed. "This morning, I was doing a stakeout when a man walking his dog knocked on my window, startling me."

"What did he want?" Quinn asked.

"He wanted to know what I was doing." She waved a hand through the air. "Sorry. The man and his dog have no relevance to your question. My brain is foggy."

"You're fine," Detective Whitton said. "You must have brought him up for a reason. Did you get a name?"

She nodded. "Frank Petri."

A nurse entered then and started taking vitals, prompting Detective Whitton to put away his notebook before he pushed himself to his feet. "I'm going to take off now. I'll do a few drive-bys, make sure nobody is hanging around your office."

"I appreciate that."

He patted his breast pocket where he kept his notebook. "I'm also going to look into a few things. I'll let you know if I find anything."

"Thank you."

He looked over his shoulder at Quinn. "Are you staying?"

"Yes," she said. "I have a few questions for Dani too. I'll be in touch."

He smiled at Quinn and then said his goodbyes.

A few minutes after Detective Whitton left, the nurse finished what she was doing and exited the room.

Dani reached for her plastic cup and drank water through a straw, then straightened her bedcovers. Her gaze fell on Quinn, whose head was bent forward, her shoulders shaking enough to know that she was crying. "What's wrong, Quinn?"

Quinn looked up. Her eyes were red and puffy. "I know you need your rest," she told Dani, "but I need to know if you're okay . . . really okay."

"I'm fine. I really am. A slight headache is all."

"Seeing you there on the floor," Quinn said, holding a tissue to her nose. "So much blood. I couldn't get a pulse, and I thought you were dead." The tears streamed down her cheeks. "I can't lose you too."

"Oh, Quinn. I'm not going anywhere."

"But you don't really know that, do you?"

"I could get hit by a bus tomorrow or the day after, so in that sense you're right. I can't make any promises. But if this is about your mom leaving, Quinn, I can promise you I will never leave you. Never."

More tears came, and if the room wasn't spinning just the slightest bit, Dani would have gone to her, wrapped her arms around her, and held her tight.

"You are an amazing person," Dani went on, knowing she should have had a heart-to-heart with Quinn long before today. "You are smart, kind, and passionate. People make mistakes. Big ones and little ones, and there is nothing in the world that could convince me that your mom stayed away on purpose. You're special, Quinn. Something happened to stop her from returning or, at the very least, reaching out to you. I'm sure of it."

Quinn got to her feet, walked to Dani's side, and carefully wrapped her arms around Dani's upper body, then laid her head in the crook of Dani's neck. Dani held her close. Everything she had told Quinn was the truth. Knowing her story, knowing Quinn was hurting, had made it easy to connect with her over the years. They both had their own inner pain to deal with, but having each other made the world a brighter, better place.

Chapter Fifteen

After cautiously scanning the office for intruders with her pepper spray in hand, Quinn spent the morning cleaning and organizing the place, picking up papers scattered across the floor and organizing them as best she could. She then cleaned the fingerprint dusting material from both of their desks. Files had been messed with, but she and Dani would have to sort through all that later. Once everything was semiorganized and off the floor, she went to the kitchen area and grabbed a bucket and a mop. Although she could tell that Detective Whitton had cleaned up the worst of the blood, Quinn could still see a faint outline of its stain, and smudges near the door to the basement.

As she scrubbed the floor and the mop turned an ugly gray color, she thought of Dani and how awful she'd looked, lying in the hospital bed. Purplish half-moons had formed beneath swollen eyes. The top of her head, the part peeking out from thick bandages, had revealed tangled hair matted with dried blood. She'd looked a mess, but she was alive. It made Quinn's stomach churn to think she might have lost her.

Dani didn't know it, because Quinn had never told her as much, but Dani had saved her when she came into her life. Dani was a caring, gentle soul who only wanted to help people, but Quinn never allowed her to get too close. Quinn wanted to open up emotionally, but she was afraid. Afraid once she did, Dani would disappear just as her mother had done.

A knock at the door made her jump. Usually she and Dani left the door unlocked when they were here, but after what had happened, Quinn didn't feel comfortable and had locked it. Through the front window she saw Ethan. She set the mop in the bucket and went to the door to let him inside. "What's going on?"

"I was bored so I thought I would come see if you needed my help with anything." Ethan looked her over. "You look horrible."

"Thanks. I'm tired. I had a long night." She didn't need to explain further since she had texted him from the hospital.

He looked around the office. "Any idea who attacked Dani?"

Quinn shook her head. "Nobody knows."

"What's really weird," Ethan told her, "is that all day yesterday, I felt as if someone was watching me."

Chills washed over Quinn. Ethan didn't come across as paranoid. "Have you ever felt like you were being watched before?"

He shook his head. "It was after you and Mary Cross left. I had nothing to do so I rode my bike to Midtown." His eyes widened. "The hairs on the back of my neck would tingle. I'm not kidding. I kept looking over my shoulder, but nobody was ever there."

Quinn had been on edge ever since she'd found Dani lying in a puddle of blood yesterday. She wanted to tell Ethan to stay inside until they found Ali, but she knew that was ridiculous. They all needed to go on with their lives.

Easier said than done.

Quinn went to her desk to check her computer to see if any of Ali's friends had replied to messages she'd sent from the hospital, hoping to find someone willing to talk about the girl.

"Do you think Ali Cross is still alive?" Ethan asked.

"I hope so. I've been thinking that it's probably a good thing she hasn't been in the news lately."

"Why would that be a good thing?"

"Because if she is still alive, maybe whoever took her won't feel any pressure to kill her and dispose of her body."

Ethan grimaced. "You really believe that some maniac would think like that? I mean, if I were a psycho and I was going to abduct someone, I would have it all planned out. If I had half a brain, I would figure the media and the police were going to be on the lookout, and I wouldn't care because all of that comes with the territory."

"What if it wasn't preplanned, though? What if this guy just happened to be delivering a package or whatever, and then he sees this girl all by herself and he doesn't think at all? He just pounces, shoves her into the back of his van, and takes off."

"If that's the case," Ethan said, "then my guess is he's already killed her."

"It doesn't do us any good to speculate. We need to assume she's alive."

Ethan sighed. "Yeah. She's got to be alive."

"This is great," Quinn said after she read a message on her computer.

"What is it?"

"I messaged some of Ali Cross's friends on social media last night, asking if they would mind answering a few questions. Natalie Chapman just wrote back." Quinn read Natalie's reply again, glanced at the time, jumped to her feet, jotted down an address, and grabbed her purse. "I've got to go if I want to catch her before she goes to cheer practice to help train next year's squad."

"Mind if I go along?"

She wasn't sure how Dani would feel about it, but what harm could it do?

"I won't say a word," Ethan told her. "I promise."

"Okay, but we have to go right now."

Ethan followed her out the door and then waited next to her car as she locked up.

Once Quinn was in the car, she pulled up a navigation app on her iPhone and typed in Natalie's address.

It took only thirteen minutes to get to Natalie's house, a two-story Victorian in Curtis Park off Fifth Avenue. It was white with bright-blue trim. Quinn thought about asking Ethan to stay in the car, but as soon as she'd shut off the engine, he'd jumped out and was now following her up the steps to the front porch.

Quinn knocked and waited.

When the door opened, she recognized Natalie Chapman from all the selfies posted on Instagram.

"Hi," Natalie said, her voice cheerful. "You must be Quinn."

"I am. Nice to meet you."

"I'm sorry I don't have much time." Natalie's gaze fell on Ethan. "Don't I know you?"

Ethan flipped his hair out of his eyes. "Is your brother Eric?"

She smiled. "Yes! That's it! I knew I recognized you." She opened the door wider and told them to come inside. "We're still waiting for one more girl on the squad before we head out. You might as well talk to all of us at once."

"Was Ali a cheerleader?" Quinn asked as she and Ethan followed Natalie deeper into the house.

"No," she said with a laugh. "I tried to talk Ali into trying out, but she prefers to spend her time with books and her artwork."

"I saw some of her paintings," Quinn said. "She's talented."

"Yeah. She's smart and pretty and . . ." Her voice hitched. "I just can't believe she's missing. You're a private investigator, right?"

"I'm working with an investigator," Quinn told her. "It'll take me a few years to earn the title."

"Do you think you'll find her?"

"I hope so."

The house was an open-concept design with high ceilings. It was extraordinarily clean. The carpeted floors looked as if they had just been vacuumed, and the granite counters in the kitchen gleamed as they walked past.

Once they got to a family room, Natalie introduced Quinn and Ethan to three other girls, who were all dressed in various workout clothes.

"Quinn just wants to ask a couple of questions about Ali. Once Rachel arrives, we'll have to go or we'll be late."

"Hey, Ethan," a blonde with a high ponytail said. "What are you doing here? Don't you have fires to start and car parts to steal?"

Ethan merely smiled. He didn't look nervous or scared or even angry by her words.

Everyone else ignored her.

The brunette in the corner said, "My mom told me that Ali ran away."

"She didn't run away," Ethan said. "I saw a man shove her into the back of his van and drive off."

There was a collective gasp.

"No evidence has been found," Quinn told them. "Although we are treating Ali Cross's case as an abduction, I would like to know if Ali talked to any of you about running away."

"Not really," another girl said. She smiled. "I'm Stacy."

"Hi, Stacy. Did you know Ali well?"

"Definitely. Since the second grade. Whenever I would go to Ali's house, she and her mom would argue. Like all the time. I know Ali was eager to go to college so she wouldn't have to listen to her mom bitch all the time."

"She did run away once before," Natalie said, "but she told me that it was a mistake because of how it affected her little sister, Gracie."

"I remember that too," the brunette said. "I really don't think she would do that to Gracie again."

"We already talked to the police about all this, you know," the blonde told Quinn.

"But we don't mind talking to you too," Natalie said.

Quinn looked at her notes. "Did Ali ever, throughout all the years you've all known her, talk about being followed or maybe watched?"

"By a creeper?" Stacy asked, eyes wide.

"By anyone at all," Quinn said.

"Well," Natalie said, "she does get a lot of attention wherever she goes, so in a way she's always being watched."

"Remember that Brent dude?" the brunette asked the other girls. "He was a senior when we were all sophomores. He used to wait for her in the parking lot and then plead with Ali to let him take her home."

"I do remember that," Stacy said. "She always told him no."

"I forgot about him." Natalie looked at Quinn. "I was with her once when he was begging her to get in his car, and she told him 'No, thank you' and his smile disappeared instantly. I swear his face contorted—slanted brows, flared nostrils. I do remember being scared."

"Do you remember his last name?" Quinn asked.

Stacy scrolled through her phone. "Here he is. Brent Tarone. Looks like he's in some sort of heavy metal band now."

Stacy got up and walked over to Quinn to show her the picture and information she'd pulled up on Brent Tarone.

"What happened after Brent graduated from high school?" Quinn asked. "Did he leave her alone?"

"I think he just disappeared for a while," Natalie said.

"He did call her once," the brunette chimed in. "We had just started our senior year. It was totally out of the blue. Ali had no idea how he'd gotten her number, but she blocked him, and that was the last I heard of him."

The doorbell rang, and they all jumped up and started collecting their matching cardinal-red-and-white duffel bags with a lion's paw print on the side. Quinn thanked them for their help, and she and Ethan walked with them to the door.

"If I think of anything else," Natalie said to Quinn, "I'll message you." She glanced at Ethan. "I'll tell Eric you said hi!"

Ethan managed a tight smile. "Great."

"Have you talked to Dylan Rushdan?" Stacy asked, coming up from behind and following them to the sidewalk. "I know it's supposed to be a secret, but he's the one Ali was spending most of her time with before she disappeared."

"Thanks," Quinn said. "He's on my list of people to talk to."

Once they were back in the car, Quinn put on her seat belt and asked, "Are you okay?"

"Yeah, why wouldn't I be?"

"I don't know. That one girl was sort of mean to you. I wasn't sure if she hurt your feelings."

He chuckled. "It would take a lot more than that to make me feel bad. I know who I am, and I'm not the horrible kid everyone thinks. Yes, I've done some stupid things. And yes, my life is fucked up. My mom is fucked up. But she's doing her best and so am I."

Quinn was impressed and envious at the same time. Ethan was only twelve, and yet despite his struggles, he came across as confident and self-assured. He knew who he was, and so it didn't matter what others thought of him. He'd never known his father, and he'd spent half of his short life with strangers. And yet it seemed he'd come to terms with the life that was his, had made peace with it.

She turned on the engine and merged onto the street. In the rearview mirror she could see the girls they had just left, all piling into an SUV. So many people in the world, she found herself thinking. So much pain, and yet everyone dealt with that pain differently. "I guess everyone has a story," Quinn murmured, cutting into the silence.

"What do you mean?"

"Just that there are a lot of people out there who have been through tough times. Look at Dani. Her only child. Taken."

"And what about you?" he asked. "What's your story?"

She didn't like telling her story because each time she did, the emotions of loss, anger, and grief hit her hard. "In a nutshell, one day my beautiful and loving mom was helping me with my homework and telling me to clean my room, and the next day she was gone. Poof! Just like that."

"How old were you when she left?"

"Fifteen." She kept her eyes on the road as she talked. "Two years later, my dad was diagnosed with cancer so we moved in with my grandmother. Dani moved to the neighborhood at the same time, which was weird because I had just started following Tinsley Callahan's abduction."

"That's a crazy coincidence."

"Well, my mom is the reason I started keeping track of missing persons. I wanted to find her. Grandma said I was in denial, though, since I couldn't wrap my mind around the idea that Mom had left on purpose. No random visits. No phone calls." A heavy lump settled in her stomach.

"Did your dad have any idea where she might have gone?"

"Nope. But I was determined to find her. Nothing was going to stop me."

"So did you find her?"

Quinn sighed and shook her head. "It's hard to find someone who doesn't want to be found."

"Makes sense. So how is your dad doing?"

"He died six months after his diagnosis."

"That sucks."

"Yeah, and then Grandma had a stroke, and Dani, who had just moved into the neighborhood, brought me to her home for a few weeks. She was great. She didn't ask too many questions. She just let me be me. When I was on a stakeout with her, I picked up her camera and started shooting. It was exciting to see what different angles and lighting could do to a photo. I started noticing details of buildings—all the different colors and the intricacies of the smallest things, even a mere flower.

Things I hadn't been paying attention to because I was so wrapped up in all the bad stuff. Anyway, working with Dani was the best thing that ever happened to me."

There was a long pause before he said, "I get that you like Dani, but it sounds to me like you need to let go of the anger you're holding inside."

She chuckled. "I have no idea what you're talking about, Mr. Psychologist."

"I think you do."

The kid was getting on her nerves. "Okay, sure. Maybe you're right. I'm angry that Mom left. Most nights I hardly sleep. I have good days and bad days, but no matter how hard I try, I'll never be able to forgive her."

Ethan shrugged. "Go ahead, then—keep playing the role of victim, but all you're doing is giving the person that isn't even in your life the power to control you. You'll never be happy."

"I don't deserve to be happy."

"That's bullshit."

"Why?"

"Everyone deserves to be happy. But it's your choice," he said matter-of-factly, as if he didn't really care what she did or didn't do.

Ethan's phone rang and he picked up the call, said, "Yeah, yeah," and then hung up and slipped his phone back into his pocket. "Mom needs me to help her clean houses. If you could pull over and drop me off, I can hitchhike home."

"No way."

"It's not a big deal. I do it all the time."

"Not going to happen. Besides, you told me earlier that you thought you were being watched."

"I'm not a little kid."

"I didn't say you were."

He crossed his arms. "I've been taking care of myself my entire life."

"Who taught you about forgiveness?"

"I taught myself."

Quinn let it go. There was no point in saying anything. He had a chip on his shoulder, and she didn't blame him. He *had* been taking care of himself, and he didn't want anyone acting like they knew what was best for him. She knew the feeling. It sucked. Because deep down, everybody wanted to know that someone cared.

Chapter Sixteen

Dani climbed out of the taxi, paid the driver, and then slowly made her way up the walkway leading to her house. It was nearly two in the afternoon. The sky was a cloudless blue and the sun was out, its rays warming her back. Under any other circumstances she might have appreciated such a beautiful day.

Yesterday's attack had left her with blurred vision. Well into the night, she'd felt nauseous and disoriented. Now she just felt bruised and battered. Even her neck ached.

She used her key to unlock the door and pushed her way inside. She set her purse on the small table by the door, then shut and locked it. Usually when she returned home after being at work all day, she felt relaxed, safe.

Not today.

With her tiny canister of pepper spray in hand, she listened closely for any unusual sounds before making her way into the living area. She opened a coat closet and then inspected the pantry in the kitchen. She looked inside the guest room and checked the closet before making her way to her bedroom. Nobody was under the bed or in the closet or in the bathroom. She locked the bedroom door just the same, then walked into the bathroom and turned on the hot water in the shower.

While the water heated, she stripped off her clothes and then found a pair of scissors and took her time removing the tape and gauze around her head. Her face was swollen and discolored. She looked like a distant cousin of Frankenstein. She had always bled more easily than most. She gingerly brushed her fingertips over the ten small stitches at the side of her head near her left ear, where they had shaved her hair. Her doctor had said she was lucky because it could have been much worse.

She walked into the shower and fiddled with the faucet until the temperature was just right. The warm water felt good against her back as she carefully washed her hair, her head tilted to one side so she could stay away from her wound but also get all the blood out of her hair. It wasn't until she was toweling herself off that dizziness set in, forcing her to make her way to the bed, where she lay down. As she stared at the ceiling, the image of the intruder swinging an object at her made her cringe. What if Quinn had returned to the office before her and had been the one who was attacked?

The thought sickened Dani.

First thing tomorrow, she would go to the store and purchase a set of digital cameras and maybe look into installing a new heavy-duty lock at the office.

Her thoughts shifted to the attacker. What had they been looking for?

Whoever it was must have heard her come in, found the lamp, and waited. If Dani had been smart, she would have called the police first or at least readied her pepper spray. But she'd never expected to find someone waiting behind the door. Who had hit her and why? Her mind swirled with speculation.

Fifteen minutes passed before she finally slid off the bed and pulled on a pair of soft sweatpants and a comfortable T-shirt. It took her ten minutes to comb out her hair before she walked to the kitchen to make some tea.

The sound of her doorbell sent her into a tizzy. She raced back to the bedroom to find her pepper spray, the quick movement making her feel nauseous.

The doorbell sounded again.

She peeked out the bedroom window and saw Matthew's car parked in her driveway. *Damn.* She wasn't in the mood to talk to anybody, especially her ex-husband. By the time she reached the door, he'd hit the ringer for the third time.

Exasperated, she swung open the door. "Really? Three times?"

The second he saw her face, his mouth fell open. "What happened? Are you okay?"

For a split second she'd forgotten about her bruised face and partially shaved head. "I've been better."

When she first peeked out the window and saw his car, she'd figured he must have heard about the attack. But that didn't seem to be the case. He'd obviously come to talk to her about something. "Would you like to come inside?"

"Okay. If you're sure?"

After she shut the door, she led him into the kitchen and offered him some tea since she'd already set the kettle on the burner. She pulled two random mugs from the cupboard, tossed in a tea bag, and poured the water, not waiting for the kettle to whistle.

She followed his gaze, which had settled on one of the mugs that said BEST MOM IN THE WORLD! Matthew and Tinsley had given it to her on her first Mother's Day. "Sweetener?" she asked.

"No, thanks."

She slid the plain white mug his way and then took her tea to the family room. "I need to sit down."

He followed her and took a seat on the ottoman across from her. "What happened to you?"

She gave him the quick version. The papers scattered about her office. How her worry about Quinn overtook all else as she opened the door to the basement, and bam. Lights out.

"Who would do such a thing?"

"I have no idea. The police are looking into it. Why are you here, Matthew?"

He squirmed a bit before finally spitting it all out. "I heard through the grapevine that you were talking to some of the girls at work about some random photos taken at a RAYTEX company picnic."

When he didn't go on, she said, "I called Mimi about a collage of pictures in the Annual Employee Report. Pictures taken at the last RAYTEX picnic I attended before Tinsley disappeared. In one of the photos you were talking to a woman I didn't recognize. In another, the same woman was painting Tinsley's face at one of the booths." Dani watched him closely, looking for signs of guilt.

"Why didn't you just ask me?"

"Because you've made it abundantly clear that you think our beautiful Tinsley is gone forever and that you want me to let it go. I wasn't in the mood for another lecture."

He hadn't touched his tea. His elbows were propped on his knees, his fingers entwined as he stared at the floor. She knew him well enough to know that he was stringing words together in his head, perhaps words to tell her to back off without being too harsh, considering her condition.

"There's more," Dani said.

His head came up. Instead of curious, he looked exasperated, as if he regretted stopping by and would prefer not to hear more about the pictures or Dani's fixation with finding Tinsley. But she didn't care.

"You no longer have any hold on me, Matthew. After the divorce, I thought we would be friends, but now, looking back, I don't know what I was thinking. We've never been on the same page. I wanted more children. You didn't—"

"That's not true," he said, cutting her off. "I just didn't have the energy to go through years of fertility treatments. And I'm still not willing to spend my life focused on one thing to the detriment of all else. There's a beautiful world out there, Dani. When was the last time you went to a park or a museum or had dinner with a good friend?"

"*Focused on one thing?* You mean our daughter, don't you? Do you think you're the only one who sacrificed to have Tinsley? When you put your foot down after we had Tinsley, saying you were not willing to use fertility options again, I was devastated. But I loved you, and I was determined to make our marriage work. I quit my job, a job I loved, so that I could watch my only child take her first steps. But Tinsley was never the *only* person I thought about. I thought about you too. I wanted you to be happy. I did your laundry, ironed your shirts, kept the house clean, did all the shopping, and made sure we had a date night every month. And now I am told that you and the woman in the picture were involved somehow. Is that true?"

His eyes widened, a deer caught in the headlights.

She'd known him long enough to know that look. Something had happened between him and the woman. "No wonder you're so upset that I won't let this go." She set her mug on the table, then leaned forward. "What else are you hiding from me, Matthew?"

His chin dropped, and he rubbed both hands over his face. When he finally looked up, he said, "You know I would never have betrayed you in such a way. Rebecca Carr was a flirt, hell-bent on getting the attention of any man that would look her way. That's why she was let go. She was a distraction."

Rebecca Carr. That was the name Mimi had given her on the phone. And yet she didn't have to say the name aloud for Matthew to remember it, even after all these years. He had never been good at remembering names, not unless the person meant something to him or left an impression. He kept rubbing his eyes and his face. He could hardly make eye contact.

"On the day Tinsley was taken, her teacher said that the woman who took our daughter not only looked like me but also that Tinsley seemed to know her, even looked excited to see her. Our daughter walked away with the woman, hand in hand, which tells me she knew this person or had at least met her."

Dani stared at Matthew, waiting for him to see the correlation. Why wasn't he jumping up, angry that this woman may have had something to do with their daughter's abduction?

This time when Matthew looked at her, he shook his head as if Dani had lost her mind.

"Who is she, Matthew?"

"I already told you. Rebecca Carr. That's all I know." He sighed. "You're grasping at straws."

Dani crossed her arms. "What happened to her after she left RAYTEX? Where did she go?"

"My guess is as good as yours."

"That's all you have to say about the matter?"

"I'm worried about you, Dani."

Her face softened. "If that's true, if you care at all about me, you'll help me find Rebecca Carr so I can question her. That's all I want to do. Just ask her a few questions."

Matthew stood, his arms dropping to his sides in defeat. "I give up. I'm done trying to save you from yourself."

"What does that even mean?"

"You're in denial. Intent on spending the rest of your life looking for ghosts."

"I don't have a choice," Dani said. Her head tilted to one side. "Don't you feel an overwhelming sense of injustice by what happened?"

He said nothing.

"When Tinsley disappeared," Dani told him, "all my unfulfilled dreams vanished with her. I lost a vital part of me. And the worst part is I feel responsible."

"Dani," he said. He stepped closer, as if he meant to offer her comfort. "I wish it wasn't so, but Tinsley is gone and she isn't coming back."

"Please go." Dani pointed toward the door. The only reason he'd come was because he'd been upset that she had reached out to his coworkers. As far as his relationship with Rebecca Carr, she wasn't sure what to think.

The minute he left, Dani grabbed her laptop and brought it to the family room. She logged on to one of her favorite pay databases and typed in Rebecca Carr's name. Judging from the photos she'd seen, she guessed Rebecca's age range to be between thirty-five and forty, which matched the age given by Forensics based on the video provided by the school on the day Tinsley was taken.

All she had was a name and approximate age and height. Hair color could easily be changed. She sipped her tea as she waited for the database to compile a list. It didn't take long. There were hundreds of Rebecca Carrs in the US alone. But they were all the wrong age or they had never lived in California. It was as if Rebecca Carr had never existed.

She pulled up another website that would allow her to check public records. If Rebecca had an arrest record or even a speeding ticket, she would pop up.

Two hours later, Dani's eyes blurred and her head throbbed.

Was Matthew right? Was she merely chasing ghosts?

She leaned her head back against the couch and shut her eyes.

Are you sure you know what you're getting yourself into? Those words had been the first thing PI Hugo Cavin had asked her when she'd expressed interest in buying the agency from him. He'd also said, *The job requires diligence and persistence.*

She sat up.

Goose bumps washed over every part of her. Sometimes, like now, she felt Tinsley's presence. It was as if she were pushing her to keep going, telling her to never give up. Dani wondered if all parents felt that when their child went missing.

Then she did something she'd never done before. She grabbed her phone, looked through her contacts, and called Hugo. When he didn't answer, she waited for the beep and then hung up. It was a dumb idea. She had tackled insurance fraud, infidelity, and corporate impropriety. She could do this.

CHAPTER SEVENTEEN

After dropping off Ethan at the mobile home park, Quinn made a phone call. Dylan Rushdan, a senior at McClatchy High School and Ali's boyfriend, according to Ali's little sister, picked up on the first ring.

"Hi, Dylan. My name is Quinn Sullivan. I'm working with a private investigator, Dani Callahan, and I was hoping we could meet. I have some questions regarding Ali Cross."

"I've already talked to detectives."

"Please," she said. "I promise I won't take up too much of your time."

"I'm taking classes at Sacramento City College, West Sacramento Center on West Capitol Avenue. If you want to meet me in front of the library in thirty minutes, I can spare a few minutes."

"That's great," Quinn said. "I'll be there. Look for the brunette wearing jeans and a white T-shirt."

"That narrows it down," he said with a laugh.

"I'll find you," she said. "I've seen your picture on social media."

"Then you already know everything there is to know about me."

"True, that. I'll see you soon."

Thirty minutes later, right on schedule, she spotted Dylan Rushdan standing in front of the library entrance. He was even better looking in person. Tall with dark curly hair and a nice square jaw. She waved as she got closer.

He smiled.

"We can talk right over there if you want to sit down," he said, pointing to a small grouping of tables and chairs.

Once they were seated, he said, "I hate to rush you, but I've only got five to ten minutes, tops."

"Then I'll be quick." She pulled out her notebook and pen.

"I've already talked to the police," Dylan said, "and I really don't have anything useful to tell you. If I did, they would have already found her."

She nodded, feeling the time pressure. "According to Ali's sister, Gracie, you and Ali were dating. Is that right?"

He nodded. "Ali didn't want her mom to know, but yes. We've been friends forever, but things got serious about six months ago. I love Ali and she loves me."

"Do you know if anyone had been bothering Ali—you know, before she went missing?"

"Bothering her?"

"Yes. For instance, did she ever mention anyone following her or refusing to leave her alone?"

"No. She would have told me."

"Did she have any enemies at school?"

"Not that I know of. She's a sweet girl who has nothing bad to say about anyone. Everybody loves Ali."

"I talked to some of her friends, including Natalie and Stacy. They mentioned a guy named Brent Tarone. They said there was a time when he wouldn't leave Ali alone."

"I forgot about Brent. It's true that he was obsessed with Ali, but he's harmless."

"How can you be so sure?"

"Well, for starters, he's married with a child on the way."

Quinn's eyes rounded. "Seriously? How old is he?"

"He was nineteen when he graduated, so my guess is twenty-one or twenty-two now."

Quinn didn't like spitting out the questions, but she knew Dylan would need to go soon. "Did Ali have a job? After school or on weekends?"

"No. Her job was basically watching her little sister while her mom was working." He looked at the time on his phone. "I should go."

"Just two more questions," she said. "Do you think Ali ran away from home?"

"No. I don't." His eyes watered. "Sorry. I don't mean to get emotional; it's just that I really don't know what to do or how to act. I feel like a zombie most days, taking classes here, working at Starbucks, doing chores at home. I keep expecting Ali to call me or show up at my house." He inhaled.

"What about the 'big fight' with her mother everyone is talking about?"

He shook his head slowly. "Ali has been fighting with her mom for years. She was excited about going away to college. She loves her sister. And her mom too, for that matter." He stood. Instead of just rushing off he said, "I'm sorry I'm not much help. It's frustrating."

"What is?"

"Feeling so useless. Not being able to do anything but wait and hope they find her."

She nodded. "Do you mind if I call you again if I have any further questions?"

"Call or text anytime. If there's anything I can do to help, let me know."

"Thanks. I appreciate it."

He swung his backpack onto his back and walked away.

Ali was a lucky girl, Quinn thought before the irony hit her like a brick to the head.

Chapter Eighteen

It was almost dark by the time Carlin saw Dylan Rushdan riding his bike toward him in River Walk Park. Once the sun began to set, it got cold fast. Carlin was shivering. The last group of students had passed by twenty minutes ago. He'd started to think maybe Dylan Rushdan had skipped class.

But here he was, coming his way, moving fast.

Carlin tugged on the wire he'd already secured to the tree across from him and held tight. The seconds ticked by until Dylan Rushdan's front tire made contact with the wire and sent the poor boy flying through the air.

With little time to get the job done, Carlin raced across the gravel path and cut the wire loose, then tossed it aside. Just as quickly, he hurried to Dylan Rushdan's side and held out a hand to help him up. "Whoa, man. Are you okay?"

Dylan was on his back. He looked dazed, but he took Carlin's hand and let him help him to his feet.

Dylan brushed himself off. "What the hell was that?"

Carlin shrugged. "I don't know. One minute you were speeding by, and the next you were flying through the air. Must have hit a rock."

He gave Dylan a minute to catch his breath before he pointed a finger at Dylan and wagged it at him. "I know you, don't I?"

"No," Dylan murmured. "I don't think so."

"No. I recognize you," Carlin said. "You're dating Ali Cross, aren't you?"

Dylan frowned. "Who told you that?"

"Ali Cross's sister, Gracie, did. I was doing some work at the house. Ali's little sister is quite the chatterbox."

"Yeah, we're dating." Dylan Rushdan looked around as if he was just noticing that it was dark and cold and he was talking to a complete stranger out in the middle of nowhere. He frowned. "Did you set this whole thing up?"

"What whole thing?"

"My bike. Something tripped up my front wheel." Dylan looked past Carlin, peering into the dark, trying to see the area where his bike had flipped over. Dylan then leaned down, grabbed hold of the handlebar, and pulled his bike upright.

"Ali told me the two of you were just friends."

"What is your fucking problem? She loves me and I love her, and someday we're going to get married. Does that answer your question?"

Carlin felt his blood pressure building and rising. All he could hear was a pounding in his ears. Ali had lied to him. As he reached into his back pocket, he counted to three.

"Who are you, anyway?" Dylan asked. "When did you talk to Ali?"

Carlin looked into his eyes as he plunged the knife into Dylan's chest, holding tight and staggering forward as Dylan struggled to stay upright. The knife was new and sharp, but it still surprised him how easily the blade had penetrated shirt and flesh. He'd never stabbed anyone before. It felt like a dream—fantastical and odd.

The surprise on Dylan's face was borderline comical. Despite all the warning signs, the big good-looking guy with the square jaw and brawny muscles had obviously thought he was safe. As soon as he felt Dylan Rushdan starting to lose his bearings, Carlin let go of the knife's handle. After Dylan collapsed, he pulled a rag from his back pocket and quickly wiped off his fingerprints. He stared at Dylan's face, surprised by how easy that had been. And fun. "You're not going to marry Ali Cross, after all."

Carlin's body thrummed with excitement. He wanted to take a picture for Ali but figured that wouldn't be a smart move. He was about to walk off when he noticed how close Dylan's body was to the steep slope that touched the river's edge. If he could roll him over the side, he might be able to buy himself a little more time to get out of sight. Bending forward, he wrapped the same rag as before around his hand and rolled the body toward the edge. One final push with the toe of his shoe sent Dylan Rushdan careening toward the water. He tossed the bike over the edge too. Nobody was around, so he ran back to the tree and cut the wire loose. As he walked away, he twisted the wire into a manageable ball, whistling as he went, eager to get home and tell Ali the good news. She'd probably be relieved to know she no longer had to lie to him about Dylan. Maybe he'd wait until morning, make her a stack of golden pancakes with crispy bacon on the side, and tell her then.

Chapter Nineteen

Early the next morning Dani jolted awake, sitting up in bed so fast her head spun.

She had an idea.

After the room stopped spinning, she slid off the mattress and made her way to the guest room that she also used as a home office. It was still dark out and she flicked the lights on as she went along. Once she was sitting at her desk, she began opening and closing drawers until she found what she was looking for. It was a hard drive from when she'd backed up all of her and Matthew's combined files and documents before the divorce, afraid she might need access. Fortunately the divorce had gone smoothly, each of them ending up with half of their combined assets.

She booted up her laptop. When the screen brightened, she inserted the hard drive into the USB port and gave it a few minutes to restore document files. When that was done, she went to File Explorer and then to the PDF files, where she pulled up paperless statements.

While they were married, Matthew had insisted on being in charge of paying the monthly bills, which included credit cards. Most of the higher-ups at RAYTEX were issued a credit card to use for business expenses, including hotels and dinners with clients. But the what-if question that had popped into her head and awakened her this morning was, What if Matthew had been intimate with this temporary employee? Would he have used a credit card to take her out to dinner or to a hotel?

If she did find an odd dinner charge, what then?

Would it help her locate Rebecca Carr?

The only thing a dinner charge would tell her was that Matthew probably did have a fling with this mystery woman and that he had lied about it. And for some reason, the notion hurt more than it probably should. Dani had always thought of Matthew as her friend. Even after all they'd been through together. But she'd never once thought him a liar.

With renewed urgency, wishing to know one way or another, she decided to concentrate on the four months that Rebecca Carr had worked at RAYTEX, plus the month before and after—March through August.

Matthew had been adamant when they married that they keep debt to a minimum, afraid too many credit cards would ramp up their spending. For that reason they'd had only two major credit cards: Discover and Capital One Visa. He requested paperless statements, and every month he would download the statement, pay the bill, and then file it all away under the year and month. It was all orderly and tidy, and because it was digital and kept on a portable hard drive, there was no reason to toss statements after a certain time period.

She began by clicking on the Capital One subfolder and opening the April statement. Right away she noticed a couple of regular charges from Sacramento Natural Foods Co-op, where she used to shop for groceries and still did. She noticed a charge at Mulvaney's B&L, a Sacramento restaurant that served New American fare in a converted firehouse. A personal favorite. She skipped over that charge since that was her birthday month and he took her there every year. There were charges for haircuts and a doctor's visit. And a few charges that looked wonky mostly because they used their legal corporate name instead of the actual business name. A quick internet search sorted things out as she went along.

After a while, her stomach grumbling, she had finally finished with the Capital One card and had found absolutely nothing.

She'd been so hopeful, bordering on certain, that if Matthew had been involved with someone she would find some odd charge from that time. She still had Discover charges to go through, but first she needed some caffeine and something to eat.

She went to the kitchen, where she got the coffee going, then back to the bedroom, where she slipped on a pair of jeans and a T-shirt. A quick glance in the mirror gave her a scare. The bruises around her eyes were no longer purple; they were yellow and green and two shades of red. Her hair, shaved around the ear, looked like she'd been trying for a cool new hairstyle and missed the mark. She tied back her hair with a rubber band and left it at that; the mirror was not her friend today.

After eating a piece of buttered toast and gulping down her first cup of coffee, she felt like a new person. By the time she returned to her desk, she was wound up and ready to get back to work. The April charges on the Discover card were few, but the month of May was another story.

There were charges at restaurants she'd never heard of before. When she looked them up on the web, she was 100 percent certain she'd never been there. A lot of these mysterious charges all happened to be within a seven-day time period. She analyzed each one, using the internet to verify the establishment: Ginochio's Kitchen, Lucas Wharf Restaurant & Bar, Gourmet Au Bay. The list went on. All within a five-mile radius of Bodega Bay. The biggest charge was for the inn where they had stayed. Or at least *he* had stayed.

Thinking back to that time, she used a calendar from that year to make notes of where she had been and what she had been doing. She recalled Matthew going on a business trip.

Think, Dani. Think.

She sipped her coffee, then circled Tinsley's birthday.

Los Angeles.

Her pulse rate accelerated. LA was where his business trip had been that year. She remembered because he'd made such a fuss about it at the time. He didn't want to go. Didn't want to miss Tinsley's fifth birthday. Or so he said.

The memories came rushing back in a flood of images and pieces of conversation. Matthew had complained about traffic and crowds while he packed, wishing it had been a coastal event so that they, his family, could take a much-needed vacation. She remembered suggesting he tell his boss to have someone else go in his place, but Matthew insisted it was important he be there to represent RAYTEX.

Matthew had lied to her. There was no question in her mind that he'd been having an affair. She had used every database she had to find Rebecca Carr. Was that even the woman's real name?

Dani was itching to call Matthew, tell him she knew about his week in Bodega Bay, but then decided she'd rather wait until they were face-to-face so she could see his reaction. Instead she picked up the phone and called Mimi's cell.

Mimi answered the phone on the fifth or sixth ring. "I've been asked by Matthew not to take your calls," she said, her voice low.

"He's not at your house, is he?" Dani asked since Mimi was whispering.

"No. Of course not. But my husband knows what's going on. He's been out of work for a while now, and we can't afford for me to lose my job too."

"The rumors were true. Matthew was having an affair," Dani said. "I've spent the morning analyzing old credit card statements, and it appears he took her to Bodega Bay for a week of sunshine and fine dining. But that's not why I'm calling."

"I really should go."

"Please hear me out. If you can't help me, I'll have to accept it and find another way. I have a niggling feeling that Rebecca Carr isn't the woman's real name, but I can't know for sure without a social security number, which I'm assuming she must have provided RAYTEX with when she filled out paperwork."

Silence.

"There must be a phone number or address in her file, right?" Dani asked.

"What would you do if you found her?" Mimi wanted to know.

"I would ask her about Tinsley," Dani said. "I would ask her if she was the one who picked her up from school the day she went missing."

"Oh, Dani."

"Please," Dani said. She had to think fast, find a way to get Mimi to help her. "I'll be at McKinley Park Monday at noon. Near the tennis courts. I only want to talk to the woman. That's all. Matthew doesn't ever need to know."

A heavy sigh and then: "I'll see what I can do."

The call was disconnected.

All sorts of theories about the mystery woman swirled through her mind. Tinsley would never have simply walked off with someone unless she had met the person before and felt comfortable with them. Like every other piece of information Dani had gleaned over the years, it was a long shot, but she would never have another good night's sleep if she didn't follow up.

CHAPTER TWENTY

Ali heard padded footsteps on the floor outside the door and then the key being inserted in the lock. She'd been sitting up in bed, waiting, wondering when he was going to bring her food. She'd hardly seen him yesterday, which left her with only a few snacks. It had been a while since she'd had a full meal, and she was hungry.

Carlin burst through the door with a Cheshire cat grin on his face. He clapped his hands. "I've got a surprise for you!"

She managed a tight smile. Being nice to a bona fide psycho was easier said than done.

His eyes narrowed. "I'd appreciate a little more enthusiasm. I'm going to turn around and walk out that door. Then I'm going to count to three and we're going to try it again." His dark-blue eyes pierced her own. "Words," he said in the same way someone might tell their dog to sit.

"I'm sorry. I'll do better."

"We'll see." He walked out the door and closed it. She wanted to cry out, scream at the top of her lungs and let out all the pent-up anger and frustration inside her. Her life with Mom and Gracie flashed before her eyes. All those arguments with her mom, the constant drama . . . such a waste. What was the point? She'd put so much energy into being angry with her mom for expecting her to watch

Gracie. Dad was the one who had left them, but Mom was the person she took it all out on.

"One. Two. Three," came Carlin's voice.

She hated when he counted to three, the way his voice gradually increased in volume, loud and high-pitched. It made her cringe every time.

The door opened.

Ali widened her eyes and forced the biggest smile possible. "Good morning!"

"Good morning, Ali." He clapped his hands just as he had done the first time he entered the room. "Guess what?"

She sat up a little taller in bed. "You look excited about something," she said. "What is it? I'm dying to know." It was exhausting, trying to please him.

"I've decided it's time to bring you downstairs. I have the guest room set up, and I have a few surprises in store for my beautiful Ali. I think you'll be pleased with all the effort I've put into making you happy."

"Wonderful," she said, her voice strained.

"Come on," he said, walking closer to the bed and flipping off the covers. She slid her legs to the side of the mattress, but before her good foot touched the floor, he scooped her up with a grunt and carried her out the door and to the top of the stairs. He smelled as if he'd soaked in a bath filled with fruity cologne. She wanted to gag.

"I'm going to walk down the stairs in front of you. I want you to use me and the railing as support. Okay. Here we go."

She knew if she didn't put a hand on his shoulder, he would most likely stop the entire process and start over. With her right hand on the railing and her left on his shoulder, they made their way to the bottom landing in less than a minute. Although she couldn't put any weight on her foot, it was no longer throbbing, which she took as a good sign.

He turned around, smiling when he found himself face-to-face with her, their noses nearly touching. For a heartbeat she thought he might kiss her. If he did, she was afraid she wouldn't be able to keep the act going. Instinct would set in, and she would either knee him in the groin or bite his lip. The way he was looking at her worried her—his eyes changing from overly bright to hard and cold in an instant. In the next breath, he scooped her into his arms again, talking about how busy he was yesterday as he made his way down the familiar hallway to the bedroom where she had broken a window. Iron security bars had been installed outside the large-pane window, just as he'd said.

He finally set her down in the bathroom. "Here you go! Surprise number one." He gestured toward the shower as if he were Vanna White on a game show. "I want you to take a long, hot shower and get all the stench off you. On the countertop you'll find a towel, a hairbrush, some nice-smelling lotion, and a billowy dress that will be easy for you to get in and out of. After you're cleaned up, just ring that bell sitting next to the sink. I'm going to serve you your favorite breakfast with a side of melon and blueberries."

"Thank you, Carlin." She swallowed the lump lodged in her throat and then offered a watery smile. "You've thought of everything."

He stared at her for much too long. Then, after what felt like an eternity, he walked toward the shower and got the water going. He stopped at the door leading to the bedroom and said, "Leave the door open. There's no lock and I want to be able to hear the bell if you ring me."

She nodded, practically crying with happiness when he finally walked away, and then hobbled over to the bathroom counter. The first thing she did was open the new toothbrush and toothpaste and spend the next five minutes brushing her teeth and the roof of her mouth. The image reflecting back from the mirror was unrecognizable. Her skin looked pale gray, her hair a bird's nest, her eyes blank and hollow as if someone else now resided inside her. She'd lost a lot of weight. Too much weight.

Having seen enough, she unfolded the clean towel and put it on the floor so that she wouldn't slip on her way to the shower. She stepped out of her dirty clothes, leaving them in a heap on the floor, then took hold of the bar inside the shower, using it to keep her balance. As the water drenched the top of her head and poured down her face and neck and the rest of her body, she allowed herself to cry, great gulping sobs of anguish. The water was turning cold by the time she finished. After drying off, she returned the towel to the floor and hobbled back to the sink area. As she combed the tangles from her hair, she caught a movement out of the corner of her eye.

He was watching her.

She could see his shadow standing in the bedroom where he thought he wouldn't be seen. She looked around for the dress. It was gone.

"Hey," he said, stepping into the bathroom, his gaze roaming over her, his eyes filled with lust. "I found another dress that I thought might fit you better."

She reached out for the dress, but he wasn't ready to hand it over. His gaze met hers. "Feel better after such a nice long shower?"

Maintaining eye contact, she said, "It was nice. Thank you."

"Happy, then?"

"Yes. I've never been happier."

"Good. That's what I like to hear." He let go of the fabric, and she pulled it her way and held it close to her chest. Instead of leaving, he went to collect the pile of dirty clothes from the tile floor. In the mirror she watched him look over his shoulder at her, his eyes unblinking as he took in every bit of her.

Goose bumps covered her flesh.

"Are you cold?"

She quickly raised the dress over her head, slipped her arms through the short-capped sleeves, and then yanked the fabric down toward her knees. "I'm fine," she said when she found him still staring.

More than anything in the world, she wished she could harm him in some way. Hit him with something, stab his other eye with the toothbrush, make him pay for what he was doing to her. Instead she turned back to the mirror and began brushing her hair.

With her dirty clothes piled in his arms, he finally left. She began opening drawers, looking for something she might later use as a weapon.

"What can I get for you?"

She jumped. "You scared me."

"I'm sorry."

"I'm looking for a blow-dryer."

He moved around her, rummaged through one of the cupboards, and held up the blow-dryer. "Here we go!" He plugged it in, and before she could protest, he took the round brush from her and attempted to style her hair. She kept her gaze averted downward, didn't want him to see the contempt she felt for him. Her insides trembled with hate and fear.

When he finished, he said, "Come on now. Hold on to my shoulder for support, or would you rather I carry you?"

Never again, she thought as she placed her hand on his shoulder, taking one-legged hops while doing her best to keep up as they made their way through the bedroom and down the hallway toward the kitchen. He guided her into the same chair she'd sat in when she gouged him with a fork. The table had been set with cloth napkins and plastic silverware. He disappeared for a minute, returning with a platter of golden pancakes and bacon. He went back and forth between the kitchen and the dining room table.

She sat quietly while he worked. He seemed overjoyed about something, and he kept looking her way, smiling and winking, making her want to throw up.

"Eat," he said when he sat down in the chair next to her. "I've been slaving away all morning."

She took a bite and took her sweet time chewing so as to avoid having to talk to him.

"You are a hungry hippo," he said happily when she hardly stopped to sip her water or orange juice.

She nodded, thinking what an odd man he was, definitely a psychopath. She'd learned about the brain in biology class. The prefrontal cortex was the part that had to do with empathy and guilt. With psychopaths and some people who had suffered a frontal head injury, there lacked a solid connection between the prefrontal cortex and the amygdala, which facilitates fear and anxiety. This man was hanging on to reality by a thread. Had he been born that way, or had his environment steered him into crazy land? Knowing she couldn't remain silent forever or he'd have to count to three, she decided to strike up a conversation. "Carlin. I was wondering . . . What do you do for a living?"

His eyes narrowed. "Why? I have plenty of money. Just look around you. The furniture isn't cheap, and neither is the upkeep of this place."

She forced a lighthearted laugh. "I didn't mean to offend you. I thought you wanted to get to know me and vice versa."

He squirmed a bit in his seat, then gave his head a small shake. "Yes. You're right." He shoved an entire piece of bacon into his mouth and talked while he ate. "Let's just say I provide a much-needed service for the community. I own my own business. We'll leave it at that."

She let it go, figuring he didn't want her to know what he did for a living because he didn't trust her. She forced a smile and changed the subject. "Who taught you to cook?"

"My mother."

"I am excited to meet her," she said, only because she hoped the woman would help her escape.

"She'll love you almost as much as I do." He stood and took their plates to the kitchen sink.

She glanced at the door. Her chest tightened when she noticed that there was now a heavy-duty padlock around the handle.

When he returned to the table, his eyes were as bright as ever, and his hands were behind his back. "And now for the surprise. My gift to you."

The greatest gift would be if he would fall dead at this very moment.

He showed her his gift, his eyes beaming with pleasure.

It was a metal collar lined with some sort of padding, possibly a thin layer of felt. She prayed it wasn't meant for her. He walked past her, but he stopped once he was directly behind her, his breath moving the hairs on the top of her head. "Lift your hair for me."

She looked over her shoulder at him. "Please don't put that on me. I won't run. I promise."

"Sorry. You'll have to earn my trust. Now turn around and lift your hair. I'll count to three—"

She threaded her hands behind her neck and lifted her hair to the top of her head before he could say "one."

"Very good."

His fingers lingered at her throat, his thumb brushing over the nape of her neck. It seemed like forever before she heard a click.

"There," he said happily. "Ready to go." Grasping her forearm, he forced her to stand on her one good foot before placing his hands on her face, tilting her chin upward so she had no choice but to meet his gaze. "It's a locked collar, so no use trying to pry it off. As you'll soon discover, I have set up an invisible fence like you would for a beloved pet. The fence, which is simply wires, transmits energy. Your collar is the receiver."

The excitement in his voice made her stomach clench.

"Electrically charged wires have been installed around the windows and doors. There is also a transmitter, of course. No use looking for it. I spent hours yesterday customizing and installing the wires, making sure everything was good to go."

She said nothing.

"Don't you see? You'll be free to roam the house as you see fit."

She raised a hand to her throat and touched the metal collar. "It's humiliating."

He angled his head to one side. "You want to know real humiliation? Try having your eye nearly gouged out by the love of your life! I had to run after you as I bled, and then punish you so that you would not try to escape again. Do you have any idea how much it pained me to have to hurt you like that?"

His face was red and mottled. Spittle formed at the corners of his mouth. He was deranged, and yet that hadn't stopped her from saying too much. When would she learn to keep her mouth shut?

"I have provided you with a beautiful house," he went on, his arms raised as if he were preaching to an audience of fifty instead of one. "I have cooked for you and tended to your injuries, and you're complaining?"

"I'm sorry. I wasn't thinking. I never meant to hurt your feelings after all the work you've put into this just so that I would be free to roam." Again, she touched the collar around her throat. "The truth is I can hardly feel it. It's perfect. You're amazing."

His chest rose and fell, but the lines in his face softened. Her words had done what they were supposed to do—they soothed him, calmed him down.

He exhaled, held his head a little higher, then gestured toward the door. "If you approach one of the exits, you'll feel a jolt. It won't cause you any real harm unless you hold your ground or force your way through." He cringed as if he were imagining her doing so. "I wouldn't try it." He then clapped his hands, smiling as if he hadn't been in a rage twenty seconds ago. "Any questions?"

"Will I be able to take a shower without being electrocuted?"

"Yes."

She hopped on one leg to the kitchen just to see if she would feel anything. After opening the refrigerator, she made her way to the sink and turned on the faucet. She looked over her shoulder, surprised to see he hadn't followed her. Her attention fell on a pile of mail sitting on the counter. Set to the side was an envelope with a stamp on it, ready to be mailed. It was a utility bill. An idea struck her, giving her hope.

"Isn't it wonderful?"

Startled, she put a hand to her chest.

"I should have thought of this sooner. It would have made your transition so much easier." He walked forward holding a cane. "Here. This should make getting around much easier."

"Thank you."

"Don't thank me yet. There's more! One last gift from me to you. I saved the best for last."

She waited and then remembered he wouldn't tell her what it was until she asked him. "What is it?" she asked, feigning interest.

He reached for her hand and held it in his. "I talked to Dylan Rushdan."

Her heart kick-started into high gear. *Why would Dylan bother to talk to him? Stay calm. He's just trying to scare you.*

"I know you lied to me, but I'm not going to punish you."

A growing sense of unease made her stomach quiver. "What did you and Dylan talk about?"

"You! Of course. He told me the two of you were in love and planned to marry."

She could hardly breathe.

"You never should have lied to me."

"I'm sorry," she blurted, afraid of what he might do to her.

He waved off her apology with a flip of his hand. "No matter. He's dead."

"What?" she asked, certain she'd heard him wrong.

"I killed him. Stabbed him in the heart."

No. It couldn't be true. He's messing with me. And yet . . . Carlin had been acting strange all morning. She willed her legs to hold her upright.

It was no use.

His voice faded as her knees buckled and her body hit the floor.

CHAPTER TWENTY-ONE

Just after nine o'clock on Sunday morning, Dani was in the kitchen when she heard an urgent knock on the door.

"Dani, it's me, Quinn. Open up. Please!"

Dani rushed to the door, and when she opened it, Quinn was shaking uncontrollably.

"What's wrong?" Dani asked, pulling her inside and shutting the door. "Is your grandmother okay?"

"She's fine. It's Dylan Rushdan."

Dani frowned. She recognized the name as a friend of Ali Cross's. "What about him?"

"He's dead."

Dani was stunned by the news.

"His body was found early this morning by someone boating on the river. He'd been stabbed."

"Come on," Dani said. "Let's sit down." She ushered Quinn into the main room, and they both took a seat.

"According to the news story," Quinn went on, her voice hitching, "his parents hadn't seen him since Friday morning. I might have been the last person to see him before he was killed."

That got Dani's attention. "You met with him?"

"After talking to a few of Ali's girlfriends, I called the number Ali's mom had given us when you and I paid Mary Cross a visit. Dylan didn't have much time, but he agreed to meet me at the community college in West Sacramento where he's taking extra classes to help him get into college."

Dani blew out a sigh as she tried to think.

"What if his murder has something to do with Ali?" Quinn asked.

Dani considered the question before she said, "Mary Cross said they were friends."

"And little sis said she saw them kissing. Friends don't make out with each other. And besides, Dylan told me they were in love."

Dani let it all swirl around for a bit.

"What are the odds of Ali being taken and her boyfriend being killed less than three weeks later?" Quinn asked.

"Okay. Let's go with that line of thinking and say Ali's abductor is responsible for Dylan's death. What I want to know is, why he would take such a huge risk?"

"That's easy," Quinn said. "Because he wants her all to himself."

Dani knew what needed to be done. She went to the kitchen and returned with her cell phone. "If you don't mind, I'd like to give Detective Whitton a call and tell him what you told me."

Quinn nodded.

A minute later Dani was talking to Detective Whitton, explaining what was going on. He wanted to talk to Quinn so she handed over the phone.

Dani listened to the one-sided conversation as Quinn repeated what she'd told Dani, that Dylan and Ali were in love and that despite the argument with her mother, he seemed confident that she never would have run away. Quinn also told him about a boy named Brent Tarone who was once obsessed with Ali, but Dylan thought he was harmless since he was now married with a baby on the way.

After Quinn had said goodbye and hung up, she handed the phone back to Dani. "Detective Whitton said there was no need for me to go to the station, but that he would call me if they had further questions."

Dylan Rushdan being stabbed to death was something Dani didn't want to think about. Wrong place at the wrong time? Or something else? And the most terrifying question that came to mind was whether or not his killer would strike again.

"What if Ali's abductor was following me and saw me talking to Dylan?" Quinn asked, barging into Dani's thoughts. "I could be the reason he was killed."

"You can't think that way, Quinn. You are not responsible for that boy's death."

"Ethan told me he felt as if he were being watched. And look at you," Quinn said. "What if it's all connected somehow, and the same person who stabbed Dylan was hiding out in your office, hoping to kill you too?"

"The intruder at the office was looking for something. If the person had meant to kill me, they would have."

"I get that line of thinking," Quinn said, "but then what were they looking for?"

"That's the million-dollar question."

Quinn's phone buzzed and she pulled it from her pocket. "I better pick it up. It's Mary, Ali's mom."

Dani nodded as she got to her feet and returned to the kitchen to put the kettle on the stove. When she came back to the living room, Quinn was already finished.

"Mary heard about Dylan, and she and Gracie are pretty upset," Quinn said. "They're antsy and need something to do to keep their minds off everything."

Dani nodded. "Understandable."

"Mary wants to help with the investigation. She made a list of local businesses that use cargo vans, but she doesn't know where to start. I told her I would come by. I wasn't sure if you were feeling good enough to come along?"

Dani was still standing. "I need to get out of the house for a while. Give me a few minutes to get ready."

"Great. I'll text her and let her know." Quinn jumped to her feet. "I'm also going to run home and grab my laptop. I'll be right back."

Dani returned to the kitchen and shut off the stove. She thought about Mary and what she was going through. Dani knew the feeling. When Tinsley had first gone missing, she hadn't been able to sleep or eat. If she had too much time alone, doing nothing, her mind would drift to the dark side, to all the horrid possibilities of what her daughter might be going through.

CHAPTER TWENTY-TWO

Mary Cross led Dani and Quinn into the dining room, where she had set up her laptop at the end of the long, rectangular table. A stack of notebooks and pens served as the centerpiece, along with a tray of pastries and coffee from a local café.

Ali's younger sister, Gracie, walked into the room, her eyes puffy and red from crying. Dani wasn't sure if Gracie had been crying because of what happened to Dylan or because she missed her sister and wanted her home, but it didn't matter. Dani opened her arms and Gracie headed straight for her, wrapping her skinny arms around Dani's waist. "I'm so sorry," Dani murmured.

It wasn't until she let go of Gracie that she saw a large whiteboard propped on an easel with a picture of Ali taped at the top. The setup reminded her of the type of command center detectives might use in a conference room.

"If everyone is ready to take a seat, we'll get started," Mary said.

Since opening the door to let them in, Mary had said nothing about Dylan. Nor had she commented on Dani's banged-up face. Impressed by Mary's straightforwardness and her ability to get right to it, Dani took a seat at the table and grabbed a coffee, hoping it was loaded with caffeine.

Gracie took a seat next to Dani and showed her the flyer she was designing. It was a picture of Ali, the same picture as on the whiteboard. In the top center was one word: MISSING. In the bottom center was the date she went missing and another line asking anyone with information to contact the Sacramento PD.

"I need to add the phone number," Gracie said.

Quinn suggested Gracie add more detail to the flyer—where Ali was when she disappeared, along with a description of the man Ethan saw driving a white cargo van.

Mary agreed.

Gracie looked pleased. "Mom said she would print hundreds of them, and we'll put them everywhere."

"The flyer looks great," Dani told Gracie.

Once Quinn had taken a seat across from Gracie, Mary sat down at the head of the table and got started as Dani and Quinn set up their laptops.

"Ali has been missing for nearly three weeks now," Mary said. "Hank Davine, the detective in charge of her investigation, wasn't the only one leaning toward the idea that my daughter had run away. If I hadn't met Ethan and listened to his story as he told me what he saw, I would probably still be waiting for her to walk through that door."

Dani's heart went out to Mary. When Tinsley disappeared, her case was high priority because of her age. Nobody questions whether a child ran away if they're under the age of eleven.

"Quinn had mentioned it might be helpful to the investigation if I could look for Sacramento companies that might use cargo vans." Her shoulders sagged. "Quinn was right when she'd said nearly everyone uses cargo vans these days—electricians, plumbers, construction crews." Mary handed Dani and Quinn a piece of paper with a long list of companies and phone numbers. "As you can see by the notes in the margins, I've made my way through half of the list."

"Impressive," Dani said. "This is a great start."

"Is it?" Mary asked. "It's all so overwhelming. I did find myself wondering what the point was. Even if I end up with fewer than fifty businesses that use cargo vans, what then?"

"It is tedious work," Dani said, "but it has to be done. It's a matter of checking one item off the list at a time—one person, one business, etcetera."

Quinn unfolded a piece of paper she'd pulled from her bag, smoothed it out flat, and asked Gracie if she could please tape it to the whiteboard next to Ali's photo. "This is a drawing Ethan did of the logo he saw on the van. He believes there were at least two initials that were entwined in an elegant cursive font."

Dani stared at the drawing. It almost looked like a child's scribble, but it provided them with a way to whittle down the number of companies that used white cargo vans. "We can start by using Mary's list to see if any of the businesses on the list have a logo that resembles Ethan's drawing."

"I have a laptop," Gracie said. "Can I help?"

Mary nodded and Gracie ran off to grab her computer.

As Dani sipped her coffee, her gaze roamed to the sliding glass door that led to the backyard, reminding her that the front lawn had looked newly cut.

"What about lawn maintenance?" Dani asked. "I noticed how well maintained everything was when we drove up. Do you use a service?"

"I do. Earth Green comes twice a month. They use the side gate to get to the backyard."

Dani made note of that. "Do any other maintenance people come to the house on a regular basis?"

Gracie returned with her laptop, sat down, and booted it up.

"We have a pest-control company that comes bimonthly," Mary said.

"Do you recall the company name?"

"The Pest Control Experts."

Dani made note of it. Everything about the house looked new and fresh. "Did you have work done here recently . . . more specifically, before or around the time Ali disappeared?"

Mary considered the question before shaking her head.

"The house was painted right before Christmas," Gracie said. "I remember because we didn't get a tree until after all the painting was done."

"Not this past Christmas," Mary explained to Dani and Quinn, "but the Christmas before that. So it was painted a year and a half ago, right after the floors were done."

Dani made note of that. "Do you remember who did the work?"

"Green Haven Construction." Mary shook her head. "We had the work done so long ago, I never thought to mention it."

"I understand," Dani said. "In cases like this, when evidence seems elusive, we need to think outside the box and look at every possible clue. Like I said before, it's all about ticking off the boxes, one at a time."

"I'll be right back." Mary got to her feet and walked away. She returned a few minutes later with a thick file and handed it to Dani. "Before my husband left us, we remodeled most of the house. I kept everything: pamphlets, quotes, receipts."

Quinn glanced Dani's way, a hint of excitement making her eyes gleam.

Dani could guess how Quinn might be feeling. More often than not, looking for a missing person was like finding a clean bed in a cheap motel. Almost impossible. So if and when a new lead popped up, no matter how tenuous, it could feel like striking gold.

"Should we tell them about the rats?" Gracie asked.

"I called in the exterminator six months ago." Mary blushed. "I'm embarrassed to say that Detective Davine did ask me if I'd had any repairs done recently, but it never dawned on me to go back so far in time and think about who might have been in the house that long ago."

"It's okay," Dani said. "I'm sure you were in shock. Why don't you make a list of any repairs that were done during the remodel? The rest of us will start looking at company logos on the internet."

Everyone agreed.

"I did talk to the principal at Ali's school the other day," Mary said as she looked through a thirty-six-month pocket calendar she had pulled from her purse, "and she invited me to talk before the next sporting event and ask the community for their help."

"Whenever you can get the public involved," Dani said, "that's a good thing. It might also be helpful to post information about Ali in the newspaper. Tell the reader a little bit about Ali, her plans for the future, her hobbies, anything to make the reader feel like they know her."

"Make sure to include where and when she was last seen," Quinn added.

"Where should I put my flyers after they're printed?" Gracie asked.

While they searched companies from the list Mary had made, looking for logos on websites and social media that looked similar to the one Ethan had drawn, they also brainstormed places where Gracie could post flyers. Gracie stopped what she was doing so she could use a big fat red marker to make a list on the whiteboard: schools, coffee shops, telephone poles, bus shelters, hair salons, and any business that would allow a flyer to be posted.

Quiet settled around them as they worked, and the day passed quickly.

When the pastries and coffee had disappeared, Mary had made everyone tuna sandwiches and iced tea. It was five o'clock when they decided to call it quits. Many of the businesses on Mary's list didn't have a website or a social media presence, so they were moved to a different list.

For now it was decided that Dani and Quinn would focus on five companies, the first three of which had company logos with decorative swirly fonts that looked similar to Ethan's drawing. Green Haven Construction was added to the list because the company had been in charge of the remodel at Mary's house, and they hoped the foreman might remember any subcontractors or crew members who drove a white cargo van with a swirly font. The exterminator was included because the website header included a picture of a white cargo van.

1.   Grayson Electric (electrician)
2.   Designology (interior designer)
3.   Dwayne's Fine Cabinetry (cabinetmaker)
4.   Green Haven Construction (remodel)
5.   The Pest Control Experts (exterminator)

If nothing panned out, Dani and Quinn would give Mary's list another look and start the process over.

Mary and Gracie walked Dani and Quinn to the door. Everyone hugged before parting ways.

After they were buckled up in the car, Dani pulled away from the curb, surprised when Quinn said, "Thank you."

"For what?"

"For everything you've done for me. For letting me get into the nitty-gritty of this investigation. But mostly for always being there for me."

Dani swallowed a lump in her throat. Where was this all coming from? "I'm proud of you, Quinn."

"But we haven't found her yet," Quinn said. "You can't be proud of me until I find her. And Tinsley. We must find them both."

Dani wondered if Quinn's expression of gratitude had something to do with her mom. Quinn didn't often talk about that time in her life, but Dani knew, based on offhand remarks she sometimes made, that her mom's absence and the events surrounding her departure weighed heavily.

"Do you think my mom regrets leaving me?"

Well, there you go, Dani thought. *Bull's-eye.* "Definitely."

"So why didn't she ever try to contact me?"

Dani released a long sigh. "I don't know, but I wish I could give you the answers you need and deserve."

"Life really is fragile," Quinn said.

The light ahead turned red. Dani pulled to a stop and turned toward Quinn. "I'm sorry."

"Me too." Quinn's eyes appeared to be filled with pain and desperation as she said, "When we find Tinsley—because I'm certain we will, I feel it in my gut—I'm going to make sure she knows how lucky she is to have you as a mother. You've never given up on your search for her. Not once. And you never will. I'm going to make sure Tinsley knows that her mom would have stopped at nothing to find her."

Dani swallowed a knot in her throat. "I'm lucky to have found you."

"Sort of a silver lining?" Quinn asked, looking more vulnerable than Dani had ever seen her in all the years they had known each other.

"Definitely a silver lining," Dani said. "When we do find Tinsley, you're going to make a wonderful big sister."

The corners of Quinn's mouth turned upward. "Really? You think so?"

"I know so."

The light turned green and Dani drove onward.

"I *have* come to realize that, despite the pain and struggles," Quinn said, her voice low and thoughtful, "life is a gift. A random gift that we're all given. One gift."

Dani made a right, keeping her eyes on the road, saying nothing, hoping to give Quinn a chance to let it all out.

"My mom may have left me," Quinn continued, "but she gave me life, and for that I am grateful."

Quinn was her gift, Dani thought as she neared home, knowing that the two of them would be forever connected by loss and the persistent hope for the return of a loved one.

CHAPTER TWENTY-THREE

Carlin had spent most of the night thinking about whether he might have mistakenly left any evidence near the river. Confident he had done no such thing, his mind began to race anew with thoughts about Ethan Grant. Finally he had given up on sleep, gotten out of bed, and hopped in the shower. He needed to know what the kid knew, if anything.

When he had left the house, Ali was still asleep. He would return in an hour or two to make her breakfast. At the moment, though, he was parked outside the Hawkeye Mobile Home Park, wondering if he should knock on the kid's front door or wait a little longer. The decision was made for him when, minutes later, the kid appeared on his bike, did a wheelie off the curb, and rode off.

Jesus, kid. Wait for me.

He pushed the start button and drove after him. *What are you up to today, Ethan Grant?*

As he followed the kid, careful to keep some distance between them, he thought of Ali and how surprised she'd been by his declaration. He wasn't stupid. He hadn't really expected her to be elated, but he had hoped they could have a grown-up conversation about the fact that she'd lied to him. The last thing he'd expected was for her to crumple to the ground. The sound of her head hitting the floor had been brutal. Lifting her from the ground and carrying her to the couch hadn't been easy. A part of him, a small part, was beginning to wonder if she was worth all the trouble.

Women. They were put on this earth to serve men and to procreate. And yet here he was, in the prime of his life, practically begging another female to love him.

He'd thought his mother loved him until he realized that sex wasn't love. Sex was sex. If he hadn't done everything his mother had asked, he'd paid the price. Sometimes she would feel badly about punishing him for doing an inadequate job when it came to pleasing her, but more often than not, she'd bitched and moaned and called him names. It wasn't until she had met a rich old man with blood-veined eyes, misshapen hands, and an unsteady gait that he'd caught a break. To this day it shocked Carlin that she'd gone off with the old guy. She had told Carlin she wanted to be exposed to new places, people, and cultures, to develop a wider worldview. And her number one reason for leaving . . . Drum roll, please: she'd wanted to find herself.

But the opposite had happened.

Carlin was the one who had found himself, while his mom had come back looking like something the cat had dragged in. Although, thinking back on it, there was no way a cat, let alone forty cats, could have dragged her anywhere. Not after her having eaten her way through London, Paris, Rome, Barcelona, Amsterdam, and every other city she and the old geezer had stopped at. Less than a week after Carlin had received a postcard letting him know she was heading for Dubai for who knows how long, she'd returned.

Apparently the rheumy-eyed sucker had kicked the bucket.

Mom had dropped her luggage at Carlin's feet, stripped naked, and demanded a bath.

Being the dutiful son he'd always been, he got right to it. Filled the tub with hot water and a dash of orange blossom bath oil. She climbed in, lifting one heavy thigh and then the other. Half the water sloshed over the edge when she finally managed to squeeze herself all the way in. Then she looked up at him and patted the water just like she used to do. Without any preplanning on his part, he'd stepped into the bath, his legs straddling her ample waist, which was no easy feat, placed both hands on her head, and pushed her down under the water, watching her watch him as the bubbles rose from between her lips.

Judging by the look in her eyes and how long it took for them to open wide beneath the water, she hadn't seemed to understand his intentions until the moment she'd begun to struggle. Her clawlike nails had dug into his hands but had done her no good.

The funny thing was, he loved his mom. For all those years she'd kept a roof over his head, which was why he'd made sure to do the same for her. When she finally stopped fighting him and the bubbles no longer floated upward, he'd climbed out of the tub, drained the water, and dried her off. It had taken him hours to do her hair and dress her in one of the plus-size muumuus he'd found inside her luggage.

The loud rumble of an engine as a car cut in front of him brought him back to the present. Carlin slammed on his brakes, tires squealing in protest. His heart spiraled out of control, making his chest feel like it had a miniature jackhammer inside of it. At least he hadn't hit the car. The driver looked at him through the rearview mirror and gave a wave as some sort of half-assed apology.

Two blocks ahead Carlin saw the kid take a right. He needed to focus.

By the time he caught up to Ethan Grant he realized the kid was headed for Ali Cross's house, the one she'd shared with her mom and sister before she'd moved in with him.

After the kid dropped his bike on the lawn, Carlin parked on the opposite side of the street from the house and watched Ethan make his way to the front door and ring the bell. Gracie answered the door and they both disappeared inside.

Carlin didn't like being out of the loop. What were they discussing? He drummed his fingers against the steering wheel and sucked in a breath to calm himself. There was nothing he could do.

Ethan returned a few minutes later, holding a stack of papers to his chest and waving goodbye, before Carlin's imagination had a chance to get the best of him.

After the kid rode his bike into town and stapled one of the papers he'd picked up from Ali's sister onto a telephone pole, Carlin waited until Ethan was out of sight before he climbed out of the car and ripped down the flyer. Ali's picture was on it, along with details about what had happened to her: a slender white man, driving a white cargo van, was seen pushing Ali Cross into the back of his van before speeding off. There was a date, time, and place where the van had been seen.

His skin tingled.

He needed to get rid of the van.

But first he needed to figure out how he was going to rid himself of Ethan Grant.

Chapter Twenty-Four

After tossing and turning all night, praying Carlin had lied to her and Dylan was alive, Ali feigned sleep when the door opened and light spilled across the floor.

"I was out for a while," Carlin said, "but I came back to check on you before I left for work."

Instead of leaving, he came forward and brushed the back of his hand over her forehead, reminding her that this nightmare might never end.

"Are you awake, Ali?"

There was no use pretending. He was stubborn, and she knew he wouldn't leave her the hell alone until he told her whatever it was he had to say. Holding the blankets close, she pushed herself upward, her back against the headboard. "What do you want?"

"It's ten o'clock. I was worried."

The time of day surprised her. She'd thought it was much earlier, but she said nothing, didn't care if he demanded she talk or gave her until the count of three. He did neither of those things.

"I let you sleep in my bed, and I slept upstairs."

A regular Prince Charming.

He gestured toward the chair in the corner of the room where she saw a pile of neatly folded clothes. "I rustled up a few outfits I thought you might like to wear."

She could see that her silence was getting to him. His eyes narrowed slightly and a tic set in his jaw. She was testing him, probably to her own detriment, but the hatred she felt for him was bubbling over and she was afraid if she opened her mouth she might tell him what she was thinking.

"I made you an omelet and some fresh fruit," he went on. "Your plate is on the table."

"Thank you." No need to push him over the brink, she decided. She just wanted him to leave.

"Are you okay?"

"I'm fine."

"No hard feelings?"

"None."

"That's my girl. I'll be back around two, so don't do anything I wouldn't do." His cruel smile and lifeless eyes made him look clownish. "In the family room you'll find some books that I brought up from the basement. I also found a sketchbook and colored pencils."

One "thank you" had been enough. She merely stared at him.

And then it happened.

He left the room.

She leaned her head back against the pillows and closed her eyes. Only then did she realize how stupid she'd been to push him like that. No telling what he would do to her the next time his rage got the best of him.

She didn't dare move until she heard the familiar sounds of receding footfalls, the click of the door opening and closing, and finally the whirr of a car's engine. She moved quickly, as quickly as she could with a bum foot. Sliding her legs over the mattress, she reached for her cane and used it to make her way to the bathroom, moving the cane forward with each step.

If she was going to go through with the plan she'd concocted the moment she'd seen the pile of mail on the kitchen counter, she needed to work fast. The freak would be back in four hours.

She stared at her reflection as she washed her hands and face. Dark shadows circled her eyes. She looked thinner and older. After drying her hands, she tugged at the dog collar around her neck and fiddled with the lock as she had done throughout the night. It was no use trying to get it off.

Just as Carlin said, breakfast was waiting for her. She sat down at the table and took a couple of bites, but she'd lost her appetite. Back on her feet, she hobbled to the front door, close enough to poke at the lock with her cane until her arm ached. Next, she focused on the chain at the bottom of the door, tried to push the end of the chain to the right. She almost had it, but then the tip of the cane fell to the ground.

Shit. The cane would never work for all those locks. Instead, she reached her hand to the doorknob and pulled it back the second she felt a vibration.

Sweat gathered on her brow. She inhaled. *You can do this.*

This time she stepped forward, yanked one of the latches open, and gritted her teeth as a nasty tingling sensation swam down her arm. She went for the latch on the bottom next, cried out, and finally hopped away from the door, almost losing her balance. Her right side felt numb, the pain running through her body excruciating.

It was no use.

Her posture stiff, every muscle rigid, she wanted to scream at the top of her lungs.

The clock was ticking.

She made her way to the family room and sat in front of the table where he'd left the sketchbooks and pencils. With pencil in hand, she wrote, *"My name is Ali Cross. Call the police! I'm being held captive by a man named Carlin Reed in Sacramento, California."* She set down her pencil when she realized she needed an address, a street name, something.

The cane was helpful, but moving from room to room required a lot of effort. In the kitchen, she was relieved to see he hadn't taken the utility bill with him. It still sat on the far edge of the countertop. He hadn't written the return address on the envelope, but that didn't matter. She needed to open the envelope so she could slip her note inside with the statement. After that it would be a waiting game, leaving her with nothing to do but hope and pray whoever opened the envelope and read her note would take it seriously enough to call the police.

She looked through the kitchen drawers, which were mostly empty. He might be crazy, but he was smart enough to know he couldn't trust her with a sharp knife. She considered using a plastic knife, but knew if she damaged the envelope he would know.

Stick with the plan.

After opening nearly every drawer, she found a box of plastic wrap. Her hands shook as she pulled off enough to cover the utility bill. She stuck it inside the freezer, where she would leave it for at least an hour. She'd read about the hack in a magazine at the dentist's office. Freezing a sealed envelope worked better than steam.

With that done, she made her way back to the family room and tucked the note inside the midsection of the sketchbook, where it would have to stay until it was time to open the utility bill.

She took a seat on the couch, grabbed one of the books he'd left for her, and began to read. It was no use. She couldn't concentrate. A noise prompted her to look up and listen.

She heard the pitter-patter of tiny feet on the roof. A squirrel, no doubt.

Every muscle in her body felt quivery and twitchy. Her nerves were shot.

After reading the first page three times and having no idea what she'd read, she gave up. Using her cane to push herself upward, she made her way to the front window, mindful to stand far enough back so she wouldn't be shocked.

She stared out past the front lawn and chain-link fence covered with poison ivy to the empty lot across the street, wishing there was a house filled with children. Maybe then they would be playing outside and somebody would notice the chain-link fence and iron bars over the windows and—

And most likely do nothing.

Her heart sank.

Most people in their neighborhoods didn't have a clue what was going on in the house next door. The thirteen Turpin children were a pretty good example of that. Thirteen children held captive in their own picturesque suburban home, many found chained to their beds. They had been beaten, starved, tortured, and shackled. Neighbors were unaware the Turpins had that many children. Another neighbor whose yard connected to the Turpins' backyard said the place looked unkempt but was quiet. Ali still remembered how the story had shocked her. How could so many people in the community have been unaware of what was going on?

Easy. People minded their own business. She thought of all the times she'd heard the screams of a child down the street and assumed the kid was playing and probably fell down and skinned their knee. How many times did people hear others fighting or watch an unfamiliar car drive around the neighborhood day after day? Most people didn't take suspicious behavior seriously.

If she ever escaped, she would bring awareness to the importance of neighborhood watch programs. Not just to reduce burglaries and vandalism, but to make people see how important it was to look out for one another. They could have block parties to teach children what to do in emergency situations.

She hobbled back to the kitchen and let out a heavy breath when she saw that only twenty minutes had passed.

Back in the family room, she used the remote to turn on the television and scroll through the channels. All the news channels had been blocked, leaving only soap operas, *Sesame Street* reruns, and game shows. She wanted to be able to hear Carlin's return, so she shut off the TV. He said he would be home at two, but what if he'd only said that so he could drop in for a surprise visit to check up on her?

Looking around, she told herself she wasn't trying hard enough. There had to be a way to escape. She just hadn't thought of it yet. Maybe he had lied about the dangers of going through the door or window with the shock collar on. Maybe it would be painful but wouldn't cause her any real harm. The problem would be getting over the chain-link fence, if she even made it that far. She wasn't strong enough to pull herself up and over, especially with one useless foot.

She pivoted on her good foot and made her way past the dining room table to the side door that led to the shed. From where she stood she could see, through one of the barred windows, the small building where she'd been kept. Chills washed over her at the thought of being trapped inside again. She'd been so cold and hungry, and yet it seemed like her time in the shed had happened another lifetime ago.

She stood there for a moment, thinking. If he caught her trying to escape, what would her punishment be this time? Would he toss her in the shed? Break her other foot? Kill her?

The alternative was living with the madman for how long? What was his plan? He'd told her they would be married and hinted at taking their relationship to the next level. Was he was going to rape her? Her skin crawled at the thought.

Surely someone would find her before too long.

Who? Who would find her?

A sob erupted at the thought of Dylan. He had to be alive. She couldn't think any other way.

The boy on the bike truly might be her only hope. He'd seen Carlin push her into the back of his van. Had he gotten the license plate number? If so, why hadn't the police knocked on Carlin's door?

Her shoulders sagged. Nobody was coming.

She hobbled closer to the side door leading to the backyard, inch by inch until she felt a jolt. She hopped backward. Her hand caressed her throat. It had been more of a surprise than anything else. Again, she moved closer. This time she ignored the initial shock and kept going until she was close enough to place her hand on the doorknob. Her teeth ground together as she felt her muscles buzzing and tingling as if something inside her might snap.

She fell backward, landing hard on her buttocks.

The cane clattered against the ground.

Don't cry. You can't give up.

She remained on the ground as she caught her breath. If it was just a matter of turning the knob and hopping outside, she might be able to do it. But he had installed an extra lock, which would require her to pick two locks instead of one. She might be dead by the time she got the door open.

Five minutes passed before she began the struggle to get to her feet again and make her way back to the kitchen. It had been forty-five minutes since she'd put the envelope in the freezer. Impatient, she returned to the kitchen and pulled it from the freezer, unwrapped it, and held her breath as she slipped a fingernail under the flap.

It opened. It worked!

Swallowing her glee, she took the envelope to the family room, sat down, and pulled her partially written note from its hiding place. Very carefully, she slid the utility bill out of the envelope and copied the address onto her note. She finished it with, *Please help me! Ali Cross.*

Carlin hadn't left any scissors about so she carefully tore the edges of the paper so the envelope wouldn't be too thick when she closed it back up. Making sure the note was well hidden within the statement, she slipped everything back into the envelope.

She spent the next fifteen minutes stumbling around the house looking for glue. There was none to be found. Flour and water! She would make a paste. She needed to hurry so it would have time to dry.

Back in the kitchen, she found the flour easy enough except it was inside a cupboard too high for her to reach.

She looked at the clock on the kitchen wall. Two hours had passed. Desperate, she used the cane to move the bag of flour until it finally fell to the ground with a thud and sent a white cloud exploding around her.

Shit.

There was flour everywhere, on the cabinets and the floor and on her. She leaned over, holding on to the counter for support, and scooped flour into a small bowl. Adrenaline pumping, she added a few drops of water, and used her finger to stir it together. She quickly washed and dried her hands before picking up the envelope. Using the tip of her finger, she applied the paste sparingly to the back of the envelope and sealed it closed again. She then placed it under a stack of bowls to keep it from coming apart, found a dish towel, ran it under the faucet, and got down on all fours and started cleaning.

CHAPTER TWENTY-FIVE

Dani stared at her reflection as she brushed her teeth.

She hardly recognized the woman peering back at her. The bruises were now a light shade of yellow. Her cheeks looked hollow, and the half-shaved head was not a good look on her. She'd hardly slept last night, which was nothing new. Every time she closed her eyes, a black-clad figure appeared, swinging the base of a lamp.

She found herself thinking of Matthew, which was really weird, since she usually only thought about him when he got right up in her face and lectured her about Tinsley. For quite possibly the first time since they'd divorced, she looked inside herself, questioning what had happened to them. Their life together was blurry, like most people's memories from the ages of one to six—unsure of what parts had been real. If a moment in time together popped into her head, she wasn't sure if it was a recollection or something she'd seen in an old photo.

They had been in love once, hadn't they?

She tried to imagine them out to dinner on her birthday, an annual tradition, and the only thing that came to mind was how antsy she'd felt whenever they did go out, always ready to call it a night and get back to Tinsley.

After rinsing her mouth, she splashed cool water on her face and grabbed blindly for a towel to dry off. Enough of that. No more strolling down memory lane. It wasn't any fun.

She put on her shoes and made her way to the kitchen to make some coffee. She knew she should go to the office, but she hadn't been there since the attack. At some point she would need to get back on the horse, so to speak.

It was nearing ten. She needed to be at McKinley Park by noon in case Mimi showed up with information on Rebecca Carr.

She checked her messages, surprised to see a voice message from Cameron Bennington. She'd forgotten she'd given Cameron her cell phone number. Dani thumbed the tiny arrow and listened to Cameron apologize for calling so late, explaining how she'd returned home after midnight and noticed someone had been trying on her clothes and rearranging her toiletries in the master bedroom. Cameron ended the call by saying she had a meeting in the morning and had to be at the office by eight, but was hoping Dani wouldn't mind having a look around. She left her a six-digit keyless code to get inside, another gadget she'd had installed in hopes of stopping the intruder from getting inside.

A part of her wanted to pass Cameron's case to another investigator, someone who could devote more time to the situation. But doing so would probably be more work than just getting the job done. Whoever was snooping around Cameron's house couldn't possibly be coming in through the front door. Otherwise they would have been captured on the security camera. The house did not have a basement, and the garage was detached. When they had first met, Cameron had taken Dani on a tour. There was an aluminum bar to secure the sliding glass door, and Cameron had had a latch with a chain installed on the laundry room door leading to the backyard. The house had been secure.

If she left now, Dani figured she could have a look around before heading for McKinley Park. She grabbed a sweater and her purse. She would pick up a coffee on her way.

The first thing she did when she arrived at Cameron's house twenty-five minutes later with a half-empty vanilla latte in hand was to do what she always did: she used her binoculars to scan the neighborhood to see if anyone was peering out curtains or sitting in their car.

The street was quiet, but the sun was already bright. It was going to be another hot day. Dani didn't have a whole lot of time. She texted Cameron to let her know she was going to take a look around inside the house. Two seconds later, she got a thumbs-up emoji.

Dani got out of the car, looked both ways before crossing the road, and headed up the walkway to the front door. A little more paranoid than usual, she glanced over her shoulder before punching in the code. The keyless lock beeped and whirred before she pushed it open.

Cool air greeted her when she stepped inside. The trees surrounding the property did a good job of protecting the interior of the home from the sun. After shutting the door, she walked into the family room and looked around, spotting a camera on the bookshelf. The problem with the placement was that it wouldn't capture anyone going up the stairs. Nevertheless, she waved, then continued on through the dining room and into the kitchen. A large-pane window above the sink gave her a clear view of the yard, which was basically one square consisting of a wood deck and a patch of lawn. Fuchsia-colored bougainvillea covered the back fence.

Again she looked around for a security camera, finally spotting one above a high cabinet. She didn't bother checking out smaller spaces like the pantry or coat closet, but she did take a look in the laundry room to make sure the chain was latched before heading upstairs. When she reached the landing at the top of the stairs, her phone buzzed. She saw that it was Cameron and picked up the call.

"Hi, Dani. I had a minute and thought I'd let you know I received two alerts and I was able to see you walk through the living room and the kitchen."

"Where am I now?" Dani asked.

"I'm not sure."

"Are there cameras upstairs?"

"No. I figured if we caught the intruder coming in that would be good enough."

"I'm going to angle the camera in the living room so the viewer will catch anyone going upstairs."

"Thanks for taking a look around."

"No problem. I'll text you when I'm finished."

They hung up and Dani inwardly scolded herself for not insisting she have someone do the installation from the start. Cameron had wanted to save money by doing it herself, which was costing her more money in the long run.

There were three bedrooms upstairs, two to the left, both with windows overlooking the street. One appeared to be used as an office, and the other room was obviously being used for storage since it was stacked with plastic bins. Once she was done inspecting both rooms to the left, she headed for the main bedroom, making her way straight to the walk-in closet where Cameron had said her clothes had been disturbed.

The french doors leading into the closet were latticed. She opened them wide and stepped inside, impressed by the perfectly organized shoes and hats and rows of color-coordinated clothes. No wonder Cameron knew exactly what was missing and which pieces had been tampered with. If someone ever rummaged through Dani's clothes, she'd be none the wiser.

She closed the closet doors and made a quick pass through the bathroom before coming back to stand in front of the bedroom window that provided a bird's-eye view of the backyard. If ever there was a mystery, this was it. She plunked her hands on her hips and pivoted on her feet, taking it all in. She was about to sit on the light-blue velvet settee when something caught her eye. The floors upstairs were all carpeted with a thick, natural-colored Berber. But the floor wasn't her concern. There were hairs on the settee. Not a lot. But enough to stand out.

Cameron was a brunette, and she didn't have a dog or a cat.

Dani got down on her knees to get a closer view of the hairs. They weren't all over the settee, which is why they hadn't stood out at first. If she had to guess she would say someone noticed it and attempted to wipe the settee clean. But whoever had done so had missed a spot.

With the sun shining brightly through the window, it was clear they were short blond hairs—dog hairs.

Dog hairs that looked as if they might have come from a white lab. A white lab named Sadie, who belonged to a man named Frank Petri.

Everyone knew a dog couldn't rearrange furniture and try on clothes. But the animal could sit on the settee and wag its tail while it watched its owner do his thing. Dogs were funny that way. No judgment. Just pure, unconditional love.

She pulled her phone from her pocket and sent Cameron a text: I think I know who your intruder is.

CHAPTER
TWENTY-SIX

Quinn pulled up behind a flatbed truck delivering supplies to the construction site in Sacramento near Tahoe Park. From the looks of it, they were building at least a dozen look-alike homes, all at once. An explosion of sounds greeted her when she stepped out of the car: the whine of an air compressor and the pop, pop, pop of numerous nail guns while men shouted to be heard above the din.

She'd already been to Grayson Electric, where she'd learned they only used their logo on business letterhead and their website, not on their vehicles. Quinn had made note of that and headed for number four on the list since numbers two and three had later office hours.

The woman managing Green Haven Construction's main office was busy, buried behind stacks of files and invoices. She didn't recognize the logos Quinn showed her and made it clear the only person worth talking to would be her boss, Ed Hoffman. He had a memory like an elephant, she'd said before sending Quinn off with the address of the construction site, telling her to look for the guy with the long white beard wearing a red hard hat that said Boss.

Quinn stood in place, looking from half-framed house to half-framed house, and spotted him two doors down. The ground was covered with sawdust, bent nails, and cigarette butts. Nobody paid her any mind as she walked past buckets of nails and stacks of lumber. Ed Hoffman was a big burly guy with a ruddy face. As she approached him, she waved. He frowned.

They met each other halfway.

"You can't be walking around here. I'm going to have to ask you to leave."

"I was just at your main office, and they told me where I could find you. I need only a few minutes of your time."

"I'll be with you in a minute, Jimmy," he shouted to a man holding blueprints.

"It's about a missing girl," Quinn said. "It could be a matter of life and death." She knew she was being dramatic, but if Ali had been kidnapped and was still alive, they needed to find her sooner rather than later. And besides, the life-and-death thing had softened his expression somewhat.

Quinn opened her slim manila file and showed him the logos they had enlarged and printed at Mary's house. "Recognize any of these? We have reason to believe it's the vehicle lettering on the suspect's white cargo van. We think he's a tradesman."

While he looked closer, she pointed to Ethan's drawing in the file. He used his free hand to scratch his neck as he looked at it.

Quinn gritted her teeth at the nerve-racking sound of a jackhammer somewhere close.

"This one," he said, tapping a finger on Ethan's drawing of a swirly logo.

"You recognize it?"

"Yeah. It looks familiar."

She had to tamp down the giddiness threatening to consume her.

He kept nodding. "I've seen this design on a white cargo van." He dug his meaty fingers into his beard and scratched his chin while he thought.

"Do you remember the company name or what line of work he might have been in?"

"I've been using a lot of the same guys for years. It's not my electrician," he murmured, "or the roofer."

Someone called his name and the light went out of his eyes. He returned her file. "Sorry. Can't remember off the top of my head, and I gotta go."

In a heartbeat her excitement had been extinguished. Quinn handed him a card with her name and number. "If it comes to you, please call me. Any time, day or night."

He tucked the card into his back pocket. "Good luck to you." He waggled a finger at the ground. "Watch where you step."

Once she was in her car, she took a closer look at Ethan's drawing, shaking her head all the while. There was an *S*, and possibly a *C*, but for the most part it looked like nothing more than random scribbles. She set aside the paper, pulled out her phone, and sent Ethan a text to let him know she was on her way.

As she drove, she tried to stay positive. Ed Hoffman would call her if it came to him. They just had to keep going, keep ticking off the boxes, as Dani liked to say.

When Quinn arrived at the Hawkeye Mobile Home Park, Ethan was out front, leaning against a five-foot, crumbling cobblestone wall, smoking. Quinn was about to beep the horn when Ethan straightened, snuffed out his cigarette, and swaggered her way.

The cool kid, she thought. Every school had one.

He opened the passenger door, picked up the papers on the seat so he wouldn't sit on them, and hopped in. "What's all this?"

"Mary and Gracie Cross helped Dani and I come up with a list of companies we're looking into. It turns out Mary had some work done on the house. I went to a construction site just before I texted you and talked to the owner of the Green Haven Construction Company, who also happens to be the foreman, and he remembers seeing a logo on a white cargo van that looks similar to your drawing."

"Well, who is it?" he asked with raised eyebrows. "Do you have a name? Did you call the police?"

"No. Not yet. He couldn't recall the name of the company, but said he would call if it came to him."

Ethan didn't respond. He didn't have to. Unless Ed Hoffman had a sudden breakthrough, it was basically another dead end.

Ethan put the file and papers on the back seat and asked, "Where's Dani?"

"She's busy with another case."

"My mom told me about Ali's friend, Dylan Rushdan. She's worried there might be a connection. She made me promise I would stay away from you and Dani."

Quinn's fingers curled around the steering wheel. "She's right, you know. Maybe you should lay low for a bit."

He crossed his arms over his chest. "Don't treat me like a kid, okay?"

Her first thought was that he was a kid, but she said, "Okay." She sniffed the air. "When are you going to quit smoking? You smell. And it's an expensive habit, isn't it?"

He shrugged. "I know where Mom hides her cigarettes."

"That's stealing," she told him. "It doesn't matter if it's your mom. In fact, that's even worse."

"You sound just like her." He stretched the belt over his lap and snapped it into place.

"I'm flattered." Quinn merged onto the road.

"You shouldn't be."

"Why not? She obviously loves you."

"How would you know?"

"Because I'm a PI."

He chuckled as he stretched out his legs.

"Laugh all you want, but it's true. I know things. Your father left when you were two. Your mom went to jail for a bit, but at least she came back."

"Then you also know she loved me so much she almost went back to jail."

"But she didn't go back to jail, did she? She was selling weed. Everyone smokes weed or uses one of those medicinal cards to get edibles these days. It's not easy being a single mother."

"How would you know?"

"I guess I wouldn't. But I took care of a neighbor's new puppy for a week one time, and it was the most difficult week of my life."

He laughed.

"I'm serious. That puppy chewed on wires and tanbark and plastic wrappings, anything he could get hold of. I had to watch him like a hawk. I would think taking care of a baby would be a hundred times harder."

He said nothing.

Quinn sighed inwardly. Ethan seemed off today. She didn't want to make too much of it, but she wished he could see what she and Dani saw, a good kid who probably just needed a little push in the right direction. "Babies and puppies aside, I hope you realize you're smart and kind—"

"I'm neither of those things."

"You're wrong. Everyone who has met you—Dani, me, and Mary, for starters—has seen firsthand that you're a good person. You came forward, despite your mom's situation, because you saw a girl tossed in a van. You knew she needed help. You could have ridden away on your bike and never said a word, but you didn't."

He grunted, unwilling to take any sort of praise.

"You're still young. Don't throw it all away because you have a shit dad. Use that brain of yours to do the right thing. Go to school. Make something of yourself and show your mom what a real man does for his family."

It was quiet for a long while before Quinn asked him if he had any flyers left. If not, they would stop by Mary Cross's house to grab more.

He leaned over and pulled them out of the backpack he'd thrown on the floor by his feet. "I posted all but fifty, concentrating on the area where Ali disappeared."

"Great. What about Midtown?"

"Sounds good."

After finding parking on Sixteenth, they split up and posted flyers wherever the store owner would give them permission—Temple Coffee Roasters, Device Brewing Company, Urban Roots, Mendocino Farms, the Mill, and Magpie Café. From there they headed up Seventeenth, Eighteenth, and Nineteenth, hitting up Safeway and a bookstore. They grabbed bottled water and a delicious ice cream cookie at Ginger Elizabeth Chocolates. By the time they reached Peet's Coffee on J Street, they only had a couple of flyers left, which was a good thing because the heat was becoming unbearable.

"I'll go and get the car, then text you on my way back so you can tell me where you're at," Quinn told Ethan as she fished around in her bag for her keys, wishing Grandma drove one of those newfangled cars with the fob instead of a key. Her bag slipped out of her grasp, and the keys she'd been looking for, along with a pen and her phone and an assortment of odds and ends, rolled out onto the cement around her feet.

Ethan bent down to help her.

The sun's rays reflected off her key and hit Ethan in the face. He put his hands over his eyes. When he pulled his hands away, his eyes were wide and his mouth hung open.

"Are you okay?" Quinn asked.

"Keys!"

"What?"

"Remember when we sat for three whole days in the same spot where I had seen Ali Cross abducted, and you were badgering me about what I had seen, asking me the same questions over and over again until my head pounded?"

"Sure. Yeah. What about it?"

"Remember when I told you the sun was bouncing off something inside the guy's van and blinding me?"

"I do," she said, waiting, trying to be patient.

"The sun's rays were reflecting off keys, lots of them. They were hanging off a giant pegboard that was at the back of his van. The guy must be one of those—"

"A locksmith," Quinn blurted excitedly.

"Yes! Do you think he was visiting one of those stores to put in a new lock?"

"I don't know," Quinn said, "but we're going to find out. I'll get my car and be right back."

———

Carlin's morning had been spent sitting in his car a block away from the Hawkeye Mobile Home Park. The moment he saw Ethan Grant stroll out and light up a cigarette, he felt a lightness in his chest that quickly turned into a block of cement when the same young woman he'd seen the last time he was here drove up minutes later, ruining what could have been a slam dunk.

After seeing her with the boy and Ali's mom the other day, he'd done some research and learned her name. Quinn Sullivan worked for Dani Callahan.

Carlin had also found an obituary for Quinn's old man, and he knew she lived with her grandma, but her mother was a mystery.

He kept a good distance away as he followed the old clunker that the wannabe investigator drove from West Sacramento to Midtown. It wasn't too surprising to watch them park and begin to post more damn flyers. If their big priority was tacking flyers to telephone poles, that told him they probably didn't know much, not enough to make him sweat.

He thought about heading home early.

And yet . . . he couldn't let it go. The kid might have seen his face. He was the only person in the world who could point him out in a lineup. For some reason that made him laugh. The thought of standing against a wall next to four other guys while someone spied them through one-way glass seemed silly. He'd never once been in trouble with the law.

But still.

He couldn't let it go.

For the next hour he would park his car in some random spot, wait for the two of them to get a few blocks ahead of him, and then seek them out again.

He found another spot, not bothering to put money in the meter as he waited to see where they would go next. He was hungry, and it pissed him off that he hadn't asked Ali to make him a bag lunch, like his mom used to do for him when he was a young boy. The thought lifted his spirits and reminded him that he could check in on her anytime without her knowing. He pulled out his phone, hit the camera app, and watched at least a dozen videos pop up.

Ali had been busy.

He grimaced as he watched her try to get through the door, then fall back on her butt.

I warned you.

The videos were set to record movement for thirty seconds. He randomly selected another video and saw her on all fours in the kitchen cleaning the floor. It looked like flour. He wondered if she was making cookies, or maybe a cake, hoping to surprise him. He clicked on another one. In this video she was fiddling with his mail, which worried him, making him wonder what the hell she was doing. By the time he watched a few more clips, he knew exactly what she was up to.

He took slow, steady breaths.

Ali had been so sweet and nice lately. Too nice. It saddened him to think he couldn't trust her, after all. He was about to pull out of his spot and drive off when he saw Quinn walking away, leaving the boy on his own.

He swallowed a laugh. He'd have to deal with Ali later.

It was somewhat nerve-racking, following the kid now that traffic had thickened, making it impossible to go too fast or too slow. More than once, he had to circle around, which was frustrating since he figured Quinn might come back for the kid and he didn't have much time. Even so, he managed to trail Ethan all the way to Capitol Ace Hardware on I Street, where the boy took a seat on the sidewalk out front.

This was it. Go time. He had to hurry. He pulled into the nearly empty Ace Hardware parking lot, drove around to the back of the building, left the engine running, and hopped out. He ran around to the back and opened the trunk. Working fast, he grabbed a rag and soaked it in chloroform before putting on the act of his life.

Wearing a baseball cap and sunglasses, he ran around to the front entrance, only a few feet away from where the boy sat, and yelled loud enough for the kid to hear him. "Help! Please help!"

The boy stood up, looked at him.

"My dog! I think it's heatstroke!"

The boy held up his water. "Maybe this will help."

"Yes!" he said. "Hurry!"

He didn't look over his shoulder to see if the kid was following him, not until he rounded the corner where he could see his car. As soon as the kid caught up, he grabbed him and held the cloth over his nose and mouth. The boy struggled. He was strong, but he weighed nothing. The kid finally fell unconscious, dangling from his arms. His phone dropped to the ground.

Carlin tossed him into the trunk, threw the rag inside with him, and slammed it shut. He then ran back for the phone and scooped it up from the ground.

Nobody was around when he made a right out of the parking lot and drove away. He should have been shaking with excitement now that his biggest problem was stashed in his trunk.

Instead, the video clips he'd watched of Ali played havoc with his mind and soul, creating a feeling of extreme disappointment weighed down by the realization that she would need to be punished.

CHAPTER
TWENTY-SEVEN

Dani arrived at McKinley Park ten minutes early. Right or wrong, Cameron's problems would have to be put on the back burner for now. At the moment, her only thought was of the mystery woman who had been at the last RAYTEX picnic before Tinsley disappeared. The anticipation was making her crazy, her mind creating a fantasy so beyond reality she could hardly breathe.

But what if? What if she had found a connection to Tinsley?

Despite Matthew's worries, despite a prisoner's confession that he'd killed her daughter, Dani needed to talk to the woman who called herself Rebecca Carr. She couldn't let it go. Why would Rebecca Carr use an alias? If the woman wore the right clothes and a hat and sunglasses to cover her face, she easily could have passed for Dani.

She opened the door and stepped outside, brushing a wrinkle from her pants before walking across a large expanse of grass toward the tennis courts. If Mimi had been able to find a social security number or Rebecca Carr's real name, anything that might lead Dani to the woman, she might be one step closer to finding out what happened to Tinsley.

Even on a Monday afternoon, the park was bustling. A large group of people huddled around two picnic tables under a shade tree where colorful balloons and streamers hung from every branch. A couple in the middle of the park tossed a Frisbee back and forth. There were joggers and dog walkers. More than one young mother could be seen pushing a stroller around the perimeter of the park.

Dani found an empty bench, took a seat, and checked for messages on her cell phone. There were none. She kept her phone out in case Mimi called.

As she put her face to the sun, an odd sensation washed over her. Her skin prickled, the sort of feeling one got when they felt they were being watched. She glanced over her shoulder in time to catch sight of a man with his dog.

Frank Petri.

A coincidence?

Had he followed her to the park?

She had no idea, but she planned on finding out. She stood, slipped her phone into her purse, and walked briskly toward him.

A glance over his shoulder prompted him to step up his pace.

He definitely appeared to have seen her. When she broke into a jog, he started to run with the dog at his side, disappearing behind the public bathrooms. By the time she got to a spot where she could see both sides of the park, he was gone. She looked around, past the tennis courts and across the street at a row of two-story houses. Nothing. *Damn.*

What was going on? Had he seen her enter Cameron's house and followed her here?

She took a moment to catch her breath before heading back to the bench, where she forced herself to forget all about Frank Petri and his dog. He had seemed harmless enough when she'd met him. Her only concern at this moment was whether or not Mimi had information. Dani hoped Mimi hadn't changed her mind about coming to the park.

No sooner had the thought entered her mind than she spotted Mimi walking her way.

Mimi's mouth dropped open when she drew near. "What happened to you?"

"I was caught off guard and attacked by an intruder in my office. I'll be fine."

"Who would do such a thing?"

"We don't know. Detective James Whitton is looking into the matter."

Mimi took a seat on the bench beside her. "I wasn't going to come," she admitted. "But I put myself in your shoes for a minute and thought of my own daughter and granddaughter. I can't imagine what you must have gone through and are still going through. The not knowing. So I called the temp agency and made up a story about needing to talk to Rebecca Carr about a project she worked on when she was at RAYTEX." Mimi exhaled. "I'm sorry to say she's no longer at the agency. I asked for a social security number, but they said they couldn't give me that sort of information. I was able to get a telephone number and address, but when I called the number, I got a recording telling me the number has been disconnected." She handed Dani a piece of paper. "I wrote down the address, which appears to be an apartment complex in Carmichael."

"Thank you," Dani said.

Mimi stood, looked around.

"It means a lot to me that you went out of your way to help. I'm sorry I put you in an uncomfortable position, but—" Dani shook her head. "Nothing. Just thank you."

Mimi nodded. "Good luck. I do hope you can find peace."

———

The apartment complex in Carmichael had seen better days. Trash bins in the parking lot overflowed with garbage. The walls were cracked and the building could use fresh paint. More importantly, if Rebecca Carr still resided in apartment 29 B, would she even talk to Dani?

It was time to find out.

She headed up the stairs, following the signage with apartment numbers and arrows, until she was standing in front of the door. Without wasting another second, she knocked.

A child, maybe three years old, opened the door. Dani smiled at her. "Is your mom home?"

The child had a round face and adorable chubby cheeks. The little girl shook her head, which worried Dani until a man in his late twenties peeked out from a room inside the apartment. His eyes grew wide. "Sophie! What are you doing?"

When Sophie smiled, a dimple appeared.

The man frowned at Dani as he approached and took the child into his arms. "Can I help you?"

"I'm looking for a woman named Rebecca Carr, dark hair, about my height."

"Sorry. Nobody here named Rebecca."

"She lived here five years ago."

"Oh, well, good luck with that. I've only been here for six months, and my wife and I are already thinking about leaving. The place is falling apart."

"I'm sorry."

He shrugged. "That's life, I guess. You might want to talk to management," he said. "Not that they'll be helpful."

"Thank you. I'll do that."

He shut the door, and Dani went to the main office, where she was bluntly told that they did not keep records of tenants who were no longer living in their complex. That was it. Sophie's dad had been right. Management was less than helpful.

As she drove back to her office, her thoughts meandered. She needed to find Rebecca Carr, and she needed help. With that thought in mind, she made a U-turn at the light and headed for the police department on Franklin Boulevard.

She lucked out when she caught Detective Whitton on his way into the building after taking a lunch break. She knew this because he had a spot of mustard on his shirt.

"Hey," he said when he noticed her. "What are you doing here?" He angled his head. "The bruises are fading. Lookin' good."

She snorted. "I need to talk to you inside, if that's okay?"

He signed her in at the front desk. The waiting room was filled to capacity. She followed Detective Whitton to his office, weaving around cubicles where uniformed officers waded in paperwork, past rows of file cabinets and interview rooms. The place clamored with activity and noise: police radios squawking, keyboards clicking, and the low murmurs of dispatchers at their stations and citizens filing complaints.

He was one of the lucky few with a private office. He told her to take a seat, then offered her coffee, which she declined. Once he was seated, he gave her a long, hard look, his head tilted to one side, and said, "What are you going to do when I retire?"

"Are you really retiring this time?"

He chuckled. "You sound like my wife. But the answer is yes. I'd like to spend more time tinkering in my woodshop and maybe take Teresa on a cruise."

She smiled, trying to think of how to ask him for yet another favor.

"What is it?" he asked. "You've got that look on your face. Even through the rainbow of bruises, I can see it. What do you need?"

"Before I get to the reason I came, any updates regarding the Dylan Rushdan murder?"

He shook his head. "No fingerprints. No witnesses."

She didn't press him further. It was an open case, and if there was anything he thought she should know, he would tell her. Reaching into her purse, she pulled out a piece of paper and slid it across his desk. Written in all caps was Rebecca Carr's name, along with "Skyler Temp Agency," where Rebecca had worked five years ago. "Rebecca Carr is the woman I mentioned when you paid me a visit at the hospital—the woman in the pictures taken at my ex-husband's company picnic before Tinsley was abducted."

He glanced at the paper as she talked.

"I've used all my usual databases and techniques to locate her, but Rebecca Carr doesn't seem to exist," Dani explained. "She must have changed her name. I was able to get a number and an address where she resided at the time, but the number has been disconnected and she's no longer living at the apartment."

"And . . . ?"

"And so, once again I am at your mercy. I need your help, and I was hoping you could do some digging for me. The temp agency should have her social security number on file. I would think they would have done a background check. If not, wouldn't they need her SSN for wage-reporting purposes?"

Elbows propped on his desk, he made a steeple with his fingers. "I'll do what I can, but only under one condition."

"What's that?"

"Promise me you'll go straight home and get some rest."

"I thought you said I was looking good."

"I lied."

She laughed. "Okay. I promise."

"I don't believe you'll do any such thing."

She chuckled. "I don't know what I'll do if you ever really do retire."

"You'll be fine, Dani. You'll be fine."

CHAPTER TWENTY-EIGHT

Ali stiffened when she heard a car pull into the garage. Time held still until keys jingled outside the front door. Straightening her spine, she finger-brushed her hair, trying to appear relaxed, which was far from reality. Her heart pounded as if a herd of horses were galloping within her chest. Looking down at the book in her lap, she turned the page and continued to read.

The door clicked open and then closed, followed by the clicks and snaps of too many locks. When Carlin stepped into the family room, she looked up and smiled brightly.

He smiled back at her. "You look happy. Did you have a good day?"

"I did."

"I haven't had lunch. I'm starved. I'll make us both something."

Her body tensed as she watched him head straight for the kitchen. Seconds later he returned, holding up the envelope she'd worked so hard on.

Her stomach dropped.

He knew. How could that be?

"Remind me to take this with me when I leave in the morning. Otherwise the lights might be shut off," he said with a laugh.

She laughed too, a little too heartily.

"Are you sure you're okay? You don't look well." He set the envelope on the table and stepped close enough so that he could put the back of his palm against her forehead. "You're clammy. I'll get the thermometer so we can take your temperature and make sure you don't have a fever."

"I'm fine. Really. It's my foot. It's been aching all day."

"I'll make us a sandwich. Do you like tuna?"

"That sounds good. Would you like me to help?"

"No. No," he said. "Don't get up. I want you to rest."

Her insides churned as she listened to all the sounds coming from the kitchen. The minutes ticked by, slowly. She kept reading her book, turning the pages without comprehension. Every so often she would look at the envelope, stare at it as if it were a snake that might strike at any moment.

Regret had set in. She never should have attempted such a stunt. Not today. It was too soon, too risky. His mother would be visiting soon. She should have waited until the woman came and left.

Too late now.

He entered the room holding a tray and set it on the table next to the envelope. He took a seat next to her, so close she could smell the same sickly aftershave he always wore. He removed the book from her lap before handing her one of the plates from the tray. "Here. Eat. You'll feel better afterward."

She took a bite, chewing slowly, her nerves making it difficult to eat.

He gobbled down half of his sandwich. "Did you use your sketch-book to draw anything?"

She shook her head.

"So what did you do all day?"

"I watched a little television and did some reading."

"What's the book about?"

She shrugged. "It's a romance. Two people meeting and falling in love."

"Sort of like us."

She took another bite of her sandwich.

He reached into his pocket and pulled out his phone. "I have something I want you to watch." Gesturing toward the remote, he asked her to turn on the TV. She did as he asked, wondering what he was up to, since she noticed a sudden stiffness in his upper body as he fiddled with his phone.

She saw him click on an app on his phone and then input a passcode.

"There," he said, prompting her to look at the TV screen.

It was a black-and-white picture of the inside of his house. She recognized his front door and knew the video was taken recently because she could see the new latches. She thought it was a still image until she walked into view.

The silence was maddening as they both watched her attempts to move toward the door and then hop backward out of harm's way.

Carlin fiddled with his phone. The screen flashed, went dark, before another camera view appeared showing her making her way into the family room, opening the sketch pad, and ripping out a page.

"I thought you didn't draw anything?"

"A few doodles," she said, feeling like she might be sick, praying the video would go black and it would only be a matter of convincing him she did nothing wrong. But the video clips didn't end. They were never-ending, like her time in captivity. Cameras were hidden everywhere, tracking her every move. When they got to the part where she was on the floor, scrubbing it clean, he leaned over and picked up the envelope. He examined it closely, turning it this way and that, even went so far as to bring it to his nose and sniff.

She tried to swallow, but her mouth was dry.

With a dramatic flourish, he ripped open the envelope and pulled out the statement. The note she'd written fell to his lap.

"What is this, I wonder?"

She said nothing.

"Words," he said.

"It's a mistake," she told him. "I made a mistake. Please forgive me."

He seemed to contemplate her words. His face had not reddened as it did when he was angry. He unfolded the note and read it, placed it on the table. Very carefully, he removed the plate from her lap and put it back on the tray.

"You want forgiveness?" he asked.

She nodded.

"Show me." He took her hand and placed it on his crotch. "Show me how sorry you are."

The second he removed his hand from hers she snatched her hand back to her lap. He was gross. She was going to be sick.

"Stand up and take off your dress. Maybe do a little dance for me. That would be a good start."

She couldn't breathe. The thrashing sound of her heartbeat in her ears made it impossible to think. "I can't."

"You mean you won't."

"Please. I said I was sorry. I won't ever betray you again. I swear."

He jumped to his feet, grabbed both her arms, and yanked her from the couch. She hit her head on the table on her way to the ground, knocking the tray to the floor.

She screamed as he dragged her past the front entrance and down the hall to the same room he'd taken her into before. The room with the chair. The torture room.

"No! Let me go!"

He dropped her arms and gave her a swift kick to the stomach. "Shut up!"

She grunted.

When he turned away, she quickly belly crawled her way out of the room, making her way down the hallway, clawing and pushing with her good foot. If she could reach the bedroom, she could try to lock him out.

"Not so fast, Ali." He grabbed a handful of her hair and pulled her around and dragged her back to the room. Scooping her into his arms, he plopped her into the chair. She reached for him, clawed at his face, her jagged nails leaving trails of blood across his jaw.

He punched her in the chest and then the gut, leaving her gasping for air as he reached for something on the metal tray beside him. She felt a pinch and then saw the syringe. Within seconds her head grew foggy and her vision blurred. She prayed she would pass out.

He pulled the straps tight around her arms and legs, the leather digging into her flesh. After strapping down her head, he gave each strap a tug. He let his hand linger on her bandaged leg before he squeezed.

She howled in pain, wishing he would kill her and be done with it.

Again, he reached toward the worktable. This time he held up a drill for her to see. "My mom used to call me a jack-of-all-trades. I always wanted to be a dentist, but that would have taken *so* many years of hard work." He shook his head. "I just couldn't commit. And dental school doesn't come cheap, you know."

"Please, Carlin," she said, her voice hardly more than a whisper. "Give me one more chance."

"You were warned, Ali. No more chances. You could have had it all." He held up a stainless steel utensil that was as long as a pencil and had two sharp ends. "I believe this is called a probe, which is fitting, don't you think?" He set it down. Whistling while he worked, he used what looked like a shoehorn to pry her mouth apart so that he could insert a block to keep her mouth open. He hummed to himself as he tapped the metal end to her teeth and jabbed the sharp tip into her gums. "Oops!"

She tasted blood.

The lines in his forehead deepened. "Bad news, Ali. It looks like you're going to need a root canal. The problem is, I don't have any Novocain."

His eyes danced, and his body shook with excitement. What made a human being torture someone and take pleasure from the act? For the first time since she'd been held captive, she wondered what had happened to him to make him this way.

As soon as he walked to the other side of the room, she tried to wriggle her arms free, but it was no use. Her lips trembled as she watched him fiddle with a stool before rolling it her way. He sat. "Much better. My back was getting sore."

Her inability to speak coherently, now that the block had been inserted, prevented her from pleading and begging for him to stop. Her heart hammered against her chest. Her arms and legs shook.

He grabbed hold of a drill, brought it close to her ear so that she heard the buzz, buzz, buzz as he used the foot pedal to turn it on and off. And then he brought the drill to her wide-open mouth and got started.

CHAPTER
TWENTY-NINE

For the first time since being attacked, Dani returned to the office. She entered with her arm held straight ahead, a can of pepper spray in her grasp and her thumb on the nozzle as she walked past her desk, making her way to the kitchen.

From the looks of things, someone had cleaned up the place. When she went to open the door to the basement, she hesitated, relieved to find a dark, empty space. The stairs were solid beneath her feet as she made her way down to the basement to make sure nobody was hiding out.

Back on the main floor, she didn't like the rock-hard feeling in her stomach or the way she subconsciously held her breath as she took a seat at her desk, fearing someone might pop out at any moment.

A few minutes passed before she powered on her computer. Once the screen brightened, she searched social media sites to see if Frank Petri had a presence. Nothing turned up on Instagram or Twitter, but when she logged on to Facebook and typed his name into the browser, she hit the jackpot. Frank's picture had recently been updated. He was sitting on a bench under the shade of a willow tree, his dog, Sadie, at his side. She scrolled through his posts. His wife had passed away unexpectedly six months ago.

Dani looked at her calendar, taking note that two months after his wife died, Cameron Bennington had begun to notice strange things happening inside her home.

Dani grabbed a pad of paper and wrote down his birthdate. When people like Frank shared their private information with friends and family, they were also sharing it with hackers and scammers and people like her who needed information. Once that material was out there, there was no reeling it back in.

By the time she was finished, she knew Frank Petri as well as she knew most acquaintances. But she still needed an address. And to get that, she would need to use one of her pay databases. The more information she could gather on Frank Petri, the better. A social security number was always ideal as far as collecting information, especially when looking for someone with a common surname like Brown or Smith. But in Frank Petri's case Dani could only type his name, date of birth, and the Sacramento region and hope for a match.

The pinwheel spun while the machine worked its magic. Seconds later, she had an address. Next, using a new tab, she opened Google Maps, entered Frank's address, and asked for directions to Cameron Bennington's home address.

Interesting, but not too surprising, Frank Petri lived two blocks away from Cameron.

Now that she knew where he lived and had an idea of who Frank Petri was, she thought about what might be the best way to handle the man. Without proof of him entering and exiting Cameron's house, no arrest would be possible. And without consequences for his actions, there would be no reason for Frank Petri to stop what he was doing.

She could contact Detective Whitton, who might be able to bring him in for questioning, but not much more than that.

Her phone vibrated. It was Quinn.

"Ethan is missing!" Quinn said when she picked up the call.

"Hold on," Dani said. "Take a breath and tell me why you think he's missing."

"We spent all morning posting flyers in Midtown. Once we were nearly done, I told him to wait while I backtracked to get my car. When I returned, he was gone. I've tried to call him multiple times, but his phone has been shut off."

That same feeling she'd had when she went to the school to pick up Tinsley and discovered she was gone swept over Dani—a surreal, out-of-body experience as fear took over. *Don't go there,* she told herself. *Stay calm. Ethan is tough, street smart.* "It's okay," Dani said. "Ethan probably got bored, started checking out a few stores. Where are you now?"

"On my way to the office."

"That's where I'm at," Dani told her. "Let's talk when you get here."

While she waited for Quinn to arrive, Dani searched for Ethan's home phone number. She'd already done some research on Ethan, and it didn't take long to find what she was looking for. She called the number, and after a good amount of ringing, there was a beep. Dani left her name and number, told Ethan's mom she wanted to make sure Ethan had made it home. She left her name and number and asked her to call.

Quinn walked through the door minutes later, her face flushed, and dropped into the chair in front of Dani's desk.

"Do you need some water?"

"No," Quinn said. "I just need to find Ethan."

"Tell me again what happened."

Quinn told her everything, starting with the moment she picked up Ethan that morning. When she got to the part where she had dropped her purse and Ethan saw the way the sun reflected off her keys, reminding him of what he'd seen in the back of the van when Ali was abducted, Dani's stomach clenched.

"Let me get this straight," Dani said. "Before you left Ethan to get your car, the plan was for you to pick him up and drive to the shopping center where Ethan had seen Ali pushed into the van. Is that right?"

"Yes."

"Maybe that's where Ethan went."

A frown creased Quinn's brow. "But why wouldn't he answer his phone?"

"Maybe it ran out of juice." As Dani came to her feet, she told Quinn that she'd left a message with Ethan's mom. Certainly if Ethan wasn't home when she finished cleaning houses, she would return Dani's call.

As they drove, Quinn updated Dani on her visit to Grayson Electric and her talk with the owner of Green Haven Construction. Unless Ed Hoffman called her back with information, number one and number four would have to be crossed off their list.

It didn't take long to get where they were going. Quinn pointed out the spot behind the tiny shopping center where Ethan had seen Ali disappear. After Dani parked, they both stepped out. The extreme dryness and heat sucked the moisture from Dani's skin as she walked to the front of the car where Quinn was waiting.

"I'll check the sandwich shop, the hair salon, and the florist," Quinn said.

Dani did a double take. There was something different about Quinn. The hair was the same. No makeup, jeans, and a black V-neck T-shirt emblazoned with the words Be Kind—all the same. But the confidence was new. She seemed focused, decisive, and composed.

Quinn gestured to another group of retail shops close by. "You can start over there." She used a tissue to wipe sweat from her face. "While we're looking for Ethan, we might as well ask the shop owners if they have used a locksmith in the past two months. Meet me back here when you're done."

Dani wasn't used to taking direction, but she headed off just the same, wishing she'd worn a hat to protect her from the sun. She started with the antique shop, as advised. Bells chimed when she walked in, and the smell of musty cloth and dust greeted her.

She wove her way between narrow aisles crowded with glass display cases and tables loaded with jewelry and vintage glassware. A beautiful grandfather clock caught her eye. The place was big on wartime paraphernalia—everything you could ever want.

But no Ethan.

She smiled at the woman behind the register, wondered how she moved around without knocking something over. "Hi. My name is Dani, and I'm looking for a twelve-year-old boy."

When the woman shook her head, the long crystal earrings moved with her. "It's been slow," the woman said. "I would have seen him. Sorry."

"I'm also looking for a man—"

"Aren't we all, honey. Aren't we all."

Dani smiled. "He's a locksmith, and I heard he did some work for one of the businesses in this shopping center. I was hoping maybe you would know who might have been in need of that kind of work. Maybe a new shop owner?"

"Sorry. I wish I could help you, but I don't know of anyone who used a locksmith."

"Thanks anyway," Dani said. "I love your store. I'll have to come back when I have more time."

The woman wasn't paying her any mind. She'd probably heard it all before, customers who promised to come back but never did.

Dani stepped outside. It was too hot to be picky about which store she walked into next, so she chose the closest one and stepped inside. There were three customers waiting at the cash register, so she got in line.

It was one of those places where people traded their used clothes for cash or other used clothes. She'd never been to one before. She found herself wondering if this was the type of store Tinsley would have enjoyed. She always loved playing dress-up. The more frills and lace and color, the better. Dani pulled out her phone and checked to see if there were any messages from Detective Whitton about Rebecca Carr. Nothing yet.

Sweat trickled down the back of Dani's neck by the time the woman with long, straight white-gray hair waved her forward. Her name tag said HEATHER.

"I don't have any clothes to trade," Dani explained, "just a quick question. I'm looking for a particular tradesman who might have been in the area, and I was wondering if you guys might have used a locksmith recently."

Heather turned toward another staff member working in the back and called out to her. "Hey, Sheila! Did we have any locks in the past month that needed to be fixed or replaced around here?"

"Not that I know of," Sheila responded.

Heather shrugged. "Sorry."

Dani thanked her and left the store. The pet shop next door resulted in more of the same. Nobody knew anything about a locksmith, and Ethan was nowhere to be seen. The temperature outside had risen another five degrees, at least. She could see heat waves coming off the asphalt.

"Dani!" Quinn was walking her way. "Any luck?"

"Not so far. How about you?"

She shook her head. "What are we going to do about Ethan?"

"We'll drive to his home and see if he's there. If not, we go back to the office and regroup."

"I feel like I've wasted so much time," Quinn said. "Three steps forward, five steps backward. I'm supposed to find people, not lose them. If something happened to Ethan, I'll never be able to forgive myself."

Dani wanted to wrap her arms around Quinn and tell her everything would be okay, that no matter what happened it wasn't her fault, chin up and all that good stuff, but she knew Quinn would take it as a sign of weakness on her part. Quinn needed a win like an alcoholic needed a shot of vodka. Although she'd never said the words outright, Quinn had gotten into this business because she thought that if she could help find missing people, maybe she could reunite families and friends and take away their pain, and hopefully some of her pain too. "Come on," Dani offered, instead of the well-intended-but-hollow, pump-her-up, feel-good speech. "Let's get out of this heat."

Chapter Thirty

Carlin carried an armful of blankets down to the basement. It was time to get everything in order so he could finally introduce his mother to Ali, let Mother decide if she was worth salvaging. He'd known all along it would take some time to earn Ali's trust, but her inability to cooperate worried him. How could he go about his business if she wasn't even willing to try?

Not once had he questioned his love for Ali and all the possibilities that lay ahead of them. Not until he watched her attempts to leave the house, again and again, despite the obvious pain it must have caused her. The note she'd slipped in with a utility bill, though, was the worst kind of betrayal.

It made no sense.

He was offering her the world—a beautiful house and his complete and utter devotion. Wasn't that what all women wanted? To be loved and cherished and treated like the delicate flower that they were?

He flicked on the light and set the blankets on a cot where his mother used to sleep until she badgered Carlin enough to make him bring down a table and a couple of chairs so she could sit up.

Mother was sitting at a small rustic wood table, right where she always was, her body tilting to the left. Her hair could use some attention, and it was probably time to change the flowery muumuu that hung loose, like the skin on her face. But overall she looked pretty good, considering she'd been sitting down here in the basement for quite some time.

After he'd drowned her, he'd placed her lovingly on her bed upstairs. It had been fascinating, watching the stiffening of her muscles, but after three days the pungent odors became too much. That's when he'd invested in the dental equipment, including the chair. He hadn't added the straps until later, of course, but Mother had always wanted him to be a doctor or dentist, so he figured he could practice dentistry on his mother without all the schooling. But first he'd had to learn how to embalm a body to get rid of all the horrid bodily fluids that were making it hard to breathe around her.

It was amazing what a person could learn on the internet. He'd used a scalpel to make incisions in her carotid artery and internal jugular vein, but without the machine embalmers used, he'd had to make all sorts of incisions and then massage her obese body for days on end just to drain most of the blood without making a huge mess. Once that was done, embalmers would usually distribute the embalming fluid and then suction fluid from the organs using some other fancy machine he didn't have. Instead, he'd sliced Mother open and burned most of her organs out back. He could have bought formaldehyde-based chemicals, but it would have been too much work. Instead he did what taxidermists did and scraped the fat from the underside of her skin, rubbed her with borax to help the skin dry, then stuffed her with cotton and sewed her back up. After that he carefully washed her body and then her hair, combing it back nicely. He even applied some lipstick.

The whole process had taken him weeks. By the time he started working on her teeth, some of them had fallen out.

"You're looking good, Mother. Sorry about the racket upstairs. You've probably been wondering what I've been up to."

He dropped down into the seat across from her and folded his hands on the table. "No. I'm not going to give you a bath. Those days are over. Thank God. That was wrong of you to touch me improperly. In fact, you're lucky I've kept you here with me all these years."

He listened to her rattle on about it being her house and her money. It was true. Even though he had his own business, her social security checks were still deposited into their combined checking account every month, which covered most of the bills and then some.

His fist came down hard on the table in front of him, startling her. Finally, she was quiet. "I'm going upstairs to get Ali. But you have to promise to behave."

She nodded, even tried to be cute with a pinky swear for good measure, but he just rolled his eyes and headed back upstairs.

Ali hung in his arms like a rag doll as he headed back to the basement. She'd lost some weight, which was a good thing because otherwise he might have tweaked his back. He wondered if he'd given her too many drugs. She looked comatose. He put her down on the cot, felt for a pulse.

Mother started nagging immediately, afraid he'd killed the girl.

He made sure Mother didn't see him roll his eyes before he looked her way. "When she wakes up," Carlin told Mother, "the two of you will have a chance to get acquainted. You're probably going to fall in love with her. She's stubborn and feisty like you. But I'm conflicted," he said as he walked toward Mother. "She's done some things I'm not happy about, which is why I need your help deciding whether or not she's truly the girl for me. She's beautiful, but—"

A loud thud interrupted his speech. He straightened. Listened.

The noise had come from the garage. He'd almost forgotten about the boy. Between the extreme heat and the lack of oxygen, he figured Ethan Grant might be dead by now and hadn't been in any hurry to find out. Obviously that wasn't the case. It was a good thing he kept the garage, like everything else, locked up tight. The only way Ethan Grant would be able to open the trunk or the garage door would be to pull on the emergency release cord. But Carlin had removed the cord. He wasn't stupid. He'd also removed the device inside the trunk of the car.

Maybe an animal had gotten into the garage when he'd pulled in; it had happened before. He told Mother he'd be right back, then headed up the stairs, locking the door behind him in case Mother or Ali got any grand ideas of escaping.

He marched through the kitchen to the side door that led to the garage. Again, he slipped his keys from his pocket. When he stepped inside, he listened carefully for any sound. No need to turn on a light since plenty of sunlight spilled in through the barred window. He got down on all fours and looked under the frame of the car. No critters and no kid. He pushed himself to his feet and went to stand in front of the trunk. Again, he listened, heard nothing. Not a peep. Hoping to scare the kid if he was trying to pull a fast one, he hammered a fist against the trunk. "Are you in there, kid?"

No answer.

He was about to pull out the fob and push the button to open the trunk when warning lights flickered in his brain. What if the kid was smarter than he looked? If he was alive, he could be waiting for Carlin to open the trunk just as he was about to do. Carlin's imagination ran wild. What if Ethan Grant had a grasp of his tire iron and was just waiting to bash Carlin's head in? There wasn't much space in the trunk, but the kid was small.

Two could play this game.

He made his way to the corner of the room where he kept his tools, looked around, and then grabbed the sledgehammer leaning against the wall. He then walked back to the trunk and stood far enough away that the kid would have to reveal himself before he could take a swing at him.

Carlin hit the button on the fob, pocketed the keys, then held the sledgehammer like Babe Ruth held a bat in his prime as he watched the trunk slowly open. He felt as if he were watching some sort of horror movie, waiting in anticipation for Pennywise to pop out and show himself.

He felt unreasonably let down when nothing happened.

Inching his way forward to see inside, still holding the sledgehammer, Carlin stepped close enough to see that the trunk was empty.

What the hell?

He hardly had a chance to let the empty trunk register before the kid leaped from atop a high cabinet, pouncing on him like a jungle cat taking down its prey, his scrawny legs circling his waist, squeezing tight while his hands grabbed hold of Carlin's face, his fingers poking into his eyes as he sank his teeth into Carlin's neck.

Somehow Carlin managed to stay on his feet, gritting his teeth as he pulled at the kid's arms, swiveling around and slamming his backside into a cabinet to get the kid to drop.

When that didn't work he staggered to the area where he kept his tools and reached for a hammer. The kid dropped to the ground and ran for the door. He was fast and Carlin had to leap across the space in order to grab the kid's ankle, hitting his chin on the cement floor in the process. White-hot pain shot through his jaw, but he held on tight to the boy's ankle, spittle building at the corners of his mouth as he pulled the kid toward him, inches at a time, until he had hold of the kid's waist.

The boy thrashed like a slippery fish, twisted around, and hawked a loogie that hit him square in the eye.

"I'm going to kill you, kid," Carlin said through gritted teeth. "That's a given. But if you don't stop fighting me, I'm going to kill your mother too."

It took a few seconds, but his threat worked. The kid stopped fighting him.

CHAPTER THIRTY-ONE

Dani stayed in the car and scrolled through her phone messages while Quinn knocked on the door to Ethan's home. She heard Quinn bang hard and call Ethan's name more than once before finally returning to the car and jumping into the passenger seat.

"Nobody's home. Should we call Detective Whitton?"

"It's been only a couple of hours since you saw Ethan last. James won't be able to do anything. Let's stick to the plan. We'll head back to the office and figure out where we go from here."

Quinn was quiet on the ride back to the agency.

Dani made sure to enter first, still acutely aware of what had happened. "Thanks for cleaning up the place."

"No problem." Quinn walked over to her desk and opened her computer. "I didn't have time to see how much damage, if any, was done to the basement. I'm going to take a quick look while my computer boots up."

Dani followed her downstairs. Whoever had hit her over the head had definitely been looking for something. The contents of every bin had been dumped onto the floor. She picked up a bin and started piling her things back inside.

"Do you think someone was looking for valuables?" Quinn asked as she collected scattered photos from the ground. "Or could it be linked to one of the cases?"

"I wish I knew." When Dani straightened, she found herself looking at a wall of faces. Quinn had added to the wall since Dani was down here last. Three missing persons had been circled in red marker.

Dani set down the box and stepped close enough to read the article below one of the pictures. Her name was Gretchen Myles. Her family had just moved to Sacramento when Gretchen snagged a job cutting hair at Best Cuts Salon in East Sacramento, not far from where Ali was taken. Three weeks later, at the age of seventeen, Gretchen Myles went missing.

Quinn walked up behind her. "I've been looking for missing girls who disappeared in the past three years, females who were around the same age as Ali. Gretchen's the only one who fits the criteria."

Dani nodded, her mind swirling with speculation. "Tell me what you know."

Quinn pointed to a girl named Alice Walker, fifteen, and Tanya Lee, sixteen. "These were both runaways. Both found. I've been meaning to remove them from the wall."

"What about Gretchen Myles?" Dani asked.

"I called the investigator working Ali's case to talk to him about Gretchen, but he shut me down. He told me that if old man Whitton wanted to waste his time with me that was one thing, but the more time I sucked out of his day, the less he got done. 'For every person they find,' he told me, 'another goes missing, and without a body or any tangible evidence, that missing person gets lost in the quagmire.'"

Dani had heard it all before. The enormous backlog of homicides and missing persons, along with dwindling resources, made it difficult to get the job done, which was where Dani and Quinn came into the picture. Dani tugged the article from the wall and headed upstairs.

"What are you doing?"

"Our computers should be ready to go. I'm going to see what I can find out about Gretchen."

"What about Ethan?"

Dani waved the picture above her head and kept walking. "Gretchen Myles went missing eighteen months ago, disappeared less than a mile from the spot Ethan swears he saw Ali picked up. She was seventeen, the same age as Ali. We need a connection to this guy, and Gretchen Myles could be it."

Quinn dropped the pictures she was holding into a bin and followed her up the stairs.

Once they were both seated at their desks, Quinn said, "I should have followed up on Gretchen Myles, but once Ethan Grant entered the picture, I thought the rest would be a cinch."

"Don't beat yourself up. I'd like you to look up every locksmith in a ten-mile radius from where Ali was taken, while I do a search on Gretchen Myles."

Dani clicked away at the keyboard while inwardly, she prayed for a break. They needed one fast. The girl could be fighting for her life, and now Ethan could also be at risk.

It was time to focus. For the next thirty minutes they worked in silence, the only noise the clacking of their keyboards.

The thought of Ethan possibly being scooped up by a madman added urgency to the case. The clock was ticking.

Dani glanced at the time. Four o'clock. Best Cuts Salon closed at seven. She usually got the best results when she talked to shop owners in person rather than on the phone. Talking to family was another matter, though. If she just showed up at a residence and knocked on the door, people were less likely to talk. She tapped in Gretchen's home number and waited. A young man answered on the second ring. Dani explained why she was calling and asked if anyone who knew Gretchen would be willing to answer some questions. He said he was Gretchen's brother and to go ahead and ask away.

He was friendly and easy to talk to. He missed his sister and wanted to know what happened to her.

"I realize your family had just moved to Sacramento when your sister went missing, but do you know if Gretchen had made any friends in that short time? Male or female?"

"Not really, but she seemed to like everyone at the salon where she was working." He cleared his throat. "Before you ask about her being a runaway, the answer is no. She was the one who was most excited to move from our small town of Alexander City, Alabama. I, personally, wasn't happy about the move. But go on."

Dani took notes as he talked. "Did Gretchen ever talk to anyone in the family about someone bothering her . . . asking her out, anything like that?"

"I know she was upset about two accidents that occurred at the hair salon where she worked. One lady wanted to be a blonde but walked out of the salon with orange hair. Another guy lost a part of his ear." He let out a sigh. "To tell you the truth, we were all surprised she got the job, considering she'd really only cut family's and friends' hair in Alabama. When she interviewed for the position, I think she made it sound like our little kitchen was some sort of fancy salon."

"So her clients weren't happy with her?"

"Not at all. The woman with the orange hair wanted her fired."

"What about the other guy? Was he upset?"

"I don't think so. We all laughed about it when Gretchen told us how she was the one crying and he was the one trying to make her feel better."

"And that was that?" Dani asked.

"Well, not really. Before she vanished, Mom and Dad said she was the same as always, but I noticed a change in Gretchen."

"How so?"

"She seemed less happy-go-lucky. When I asked her if she was okay, she admitted being worried about losing her job, something about a client being upset, but that's all I know."

"Did she ever mention a name?"

"No. I told her to stop worrying so much. She was getting better at hair. I even let her cut my hair." He laughed.

"Do you know if she kept clients' numbers?"

"No idea. When she disappeared, so did her phone."

Dani thanked him for his help and disconnected the call. She looked at Quinn. "How's it going?"

"Not good," Quinn said. "There are hundreds of locksmiths who do work in the Sacramento area. It will take days to look up every place, and what if this guy doesn't have a website?"

"What about the man you talked to at the construction site. Any luck?"

"He looked busy. I'll be surprised if he even remembers he talked to me, but I'll give him a call later tonight."

"Grab your bag and come with me."

As Dani drove, she told Quinn about her conversation with Gretchen Myles's brother. When Quinn failed to respond, she asked her what was wrong.

"I can't get excited anymore," Quinn said. "Every time Ethan remembered a new detail about Ali's abductor, I figured this was it! We're going to nab the sucker and bring Ali home. And then the construction guy recognized Ethan's drawing and Ethan remembered what he'd seen in the back of the van. Both times my adrenaline spiked." Quinn released a long, ponderous sigh. "I feel like I'm on the craziest roller-coaster ride of my life and I can't get off."

"Sadly," Dani admitted, "hitting roadblocks comes with the job."

"Yeah, but I wonder how many PIs can say they lost someone who was just trying to help out."

"We'll find him," Dani said, praying it was true.

Two blocks from the salon, they finally found a parking spot. Dani paid the meter and hurried to catch up to Quinn. By the time they got to their destination, sweat trickled down Dani's back.

Quinn asked the receptionist sitting at the front desk if the owner of the salon was around, explaining that they were investigators and it was very important that they speak to her.

Without a word spoken, the receptionist turned and walked away.

Dani watched her walk past a row of stylists dressed in black and wearing aprons with pockets, then disappear into a back room. She couldn't remember the last time she'd had someone cut and style her hair. She made a mental note to return once the stitches dissolved and her hair grew back.

The receptionist was already on her way back with a woman Dani assumed was the owner trailing her.

She introduced herself as Sandra Mason. Her skin and makeup were flawless. Dani wasn't a slacker when it came to working hard, but everything about the woman made Dani realize she'd been neglecting herself.

"How can I help you?"

"I have some questions about Gretchen Myles, a young woman you hired eighteen months ago. Apparently there was an unfortunate event concerning a man who came in for a haircut."

Sandra's face paled. "Is he suing?"

"No. Nothing like that."

Her hand came to rest on her chest over her heart. "Thank goodness." She glanced at the receptionist before ushering Dani and Quinn over to the waiting area, where they could speak in semiprivacy.

"By any chance," Dani asked, "do you take down the names and numbers of clients who make an appointment?"

"Absolutely."

Dani leaned in. "And how long do you keep those records?"

"Forever," Sandra said. "I'm sort of anal that way."

Dani looked at Quinn and gave her a thumbs-up.

"I don't want to jump the gun," Dani told Sandra, "but this guy could be bad news, and it's important we find him sooner rather than later."

"We get all kinds of customers, but there was something very off about that guy."

"How so?"

Sandra looked heavenward as if trying to figure out the best way to explain the guy without being offensive. Finally she met Dani's gaze and said, "He lacked social skills. Lonely, maybe stressed, the guy couldn't open his mouth without inserting his foot. I felt sort of bad for him because it seemed like he was trying so hard to be a regular guy. I hate to admit it, but nobody wanted to cut his hair so I gave him to the new girl."

"Gretchen Myles."

"Yes."

"Do you think we could take a look at your records from eighteen months ago when Gretchen was working here?" If Sandra refused, it was back to square one.

"If you swear this has nothing to do with his ear getting chopped off, I'll take you back to my office right now and let you go to town."

"Cross my heart," Dani said, leaving out the "hope to die" part.

Exactly thirty-six minutes later, Dani and Quinn left the establishment with a name and a number. The heat didn't stop them from fast-walking the entire two blocks to Dani's car. Once the engine was humming, she blasted the air-conditioning.

Neither of them said a word as Quinn pulled her laptop from the bag she carried around, flipped it open, and hit the power button. The oxygen inside the car thrummed with hope and possibilities as she used her phone as a hot spot so that she could use Google to do a search on Carlin Reed. The first link on the list was for CSR Locksmith: Fast Response.

"Click on the link," Dani said, feeling the spike of adrenaline Quinn had talked about earlier.

The website that popped up on the screen was impressive.

Have an emergency? Call us. 24-7.

There were pictures and customer testimonials. A virtual gold mine of information.

Quinn clicked on an image. "That must be him."

Dani let out a whoop of joy. "Look at the van. It's nearly the exact logo that Ethan drew."

"CSR Locksmith," Quinn said under her breath.

"Go back to the home page," Dani said. "I didn't see an address."

Quinn clicked back and scrolled through. No address. "I'll put his name into the database."

The tension was thick, the only sound the clicking of keys as Quinn pulled up a pay database and typed Carlin Reed's name into the space provided.

They both read the address out loud at the same time. "Twelve eighteen Riverside Boulevard."

Dani typed the address into her navigation system and hit "Go." "It should take us fifteen minutes from here, give or take."

"The house belongs to Marjorie Reed," Quinn said. "The satellite feature on Google Maps shows the house sitting in an unfinished development." Quinn's foot was bouncing. "Is it time to call Whitton?"

"There's nothing he can do."

"But it's him," Quinn said. "It has to be."

"All conjecture at this point. Unless Carlin Reed will give the police permission to search his property, or we can prove there's imminent danger to someone's life, police will need a warrant to search his house."

"What about Ethan?"

Dani merged into traffic. "We might not be able to get inside Carlin Reed's house, but we can do a drive-by."

CHAPTER
THIRTY-TWO

Ali Cross opened her eyes and saw nothing but blackness. She tried to move her arm, surprised to discover she wasn't constrained. She was lying on a cot, flat on her back. She reached out her arms to see if there was anything in front of her or to either side, but there was nothing but air.

Pain sizzled and popped throughout her body. She didn't think anything could hurt more than her foot, but she was wrong. She pushed herself upward until she was sitting, her legs straight out.

Her jaw hung open, saliva dripping down her chin. She put a hand to her face and gingerly felt around. Her cheeks and mouth were so swollen it was hard to tell what the freak had done to her. Recalling the drill, she inserted her index finger into her mouth.

Her heart sank.

She had gaping holes in two of her molars and spaces where at least three teeth used to be. Her tongue had been jabbed and cut, making it impossible to close her mouth. Tears slid down her face as she reached down to feel her legs. He hadn't broken anything else. Her bad foot was still wrapped in bandages.

Thinking maybe he'd thrown her back in the shed, she climbed off the cot gingerly and positioned herself onto all fours. She dragged her bad foot along as she made her way across the room, heading for the door, where she hoped to find water.

The top of her head bumped into something hard, making her wince. She reached for the object and clasped her hand around what felt like the leg of a chair or table. Slowly, using all her strength, every muscle in her body straining, she worked her way upward until she was standing on her good foot. Taking tiny hops, she followed the smooth edge of what had to be a table. It was oval-shaped. Her knee bumped into something. After pulling away, she held still, wondering if someone was in the room with her. When nothing happened, she blindly reached out, surprised when the tips of her fingers brushed against something that felt like a bird's nest, a collection of wiry and brittle—

She gasped.

The object fell toward her. She hopped backward, her eyes wide, her heart hammering wildly inside her chest. What was it? Had she felt a skull? Oh, God. It was too horrible to imagine. She began frantically hopping away, dragging her fingers across rough, jagged walls as she went, hoping to find a light switch.

A door opened. A light came on. Footfalls sounded on the stairs.

Carlin stood there, a freakish man. "I see you met my mother."

What? She looked to the area where she'd stood seconds ago and saw an old woman, skin and bones, leaning to one side. Her hair was like a cocoon around her head. Pearls hung around her neck. Her shriveled eyes bulged from dark sockets.

Ali's hands flew to her mouth as she let out a strangled cry, watching him warily as he walked across the room and propped up the thing he called his mother before kissing the top of the woman's head.

They weren't in the shed. The walls were brick and there were no windows. Ali held back a cry when he came for her, grabbed her arm, and tugged hard, making her stumble and take awkward hops back to the table, then forced her into the chair across from his mother.

Had the woman been stuffed like hunter's prey?

"Despite how it might look," Carlin said, "I loved my mother. I loved her so much I couldn't bear to live without her. She's the one who told me I needed to go out and find someone to love and cherish and grow old with."

"Why are you doing this?" she asked, her words slightly garbled.

He looked at her quizzically, as if he couldn't believe she was asking such a question. "Do you remember the first time we met?"

He was crazy. What did he want her to say? *Yes, it was wonderful. You grabbed me, put a dirty rag to my mouth, and tossed me in your van.* While these thoughts ran through her mind, she caught a glimpse of the stairs leading up to the main part of the house. No point in hobbling that way. She would never make it.

"Your mom hired me to change the locks at the house."

Her mind raced. He was lying. She'd never seen him before . . . but that wasn't true. When she'd first seen him, there was the tiniest hint of familiarity.

"I was stunned when she said she was running off to pick up her daughter from school. She left me inside the house, all alone!"

His wide grin made her shiver.

"Of course I had to take a look around. Fate brought me to your room, Ali. I even took a pair of your lacy underwear. I sleep with them under my pillow. I knew you were a snooty thing when you walked right past me without saying hello." He smiled. "You were so beautiful, though, so sure of yourself. I made an extra key, but I never used it because I was too busy following you, watching you, hanging on every comment you made on social media."

He sat quietly for a moment, one of his fingers tapping away on the tabletop.

"Sadly I don't think it's going to work out between us, Ali." He looked across the table at his mom. "Don't worry, Mother. I have another girl in mind. She's young, but she'll grow quickly. You're going to love her. Gracie is such a pretty thing. Just ask Ali."

All Ali could hear was a pounding inside her head. The room and everything in it blurred as she lunged for the monster, bringing him to the ground, her body landing on top of his. They rolled around, but she only managed to jab his side with her elbow before he had full control again.

Straddling her, holding her arms above her head and pinned against the floor, he looked into her eyes. "Tsk, tsk, tsk. You are a fiery one. If you had cooperated, I never would have needed to think about going after your sister. I was going to let Mother decide, but I've changed my mind. Although you'd definitely keep things interesting around here, I would prefer someone more docile. I've been making plans for her arrival. No shed for Gracie. She's too perfect. You'll be glad to know that I plan to treat her like royalty."

She shook her head. *No.* "I made a mistake." Her chest tightened. "I can learn to obey. I swear I can. Leave my sister alone. Please."

"Too late for that," he said. "And if you're worried about your mother being alone, don't be. I'll kill her so she won't have to spend the rest of her life looking for her girls and making my life difficult. Maybe I'll bring her down here to keep Mother company."

There was no use trying to get away. He was too strong, and exhaustion was setting in from trying to wriggle free. "You won't get away with this. They're going to catch you."

He shook his head. "It's over, Ali. Nobody is going to save you. I found your witness—the boy on the bike."

No.

"He's in your favorite chair as we speak, strapped in tight."

Carlin pushed to his feet, brushed himself off, and walked to the door. "I'm not sure how long it takes to starve to death." He frowned.

"A week or two? I think it's the dehydration that will kill you first. If I remember correctly, based on what I've read, your skin turns a bluish gray as your organs begin to shut down, especially the brain. You could end up having a stroke, which would be crazy, considering your age. But there you have it. I'm just giving it to you straight."

Sighing, he looked at his mom. "I love you, Mother. Don't take any sass from this one. I know. I know," he said to no one. "It couldn't be helped. I tried. Yes. Okay. Stop nagging. I'll bring you a change of clothes and a hairbrush. Maybe Ali can give you a makeover. I'll be back soon, but only this one time."

He flicked the light off, then on. "I think I'll leave it on for now. Mother gets lonely down here, and I'm sure she would enjoy your company while you're around."

After he shut the door and she heard the familiar click of a lock being engaged, Ali crawled to the table and pulled herself to her feet again.

Think, Ali. Think. It was impossible to do with his mother looking at her. She let out a growl and pushed the table toward the woman. Her chair toppled. What sounded like a bowling ball rolled across the floor and came to a stop at Ali's feet.

She looked down, took a hop backward, and slapped a hand over her mouth to cover a scream. Mother's head had broken loose.

Ali could hardly breathe. She needed to get out of here. She got down on all fours and crawled to where the woman's body lay in a heap on the floor. An arm bone had broken loose. Cotton spilled out of the crevices of what looked like distressed leathery skin. The tips of her bony fingers protruded from her hands.

Grabbing hold of the hem of the woman's dress, she slipped it up to her thighbones, where the flesh he'd tried to preserve had fallen off like the skin of an overcooked turkey.

She'd read in one of her schoolbooks that ancient civilizations had used bones as weapons. Daggers made from femurs were found at an archeological site and tested by scientists, who claimed they were durable and deadly. If using bones for weapons had worked for her ancestors, it could work for her too.

Unsure as to when Carlin would be back, she worked fast, positioning the skeleton just so. She then got to her feet, held on to the table, and stomped her good foot down hard on the hipbone.

The thighbone broke free.

Giddy with hope, she stomped on the kneecap next with the same results. She then stooped and picked up the femur, made her way to the brick wall, and began sanding the smaller end against the brick, back and forth. White dust sprinkled to the ground as she kept at it. If she could sand it down to a sharp point, it might just work. All she had to do was catch him off guard, then plunge his mother's bone into his heart. She was strong. She could do this.

CHAPTER
THIRTY-THREE

Dani kept her eyes on the road while Quinn put away her laptop and then pulled a Taser and a high-voltage stun gun from her bag.

"Where did you get those?" Dani asked.

"Online. I've had them for years."

"Well, you won't be needing them. We're just taking a look around. We have to be patient."

"He's dangerous. He killed a man."

"We don't know that."

The ride was fairly quick and deathly quiet.

As Dani drove slowly past the house, she could hardly believe what she was seeing. Despite having one of the few finished homes on what looked like a twenty-acre development, Carlin Reed had gone to a lot of bother to make sure nobody came onto his property. "Iron bars on every window and a chain-link fence covered in—what is that?"

"It looks like poison ivy," Quinn said. Dani pulled into a driveway two doors down. The house had been framed, but other than that, the lot was a simple square of dirt.

Quinn pocketed her weapons and climbed out of the car. "I'm going to hop the fence and knock on his door."

"Oh, no, you're not."

"If Ethan is in there and something happens to him, I'll never be able to live with myself."

"Get back in the car," Dani said, desperate to stop Quinn before she did something rash.

"I don't have a PI license. I have nothing to lose." Quinn shut the door and jogged, hunched over, toward Carlin Reed's house.

Shit. Shit. Shit. Dani shut off the engine and jumped out of the car. As she ran after Quinn, she saw her launch onto the chain-link fence and begin climbing it as if it were something she'd practiced every day of her life. She planted her right foot and then pushed off until she was able to swing her other foot upward and hook her heel over the top of the fence.

Dani tried to open the gate like a normal person, but it was locked. Quinn jumped to the ground, landing on both feet. She then ran toward the house, her body half-hidden behind the thick boxwood that lined the front of the house as she inched her way toward the front entry.

The landscaping and the house appeared to be well kept. Fresh paint. All the greenery nicely trimmed. How did a locksmith afford a house like this? she wondered.

"Hello!" Dani shouted. "Is anyone there?"

Quinn finally stopped moving.

Dani wanted to wring her neck, but there was no sense in returning to the car because nothing would stop Quinn now. Maybe if she could get Carlin Reed to come out of the house—

The door opened. "No solicitors," he said, pointing at the sign wired to the fence. It was him. The same person they had seen on the CSR Locksmith website. Just a regular-looking young man. Clean-cut. Average height.

"I need to talk to Marjorie Reed," Dani said, loud enough for him to hear.

"What for?"

"She has money coming to her, but I need to talk to her in person. There are papers to sign."

He took a step forward. "Do I know you?"

"I don't think so."

"Yeah, I do. You're that private investigator whose daughter was taken. What do you want?"

———

Quinn figured it was now or never. If she didn't do something, Ali could die. Ethan could die. She had grabbed her Taser the moment she'd heard the door open. If she could get within fifteen feet, she could immobilize him and give herself enough time to get inside the house.

With her back against the stucco wall, she waited to make her move. The second he stepped into view, she recognized him from his website and went for it, aiming the Taser and pressing the button.

He went down, his legs stiff and straight as he grimaced and then writhed in pain.

Without hesitating, she entered the house and looked from left to right before making her way farther inside. Nobody was in the kitchen or the living room. Quickening her pace, she stopped when she found stairs leading upstairs and a door leading downstairs. She went up and found herself in an attic. There was a bed and a bathroom. Nothing out of order. The room was empty.

She ran down the stairs, tried to open the door leading to a pantry or a basement. It was locked. She knocked hard. "Is there anyone in there?"

Why was the door locked? About to head off and check the rest of the house, she heard a noise and then a loud banging on the other side of the door.

"Is that you, Ali?"

"Help me!"

She was in there!

Quinn ran into the kitchen and started opening drawers, trying to find something she could use to try to unlock the door.

The front door banged shut. Quinn froze, her body flattened against the wall behind the refrigerator and prayed he wouldn't see her.

———

Dani called 9-1-1 the moment Quinn disappeared inside the house. She told the dispatcher what was happening and gave them Carlin Reed's address. A flush of adrenaline washed over her as she ran to her car, grabbed her Taser from the glove compartment and the tire iron from her trunk. She ran as fast as she could back to the same spot where she'd seen Quinn scale the fence.

She slid the tire iron through one of the holes in the fence, letting it drop to the grass before starting her climb. When she was only three-quarters of the way up, she realized she might not make it. Her biceps ached.

Quinn had made it look easy.

It pissed her off that she was this out of shape. Refusing to give up, she gritted her teeth and pulled herself upward, planted her foot, and inched her way up the fence until she was finally able to throw her leg over the top. She inhaled sharply before jumping to the grass and then dropping and rolling.

After lying there for a second, making sure nothing was broken, she got to her feet and scooped up the tire iron on her way to the door, ready to hit Carlin Reed over the head if he dared to move. But he was gone and the door was closed.

She cursed under her breath as she reached for the handle and found it locked. Scraping a hand over her face, she sucked in a breath and then shoved the thin edge of the tire iron between the door and the wood frame. A long, thin piece of wood splintered and fell to the ground.

Thoughts of Quinn and Ali and Gretchen Myles clouded her vision, making her shake as she raised the iron bar and began hammering away at the lock, over and over again. The wood was old and it cracked and splintered. After another thirty seconds of pounding, she was able to push the metal bar into the hole she'd made and pry open the door without much effort.

Pulling the Taser from her pocket, she thumbed the switch to on, then pushed her way inside, listening before following the sound of voices coming from below. The door leading to the basement was open. Adrenaline racing, she crept down the stairs, taking it slow, confused by what she saw when she looked inside the room at the bottom of the stairs. There was a girl on the floor, her face bloody and swollen. It was Ali. Her hand was clasped around a human bone, the end of it crudely sanded down. A skull with hair was on the floor, along with broken bones half-hidden beneath a moldy dress.

This was madness. The moldy smell of death made it hard to breathe.

Carlin's back was to Dani, but she caught the glimmer of a blade and could see he was threatening Quinn with a hunting knife.

Dani's heart skipped a beat as she made eye contact with Quinn.

Quinn started talking. She asked him to please spare her life, then rambled on about her grandmother and how she needed her.

Dani knew what Quinn was up to; she wanted to make sure Carlin Reed didn't hear Dani enter the room. Dani had to make her move and make it fast. With her Taser in her grasp, she held her arm ramrod straight and fired, the electrodes hitting him square in the back.

His body twitched, but nothing else happened.

The silence in the room was deafening as they all seemed to wait for something to happen. Seconds felt like hours before the knife dropped from his hand and clattered across the floor.

Quinn sprang forward and scooped it up, holding the knife in one hand and the stun gun in the other as Carlin toppled backward. His head smacked against the wall behind him on his way to the ground. His arms and legs were stiff as boards, his eyes wide open, staring at something that wasn't there.

Dani's gaze made a quick sweep around the room. She couldn't make sense out of what she was seeing. The broken skeleton, the skull with wiry hair and what looked like wrinkled grapes for eyes, and Ali's emaciated body and swollen face. What kind of horrors had she been through? And where the hell was Ethan?

A whoosh of emotion flooded her mind and body. Dani wanted to shout for Ethan, comfort Quinn and Ali, make sure they were both okay, but first she needed to take care of Carlin, find a way to make sure he couldn't do any more harm before the police arrived. "We need to tie him up," Dani said, looking around for rope or a sheet that she might be able to tear into strips of cloth.

She stopped looking when she noticed Ali crawl across broken bones to get to Carlin's side. Hovering over him, Ali reached out a hand toward Quinn and said, "Give me your Taser."

Dani opened her mouth to protest as Quinn did as Ali asked.

Ali leaned close to Carlin, her face nearly pressed against his as she looked into his eyes. "Can you see me, Carlin? I think you can. I'm going to give you to the count of three to say you're sorry."

His eyes were wide open, his teeth clamped together.

"One. Two. Three." Ali held the prongs to Carlin's chest and pulled the trigger more than once. More twitching followed. He didn't blink or scream out as his body vibrated. His eyes rolled to the back of his head.

The sounds of sirens in the distance flooded Dani with relief as she made her way to Ali's side and pried her fingers from around the stun gun, taking it from her. Ali's head dropped to her folded arms and she began to weep.

Moments later, once police arrived, they found the key ring in Carlin's pocket and were able to unlock every door inside the house.

They found Ethan strapped to a crude medieval dental chair, his eyes wide with fear, his mouth held open with a dental block.

As soon as he was free, he made a beeline for Quinn and Dani, wrapping his arms around both of them, sobbing, losing his cool for what was probably the first time in his life. Dani was glad he was getting it out. She knew how hard it was to hold back what felt like a lifetime of tears.

———

Dani saw Mary Cross and her daughter Gracie head straight through the throng of reporters before the hospital doors slid open. Dani popped out of her chair and rushed their way, giving them the floor and room number where they could find Ali. "Nobody but family is allowed inside her room. She's been through hell, but she's going to be okay," Dani told her.

Mary pulled Dani into her arms and cried, thanking her. She did the same with Quinn, who was standing a few feet away, before she took hold of Gracie's hand and rushed toward the elevators.

Dani's eyes watered at the thought of Mary being reunited with her daughter. Ali Cross was alive. She hadn't bothered to tell Mary about Ethan or that Ali's abductor was in critical condition after suffering multiple seizures. Mary would hear all about that later. Right now, Mary needed to see her daughter, let Ali know she wasn't alone, and that everything would be okay.

Quinn stood at Dani's side and said, "I feel like I could conquer the world about now."

Dani smiled. "You did good. You followed a hunch and it worked out. This time. But—"

"Too soon," Quinn said. "Can't you see I'm riding a high? No lectures until this is all over and we have a body count."

"You can't just jump over fences and tase people without knowing what you're dealing with. You could have been killed." Dani shivered at the thought.

"There was no time," Quinn said. "How long do you think Ethan had until Carlin Reed took a scalpel to him?"

Dani sighed, then bent down to scratch her ankle. A red, itchy rash had already appeared on both arms. "I think the poison ivy got me good. What about you?"

"Nope. I'm fine. It takes more than a little poison ivy to take me down."

Dani was shaking her head at Quinn when Ethan stepped out of the elevator and headed their way, walking with the same confident swagger he'd had when they first met him. Nobody else would ever know he'd spent the past few hours with a madman.

"My jaw is sore," he said as he gave it a rub, "but the doctor said I'm good to go."

There had been so much going on at Carlin Reed's home they hadn't had a chance to talk to Ethan before he was whisked away in an ambulance. "How did Carlin Reed get you into his car?" Dani asked.

"He used the old puppy trick."

Quinn looked appalled. "He asked you if you wanted to see his puppy? What are you, five years old?"

"No. It wasn't like that," Ethan said. "He told me the dog had heatstroke. The guy was panicked. I had a water bottle, so I went to see what he was talking about."

"Didn't you recognize him?"

"Not even a little bit." Ethan glanced outside at all the reporters huddled near the entrance. "I'll tell you the rest later. The nurses were gushing over me, telling me I was a hero. I better go talk to my fans."

Quinn snorted.

Dani laughed.

CHAPTER THIRTY-FOUR

Dani was awakened the next morning by a knock at her door. She buried her head under a pillow, hoping that whoever it was would go away.

No such luck. She slipped her feet over the mattress, wobbling a bit as she made her way to where her robe was slung over a chair, scratching both arms as she went.

If she'd had to guess who it might be, Matthew's wife, Carole, would not have been on the list. But that's who stood on the other side of the door when she opened it. The woman's round stomach stuck straight out, like she'd swallowed an exercise ball. In her hands, resting on her belly, was a shoebox held shut with rubber bands.

"Oh, my," Carole said, her gaze fixated on Dani's bruises and stitches. "I heard about the attack, but I had no idea how bad it was. I'm so sorry."

And here Dani had thought she was starting to look like her old self. "Thank you." Dani gestured toward the living room. "Do you want to come inside?"

"Please. I won't take too much of your time."

Dani closed the door behind her and led the way. She had no idea why Carole was here, but she figured Matthew might have sent the big guns to ask her to keep Tinsley out of the news so that reporters would stop bothering them.

Once they were seated, Dani offered her tea, but she declined. Dani clasped her hands together and said, "What can I do for you, Carole?"

"It's about Matthew."

Dani noticed how tightly she held on to the box, her hands trembling.

"He's been acting strange, and I have no one to talk to. I know I haven't gone out of my way to get to know you. I'm sorry for that, but I had to talk to you. I'm desperate."

"It's okay. Why don't you tell me what's going on?"

"You've known Matthew longer than me, and I was wondering if he's always had such an explosive side to him?"

"Explosive?"

Carole nodded. "I had Tinsley's room converted to the new baby's room. I hope you don't mind."

"It's your house now," Dani said. She felt no animosity. The house and what they did or didn't do to Tinsley's room was of no concern to her. Her daughter's memory lived in her heart. Nowhere else.

The tension seemed to leave Carole's body. "Matthew had seemed perfectly fine when I told him I was redecorating. He didn't say a word when I replaced the carpet with wood floors and had the room painted. But last night, after the furniture had been delivered and everything was perfect, I asked him to have a look." A tear slid down her face.

"What did he do?" Dani asked, growing worried, wondering where she was going with all this.

"He went ballistic. There is no other way to describe it. He looked around the room, frantically opening and closing dresser drawers. His face was crimson as he riffled through the closet, tossing baby gifts we had received into the middle of the floor. The anger made it difficult for him to speak." Carole put a hand to her chest. "I was truly frightened."

Dani couldn't remember ever seeing Matthew angry. He could be stubborn. He vented about work at times . . . but she'd never seen him lose his cool. Even so, as these thoughts entered her mind, she couldn't help but think of Rebecca Carr. "I'm so sorry," Dani said. "That doesn't sound like Matthew at all."

"It doesn't? He never went off the rails like that when you were married to him?"

"No. Never." That was the truth. No need to mention Rebecca.

"Do you think it has to do with the new baby?"

"No," Dani said without hesitation. "Whenever I talk to him, he shows nothing but concern and love for you and the baby."

Carole glanced at the box still in her lap. "When Matthew was tossing things to the floor, he wanted to know where Tinsley's things were. I didn't know what he was talking about. I had donated her clothes, with his permission of course, months before. So when he was asking about Tinsley's things, my mind drew a blank."

Dani reached for a box of tissues and handed it to her so she could wipe her eyes.

"I slept in the guest room last night," Carole said. "This morning he apologized more than once. He felt horrible, and before he left for work he assured me he would never lose his cool again."

Dani scratched her neck. "I'm glad he apologized."

Carole agreed. "It wasn't until an hour ago I remembered that I had placed what little was left of Tinsley's personal belongings in a box that I then stored in a bin in the garage to keep it safe from the elements." She exhaled. "My first thought was that I would present the box to Matthew tonight when he got home. But something stopped me. There's no way I could handle another breakdown like I saw last night. So I decided the best thing would be to give you this and let you sort through the contents and do with it what you like."

She handed Dani the box and Dani took it, unsure of what to think about all this. The random visit from Carole was strange enough, but then hearing about Matthew's outburst made it even weirder. And now all she could think about was what would cause Matthew such concern. "Thank you," Dani said. "I hope you know that I want nothing but happiness for you and Matthew and your new baby."

Carole looked down at her hands in her lap. "I'm sorry I haven't reached out to you before now."

"It's okay," Dani said, feeling a need to extend an olive branch to the woman. Maybe because she was pregnant and hormones were raging and she'd been there, done that, or maybe because Matthew had once meant the world to her and Tinsley. "Just so you know, Matthew was a great father to Tinsley. There wasn't anything he wouldn't do for her. But I might have made it hard for him to get close to Tinsley."

Carole looked up, brows furrowed. "How so?"

"I'm sure Matthew has mentioned how difficult it was for us to conceive Tinsley."

She nodded.

"It was a lot of work. Fertility injections, tests, and more tests. This went on for years, and Matthew made it clear he didn't want to go through the whole process again. Knowing Tinsley would be my only child, I became a bit obsessive, and looking back, I think I may have made him feel like an outsider, looking in." Dani sighed. "Maybe he's panicking . . . afraid you might do the same after the baby is born."

"Thank you," Carole said. "For that. For listening. For everything."

They both stood. Dani put the box on the side table and walked her to the door, taken by surprise when Carole put her arms around Dani, her extended belly making for an awkward hug. "I want you to know that I think about Tinsley often. I wish I could have met her."

After Carole drove off, Dani wondered if they had somehow bonded in that moment or if it was a one-off and she was making more out of it than it was—a need to vent. Before she could reflect further, she heard her phone buzzing in her bedroom. She was able to pick up the call. It was Quinn, calling to check on her.

Dani applied lotion to every part of her body covered with a red rash, then dressed in loose clothing and decided to continue with her plan for the day. The only way she would be able to prove that Frank Petri was the intruder would be to catch him in action, which meant they needed more digital cameras. Lots of them. She would stop at Lowe's on her way to Cameron's house and get everything she needed to do the job properly, something she should have done right from the start.

It took less than an hour to find and purchase the cameras. When she was done, she texted Cameron to let her know she would be spending a few hours inside the house. Once she arrived, she used the keyless code to enter. Everything looked the same. The place was neat and tidy, as if nobody lived here.

Dani made the rounds to make sure Frank Petri wasn't enjoying a snack in the kitchen. After double-checking that the sliding glass door was secure, she peeked into the laundry room, just as she had done the last time she was here. This time, she noticed a doggy door. Why hadn't she seen it before? She pulled out her phone and sent Cameron a text, asking her why there was a doggy door in the laundry room.

A response came back immediately: It came with the house. I never thought to remove it since I tried to crawl through it and couldn't.

Dani made sure the cameras downstairs were angled properly before heading upstairs. She was in the middle of opening one of the boxes when she heard a noise and her head snapped up. *What was that?*

She tiptoed over to the window that overlooked the backyard. Frank and his dog, Sadie, stood outside the laundry room door. Dani didn't dare step any closer to the window. Afraid Frank might see her, she stayed where she was and didn't move a muscle.

His dog disappeared.

241

Soon after, she heard the pitter-patter of paws on the tile floor. The dog was in the laundry room. What happened next defied reason. The door opened and Frank stepped inside.

What the hell?

As soon as she heard the duo make their way through the house, she knew she needed to act quickly. She grabbed her backpack and the plastic bag from Lowe's and rushed from Cameron's bedroom, down the hallway, and made her way into the guest room. Thankful that the floor was carpeted, muting her footfalls, she opened the closet just enough so she could squeeze inside and close the door quietly without being heard.

Only seconds later, Sadie was inside the guest room, sniffing right outside the closet door. She held her breath, didn't dare move.

"Sadie! Come here, girl," Frank called from the other room.

The dog ran off.

Dani sucked in some air and sank slowly to the floor, taking a second to calm herself. She couldn't stop thinking about what she had seen. Sadie had gone through the doggy door and somehow let Frank in?

How could that be?

Before coming upstairs, she'd seen the door with her own eyes. Not only was it locked but there was also a latch with a chain.

After her breathing returned to normal, she readied the video on her phone again, and walked quietly out of the room, across the hallway, and into the main bedroom.

She hit the red button. Holding the phone in front of her, she made her way past the bed and the settee and stopped in front of the closet, both doors wide open.

There he was. Frank Petri in all his glory.

He was wearing one of Cameron's dresses, a beautiful pink chiffon number with sequins across the bust. He walked toward the full-length mirror, did a twirl, then settled his gaze on his reflection and on Dani's behind him.

Turning around slowly as if he wanted to make sure he wasn't seeing things, he looked right at her. It was hard to read his expression. Was he going to laugh or cry?

He did neither.

He just stood there.

And she kept recording. "Could you please state your name?"

"Frank Petri," he said, making her job a little easier.

"Birthday? Address? Tell me about yourself, Frank."

She had been half kidding about the "tell me about yourself" part, but that didn't stop him from doing just that.

"I was bored," he said. "I had nothing to do. My wife passed away recently, you see, and my kids never come to visit. The dog—" He looked at Sadie, who was lying near the bathroom. "Come here, girl. She's all I have left."

"So you broke into Cameron Bennington's house because you were lonely and bored?"

"Yes. That's exactly what happened. She's fairly new to the area, a breath of fresh air. There was something about her that made me happy. Nothing sexual," he added quickly. "I can't really explain it except to say that she gave me a reason to live again. I was walking Sadie one day, and I saw Cameron hide the key to her house under a planter box. I grabbed the key the next day and had a duplicate made. At first, Sadie and I would just enter through the front door, take a stroll around, and check things out. I got comfortable fairly quickly. Sometimes I would move a piece of furniture." His eyes widened. "Not to scare her, but because I wanted to please her. My wife always told me I had a good instinct when it came to interior decorating. That's all I was doing, I swear."

"You took things from her refrigerator," Dani said.

"No. No. I didn't. I swear. I would go through her refrigerator, and if I found something that had gone bad, I would throw it out and wash the dishes. I never took a plate or a utensil. I never stole anything."

"Come on, Frank. You expect me to believe that?"

"It's true. I swear. Once she installed the camera out front, I knew I had to find a new way to get inside. I spent the next few months teaching Sadie to go through a doggy door and unlatch the chain. The rest was easy. She only had to rest her paw on the door handle and push down. Sadie is a very smart dog. She's a rescue." He smiled. Long enough for Dani to wonder if he was waiting for praise.

"I never meant any harm," he said before she turned off the video.

When she called the police, his face fell, and she almost felt sorry for him.

CHAPTER
THIRTY-FIVE

Two days after catching Frank Petri in action, Dani was in her bedroom getting dressed when Detective Whitton called. Hoping he had news about Rebecca Carr, she snatched up the phone and hit the talk button. "What's going on?" she asked as she plunked down on the edge of the bed.

"A couple of things," he said. "The Skyler Temp Agency where Rebecca Carr worked is playing hardball with me. I told the manager I would get a court order if I had to. Hopefully we'll hear back soon."

Her stomach rolled over. She needed to catch a break.

The detective cleared his throat. "Did you hear about Frank Petri posting bail?"

"No."

"They don't consider him to be a threat, but his court appearance won't be until next month. Let me know if you spot him lurking outside your office, and I'll have him picked up on the spot."

"Thanks," Dani said, disappointed to hear the temp agency wasn't cooperating. "Anything else?"

"The body found buried on Carlin Reed's property has been identified as Gretchen Myles."

"Not too surprising," she said. "Maybe her family can find peace, knowing she's been found."

"You know why I haven't retired yet?" Detective Whitton asked.

"Because of all the homemade treats everyone at the station brings in every day?" she teased.

"That's only part of it. The main reason—the real reason—is I wanted to find Tinsley so you could have closure and peace too."

Dani swallowed a lump in her throat. "You're a good friend, Detective Whitton. I think of you as family. You've been there for me every step of the way, but it's time for you to take a breather."

"That's why I turned in my thirty-day notice."

She tipped her head back and looked at the ceiling. "Congratulations. I'm happy for you. This is the beginning, not the end." If anyone deserved peace and quiet and time to put their feet up, it was Detective Whitton. And yet she found herself with conflicting emotions as she wondered how she would ever keep Tinsley's case alive without him.

"We'll be having lots of barbecues at the house, and I expect you to be there."

"Yes, sir."

After saying goodbye, she finished dressing, pocketed her phone, and headed for the kitchen. On her way, the shoebox Carole had left with her caught her eye. She'd been avoiding it, knowing that any little trinket would take her right back to the day Tinsley was taken from her.

Losing Tinsley had broken all the rules of life and death. Living without her was the hardest thing she'd ever had to do. There were times when she thought she couldn't go on, but someone like Detective James Whitton would come along, and then Quinn Sullivan, sparking a light inside her and showing her the way forward.

She clung to that light as she picked up the box and took a seat on the sofa. She slipped off the rubber bands and removed the lid with trepidation, as if she were expecting a jack-in-the-box to spring forward.

Nothing scary popped out at her. There were papers on top. She unfolded one, smiling at the colorful drawing Tinsley had made of her family: Mom, Dad, and Tinsley. Stick figures. There was a sun and what looked like a tree, and maybe a sliver of a moon too.

She looked at every drawing before setting them aside. Inside a plastic bag was the first tooth Tinsley had lost at the age of four. So tiny. *My baby.* Dani smiled at the Barbie-doll shoes tumbling around. There was also a dime and a nickel and a Happy Meal toy. She'd forgotten about the award Tinsley had gotten in prekindergarten for being kind. And there was a gold ribbon with tiny red hearts—Tinsley's favorite ribbon.

Teary-eyed, Dani put the ribbon to her nose to see if it smelled like her little girl. She rubbed its silkiness against her cheek. An image flashed through her mind as she recalled putting the ribbon in Tinsley's hair on her first day of school.

Her chest tightened.

If Tinsley had been wearing the ribbon, how was it possible the ribbon was here in this box?

Feeling unsettled, she started when a knock sounded at the door. A second wave of urgent knocking prompted her to set aside the box and get up. Through the peephole, she saw Frank Petri.

She whipped open the door. "What are you doing here, Frank?"

He rapidly blinked as if her bluntness startled him.

"I'm sorry to bother you. I just wanted to thank you for stopping me."

She had no idea what he was talking about, but she waited for him to elaborate.

"If not for you," he went on, "my curious behavior might have gotten out of hand."

His downturned facial features and his inability to meet her gaze made him appear so pathetic that it was difficult for her to be angry with him. She knew his story. He'd lost his wife, and in so doing had lost his mind too. A camera, a Nikon, hung around his neck, which made no sense, but seemed to fit the moment perfectly. "Your curious behavior did get out of hand, Frank."

"I know. And I have you to thank for stopping me."

"You really shouldn't be here, Frank."

"There's more I need to tell you. It's important."

She didn't think he was dangerous, but just to be safe she gestured toward the two cushioned chairs on her front porch. "Why don't we sit down while you tell me what's on your mind?"

He nodded, nervously pulling at the collar of his shirt. She wondered if he'd changed his mind about coming. Finally, he took a seat and she did the same. "So what is it you want to tell me?" Dani asked.

"I know I could never make up for what I've done—"

"What is it, Frank?" she asked impatiently. Tired, exhausted, and wanting to be alone with her melancholy thoughts, she already regretted giving him a moment of her time.

His mouth opened and closed like a goldfish trapped in a bowl. If he didn't get on with it, she was going to simply walk back into the house, lock the door behind her, and call the police.

"I know things would have gotten worse," he murmured, "because when I first noticed you watching Ms. Bennington's house, I started watching you too. I used your license plate to find out who you were and where you lived and worked."

"Oh. Yeah. That's not good, Frank."

"I know. While I was watching you, I saw some things . . . things that I should have shown you a while ago. That's why I was at the park when you spotted me, but I chickened out and ran."

Ah, so it was all starting to make sense. Sort of. Either way, she wished he would hurry things along.

"I was watching your office, waiting for you to return, the same day you were attacked."

She instantly perked up. "You were there? At the office?"

He nodded. And something must have shaken loose inside his brain because the words suddenly tumbled out. "It was the same day I approached you and introduced myself."

"I remember." She'd had to be in court and had sped off.

"After you left, I took Sadie home and then drove to your office. I was hidden behind a row of cars a few doors down when a small pickup truck pulled into the parking lot where I was hiding. The person was dressed all in black. It was a woman. I didn't think anything of it until I watched her cross the street, make a left, and head straight for your office. I was shocked when I saw where she was going. She pulled something from her pocket; I figured it was a key because she opened the door and went right in. Maybe ten minutes later, I saw you drive up. I got scared and left."

"Please don't tell me that's the end of your story. Did you get a license plate number by any chance?"

This time when he smiled, he puffed his chest. "I got better than that. I have a video of the whole thing. Her car . . . everything."

Chills washed over Dani as she leaned closer. "Show me."

Frank pulled the strap over his head, switched on the camera, and did exactly that.

Fifteen minutes later, Frank had left, but not until he handed over the memory card from his camera. Dani was sitting in front of her computer inside the house, tapping furiously at her computer keyboard, uploading the license plate number into a pay database.

The pinwheel went round and round.

Bingo!

The truck belonged to a woman named Hattie Goodwin, forty, who lived in a cabin in the woods surrounding Lake Tahoe. She had no social media presence, but Dani's breath hitched when she saw that Hattie Goodwin had a criminal record.

Public records revealed that the woman had spent most of her life in New York City. While living there she attempted to kidnap a six-month-old girl from a stroller but was stopped by a man on his way to work. All in all, Hattie Goodwin had been arrested three times and was imprisoned for four years after being convicted on second-degree kidnapping charges in 2010. Somewhere along the way she'd changed her name and moved to California.

Dani scrolled through the information until she found what she was looking for—Hattie Goodwin's mug shot.

Dani did a double take.

It was her—Hattie Goodwin was also Rebecca Carr.

Dani uploaded the video Frank Petri had taken. When it was ready, she watched it again, pausing the video and zooming in on the image where Frank had caught the woman unlocking the door. She took a screenshot of the image and did the same with the side-view mug shot so she could place the images side by side. Same elegant jawline and sharp nose.

As she stared at the images, she found herself questioning why the woman would have broken into her office. It defied reason. Why take such a risk after all these years?

Dani mentally went over the days before the break-in. The only thing that stood out was Quinn's impromptu interview with Channel 10 News.

That was it. Why hadn't she seen it before?

Quinn had looked straight into the camera and declared with confidence that they had new evidence and were close to tracking down the woman seen on the security camera at the school on the day Tinsley was abducted.

Why would Hattie Goodwin break into her office looking for evidence unless she had something to do with Tinsley's disappearance?

Her foot bounced as she called Detective Whitton. "Come on. Answer the phone." When there was no answer she left a message telling him about Frank Petri's visit, the video, and what she'd learned about Rebecca Carr/Hattie Goodwin. She told him where she was going.

He would be upset that she'd gone without backup, but there was no stopping her. She searched around the house for the Taser she'd recently used. The battery was dead, so she left it where it was. She had pepper spray in the duffel bag she kept in the car, along with water and snacks. After locking up the house, she climbed in behind the wheel of her car and keyed the Tahoe address into the navigation system.

When she hit I-80E headed toward CA-89S, her phone rang. Detective Whitton's name popped up on the screen in front of her. She hit "Talk" and said hello.

"I got your message, Dani. I also got a call back from the Skyler Temp Agency. I was able to get enough information to confirm what you already know. Rebecca Carr's real name is Hattie Goodwin. I need you to pull off at the next exit and wait for backup."

"I can't do that. I've waited too long."

"She's dangerous. You know that for a fact."

Dani's fingers tightened around the steering wheel. She couldn't think like that, couldn't let fear stop her from getting to the truth. "Hattie must have seen Quinn on TV, telling the world that we were getting closer to solving Tinsley's case. She was looking for evidence. If she had carried a gun, she would have shot me already."

"Think about what you're doing. If she takes you out and makes a run for it, we might never know what happened to Tinsley."

Dani's chest tightened. She let up on the gas but refused to pull over or turn around. Was the hope she'd been hanging on to for so long just a wild, crazy fantasy? Did all parents whose children were ripped from their lives think only of the day they were finally reunited? "Is it too much to hope that Tinsley is still alive?"

Silence was followed by, "No, Dani. It's not. But please, don't go knocking on her door. Wait for backup. We're on our way."

An hour and fifteen minutes later, Dani pulled off a main road onto a side street in serious need of surface repairs. She drove slowly, careful not to hit any of the deeper ruts. Cabins dotted the mountainside as she followed the winding road. Two-hundred-and-fifty-foot sugar pine trees, eight feet in diameter, stood like giant sentinels everywhere she looked.

Feeling nauseous, she pulled to the side of the road, rolled down her window, and inhaled the crisp, clean air. The notion that she might find out once and for all what happened to Tinsley filled her with a mixture of joy and also dread.

The thought of finding Tinsley was what got her up in the morning and kept her going, day after day. What if the truth ended up being the harsh reality that Matthew had always painted for her? What then? How would she keep going?

She let out a ponderous breath and continued on. A car came around a bend. She held her breath, peering closely at the driver as the car crept past. It was an elderly man behind the wheel of a Jeep Grand Cherokee. Neither of them waved.

A glance at her navigation system told her she had less than a mile to go. A fluttery feeling erupted inside her. Not for the first time, she considered pulling over and waiting for the cavalry, but kept going instead, driven by an invisible force.

A few minutes later, her navigation system told her she had arrived: "Your destination is ahead to the left."

It was an unmarked road covered with forest debris. At the corner was a wooden post where she could see that the signage had been removed. The notion that she might finally be closing in on the truth left her feeling anxious. Her window was still down. She inhaled the thick scent of pines.

Be patient.

How many times had she said those two words to Quinn over the past few years?

Too many times to count.

She passed by the unmarked road and pulled to the right up ahead, next to a trash bin that had a different street number and belonged to one of Hattie Goodwin's neighbors. Dani wasn't surprised when she checked her phone to see that she had no reception and wouldn't be able to call Detective Whitton and tell him she'd changed her mind.

She would do the right thing.

She would wait patiently for him and his men to arrive.

She would not give up her one chance to get this right. Not after all these years of dreaming of this day. Curiosity did win the day fifteen minutes later, though, when she got out of the car, leaving the door ajar while she crossed the street and peered down through the tall trees.

Her heart skipped a beat when she spotted the side of a tiny log cabin. It couldn't be more than nine hundred square feet. It was impossible to see much else. The thick layers of leaves and debris felt like a giant sponge beneath her as she made her way back to the car. She slipped in behind the steering wheel, sank low in her seat, and adjusted the side mirror so she would be able to see if anyone came or went.

"Are you there, Tinsley?" she asked aloud. "Do you remember me?" Her body tensed at the thought her daughter might not recognize her. She'd been five, almost six, when she was taken. For close to six years Dani had spent every waking moment with her daughter. Of course Tinsley would remember her.

The next forty-eight minutes felt like eternity. She straightened in her seat the moment she saw Detective Whitton's unmarked sedan appear in her side mirror. She jumped out and waved both arms before jogging to his open window to tell him she'd been waiting.

He nodded. "Wait in your car until we've had a chance to see if anyone's home."

She had never seen the man look so grim-faced and stern. She moved out of the way, watched his car disappear down the driveway followed by two police cruisers. As she walked back to her car, she heard the sounds of tires spitting up debris.

Dani shifted in her seat. Waiting was difficult, but the unknowing was much worse. She could be wrong about Hattie Goodwin. A zillion scenarios ran through her head. Doubt clouded her mind until she no longer knew what to think. If she closed her eyes it felt as if she were spiraling into that same deep, dark hole that was always there, its crooked finger gesturing for her to come take a closer look.

Loud knocking was followed by silence. A moment later she heard, "This is the police. Come out with your hands up."

The officer's voice was amplified through a megaphone.

What was going on? Could they see through a window? Was Hattie inside but not answering the door? So many questions. Too many questions.

The pull to run down the driveway was strong.

Unable to sit there doing nothing, knowing her daughter could be inside that cabin, she climbed out of the car, shutting the door quietly before crossing the street. She could see the side of the cabin, but not the front. She had no idea if Detective Whitton had managed to find his way inside, but she was going in.

Her mind made up, she stepped off the road and onto the sloped hillside. The earth was dark and damp, covered with pine needles and curled brown leaves.

The hill was steeper than it looked and before she knew it she was half running, half sliding downward until she reached out to grasp the trunk of a tree to stop herself from rolling to the ground.

Seconds ticked by as she caught her breath.

She could finally hear voices, but couldn't tell if they were coming from inside the cabin or the area at the front. With a good fifty feet to go before reaching the cabin, she let go of the tree and made a diagonal path down the bank, like a giant Z, to the right and then to the left. When she stopped for a second time, with less than twenty feet to go, a loud rustling of leaves stopped her cold.

She angled her head and listened closely, trying to figure out where the sound was coming from. It was much too loud to be a squirrel.

Walking into the trees had been like walking into nightfall, the branches making a canopy overhead, blocking the dawn light.

When the sounds of footfalls trudging through thick leaves grew closer, she held still, didn't move a muscle. Was it Hattie Goodwin? Had she escaped unseen? Was she making a run for it?

A flash of white fabric caught her eye as a hooded figure swept past her, weaving through the tall pines. Dani's mind raced, her heart pounding against her chest as she followed the person.

If there weren't so many trees, she might be able to better see who she was following. Keeping her gaze pinned on the white cloth, afraid of losing sight of the person, she took off, tripping over a fallen branch. She cursed under her breath, pushed herself to her feet, and continued on.

It wasn't until she reached level ground where a narrow dirt path began that she lost sight of the person. Her gaze followed the path as far as she could see. There was no way the person in white had followed the trail. If they had, she would be able to see them. Refusing to give up, she followed the path, walking slowly and trying to be stealthy as she listened.

There it was—the soft crackle of a branch snapping in two—only three feet away. She looked that way. A wisp of white peeked out from behind one of the thicker majestic pines. From the ground to the top of the head, she calculated the person to be about four foot five. It was a child.

Dani's insides vibrated.

Could it be her?

"Please don't run. My name is Dani Callahan, and I'm looking for my daughter, Tinsley Callahan, who was taken from me five years ago. I don't mean any harm," she said, her voice cracking with emotion. "I just want—"

The child stepped out from behind the tree. A long, straw-colored braid hung down over her shoulder. Their eyes met and Dani held back a sob.

It was Tinsley.

Her small nose and mossy-green eyes were the same.

It was her daughter.

For five years she'd dreamed of this moment. Her knees wobbled, threatening to give out.

There was caution in Tinsley's expression and curiosity in her eyes as she looked Dani over before meeting her gaze once more. "Is it really you?"

It took all her strength not to run to her and wrap her arms around her child. Instead, she nodded and said, "It's me."

Visibly shaking, Tinsley took a tentative step forward. "I thought you were dead?"

Dani shook her head. "I've been looking for you since the day you went missing."

Tinsley broke out into a run toward her, and Dani opened her arms. The warmth of her daughter's body enveloped in her arms was sweeter than she'd imagined. She held her daughter close, breathing her in as tears of happiness and wonder rolled down Dani's cheeks.

CHAPTER
THIRTY-SIX

Dani had always been a take-charge kind of person, able to make decisions easily and with confidence. But suddenly she was at a loss . . . unsure of what to say to Tinsley. Their journey began on the ride to the hospital, where paramedics took her blood pressure and asked Tinsley a few basic questions: *Are you hurt? When was the last time you ate and drank water?*

Detective Whitton had made sure someone drove her car back for her, and a uniformed officer handed her the keys and told her where she could find her car when they were done.

Dani stayed at Tinsley's side every step of the way, trying not to hover but finding it difficult not to stick to her like glue, unable to take her eyes off her daughter while the doctor did blood work and a body wellness check on Tinsley. No malnutrition. No dehydration. No physical signs of abuse. All good news, and yet it was the mental abuse that worried Dani most.

After the checkup Dani and Tinsley were taken to a room with colorful walls, beanbag chairs, and bins filled with toys for children much younger than Tinsley. Dani and Tinsley sat side by side on a comfortable couch while a counselor, a woman who sat across from them, explained how life would never go back to how it was before the abduction, or even how it was last week or last month. The days following would be their new normal. It would take time to heal, but they needed to be patient with each other.

The worst part for Dani was that she didn't want to fail her daughter. She felt stiff and awkward, unsure of what to say or how to say it. It was bad enough that she'd missed five years of Tinsley's life, five years she would never get back, but how could she help her heal?

Outwardly, Tinsley appeared to be handling everything so well, but Dani knew that might be wishful thinking on her part. It was late by the time they were driving home. Dani went through a drive-through and they got Whoppers, fries, and milkshakes. They were both starved. They walked into the house, went straight to the stools at the kitchen counter, and started eating. They were both stuffing their mouths with fries when they looked at each other and started laughing. It was surreal. A moment in time Dani would never forget. For years to come, if anyone asked her about this day, the first day of the rest of her life, Dani would say they gobbled down french fries and laughed.

It wasn't until they had taken showers and they were both dressed in shorts and oversize T-shirts that Dani brought out sheets and a blanket and explained that Tinsley could have her bedroom until they set up the other room.

"Why don't we both sleep in your bed? I don't want to be alone."

Dani's eyes watered, but somehow she managed to hold back a sob of happiness. Tinsley was home. Her daughter was here with her, clean and fed and safe. When they slipped under the covers, their heads on stacks of fluffy pillows, both staring up at the ceiling, Dani murmured, "Like the counselor at the hospital said, it's going to take some time for us to get to know each other, but I'm ready to listen whenever you're ready to talk."

That's all it took to open the floodgates.

It was already late, but they talked through the night to the early hours before dawn.

Tinsley told her how she'd often dreamed of Dani and would cry when she thought about her dying in a car accident as she had been told. She only knew Hattie Goodwin as Rebecca, and that's what she called her.

The thought that maybe Tinsley worried about Rebecca since she had spent the past five years with her crossed her mind, but it didn't appear to be the case. Tinsley said she didn't hate Rebecca, but she was glad to be away from her. Rebecca was easily angered and would stomp and yell, turn red in the face. Within minutes her tantrum would be over. It broke Dani's heart when Tinsley admitted she'd been lonely these past five years, and since there was no internet, no phones, and no TV, she'd done a lot of reading.

They talked about getting a puppy and what they would name him or her, which led to thirty minutes of picking silly names, like Bacon and Pup Tart. Dani mentioned her need to get fit after running after Quinn and realizing she was completely out of shape. Tinsley suggested they take their new dog to the park and throw a Frisbee. Somewhere along the way, Tinsley drifted to sleep. It wasn't until that moment that Dani realized she hadn't heard from Matthew after being assured by Detective Whitton that he would contact him. She had been so focused on making sure Tinsley was okay that nothing else had mattered. Oddly, Tinsley had never mentioned or asked about Matthew: *Where was he? Was he okay? Did he know she was here?*

CHAPTER THIRTY-SEVEN

Dani's questions about Matthew had all been answered the next morning when she got a call from Detective Whitton, giving her shocking news and telling her he would be picking her up in an hour. Luckily, Quinn was able to sit with Tinsley, no questions asked.

Dani now watched from the passenger seat of Detective Whitton's car as Matthew walked out of RAYTEX's corporate headquarters on J Street. She climbed out of the sedan. Doors opened and closed as Detective Whitton and three uniformed police officers got out of their cruisers lined up on the curb behind them.

Matthew's gaze instantly fixated on Dani. "What's going on?"

Detective Whitton and his team had spent the past twenty-four hours interrogating Hattie Goodwin, also known as Rebecca Carr. Hoping to get a lighter sentence, she told them everything, even agreed to a polygraph test that suggested she was telling the truth. "You knew that the woman known as Rebecca Carr picked up your daughter from school that day, didn't you?"

Matthew looked at Detective Whitton. "What's this all about?"

"It's over, Matthew," the detective told him.

Matthew scrubbed a hand over his face. "You can't be serious. Dani makes up alternate scenarios in her head and will never accept the truth."

"Detective Whitton and his men have arrested Rebecca Carr," Dani said, hoping they could skip the bullshit and get to the truth.

"What does that have to do with me?" Matthew wanted to know, his eyes so wide he looked silly.

"Why don't you tell us?" Dani said as she held up the gold ribbon with the tiny hearts.

"What is that?" he asked.

"The ribbon I put in Tinsley's hair before I took her to school the day she disappeared."

Matthew glanced at his watch. "I need to go."

"Rebecca told the authorities everything," Dani said, irritated by his refusal to come clean.

Matthew wagged a finger at Dani, but turned his gaze on Detective Whitton as he said, "She's crazy."

When he started walking away, Dani said, "Rebecca told them about how you came to the cabin and thought Tinsley had drowned."

He stopped. A moment passed before he looked at Detective Whitton, who merely nodded, confirming that Dani was telling the truth.

"She did drown," Matthew said, his body stiff, his tone indignant as if his declaration changed nothing. "It was an accident. I was furious with Rebecca for taking our daughter, and while we argued, Tinsley must have wandered outside. We found her facedown in the lake. I dove in, gave her CPR, did everything I could to save her, but she was gone." His face crumpled. "It was an accident."

Dani's entire body trembled with anger. In a carefully controlled tone, she said, "Listen to yourself, Matthew. You're not making sense. If it was all so innocent, why didn't you tell anyone?"

He kept shaking his head as if that might make it all go away. "Rebecca told me to go. Told me she would take care of everything."

"What did she mean by that?" Dani wanted to know.

"When I returned to the cabin—"

Dani snorted. "Days later."

"When I drove back to the cabin," he repeated, "Rebecca handed me our daughter."

"In a fucking coffin?" Dani asked.

Detective Whitton placed a hand on her shoulder, and she instantly settled down.

"Not in a coffin," he said. "She was wrapped in linen, covered from head to toe."

"She was mummified?"

"Rebecca told me she was in a terrible state. Rebecca was trying to spare me."

Dani wanted to strangle him. "Who was wrapped in linen? Say her name, dammit."

"I buried our daughter in the apple orchard where she loved to run and play hide-and-seek." His shoulders rounded as his self-confidence was replaced with repetitive swallowing and a quivering chin. "She would run as fast as she could, and when I caught up to her, I would pick her up and twirl her around and she would laugh." He was crying now. "Do you remember the orchard, Dani?"

Who is this man? Dani didn't recognize him any longer. The man she'd wanted so badly to have babies with looked pathetic and weak. She would never be able to forgive him. "You lied to me, Matthew."

He took a deep, pained breath. "I'm sorry," he said, unable to make eye contact. "I wish I could fix it." He was looking at the ground as he talked, shaking his head slowly all the while. "What I did is inexcusable. I'm so sorry."

Dani lifted her chin. "That wasn't your daughter you buried in the apple orchard."

He looked at her then. "I'm sorry, Dani, but it was. I buried her with my own hands. She's gone."

"Rebecca Carr's real name is Hattie Goodwin," she explained. "She has a history of stealing children." Dani gave Matthew a second to take it in before adding, "Tinsley didn't drown that day. Doctors believe she suffered from cold-water drowning syndrome. Although she appeared dead, she was still alive. The cold water saved her. The child you buried in the apple orchard was Kelly Rose, a four-year-old girl stolen from her grave at Old Auburn Cemetery after dying of a medical condition."

Matthew looked at Detective Whitton, mouth open, eyes wide. "Is it true?" he asked in a disbelieving voice. "Is Tinsley alive?"

Detective Whitton nodded.

Matthew turned his attention to Dani as if for confirmation. "She's home with me," Dani said. "She's safe, and under the circumstances, I'd say she's doing well."

He sank to his knees, his hands covering his face, shoulders shaking.

Detective Whitton gestured for a uniformed officer to cuff him and take him to the station.

Matthew Callahan was going to jail.

As Dani watched Matthew being led to the back of a cruiser, she felt numb by his betrayal of her trust. All these years, he'd known who had taken their daughter, and worse, he'd thought he had buried Tinsley. She tried to imagine him standing in the middle of the apple orchard she knew so well, the delicate, sweet scent of apple and flowers swirling about, dressed in suit and tie, and using the starched white shirtsleeve to wipe sweat from his brow. Had he heard the sounds of her laughter from the past as he'd stabbed the shovel into the hard dirt?

When he buried that little girl he thought was Tinsley, he had buried his soul.

Dani swallowed.

He had not taken a life.

Somehow he'd allowed himself to become entangled in a demented woman's scheme. A woman he'd wined and dined and surely taken to bed. He was ashamed. That much was obvious.

Dani knew that by forgiving him, she would be able to let go of grievances and judgments and allow herself to heal.

Maybe someday that would happen.

But not today.

EPILOGUE

One Year Later . . .

As Dani and Tinsley walked up the path toward the white Tudor home, Dani thought about the crazy whirlwind of a year it had been since Tinsley had been found. Her daughter was being tutored and would be entering sixth grade in the fall.

During that time, Dani had made a point of being in the courtroom when Hattie Goodwin was convicted of kidnapping. She would be serving twenty years in prison. Matthew wouldn't be released for another six months, after serving eighteen months in prison for making false statements and lying to the FBI. Tinsley wasn't sure if and when she would be ready to meet with him. That would be her decision. She had been talking to a therapist since coming home. She was doing well. Dani had a habit of staring at her when she wasn't looking, unable to believe her baby was home. It still didn't feel real. She no longer lived in the past. She smiled more and loved her job. For the first time in years, she was living in the present and loving every minute.

Dani and Tinsley were greeted at the door by Detective James Whitton. He took Tinsley into his arms and gave her a fierce bear hug.

"Uncle Jim," Tinsley said, laughing, "I can't breathe."

He let go and said, "Quinn is in the backyard."

After she disappeared inside the house, Dani looked Detective Whitton over. His eyes were as bright as twinkling stars, and he had a nice glow to his face. "Retirement looks good on you."

"A week in Kauai didn't hurt," he said with a smile as he ushered Dani inside and shut the door behind them. "Ethan is here, and he brought a surprise."

Dani's eyebrows arched. The boy had grown on her and Quinn. They'd thought he might not come around anymore after Ali was found, but they'd been wrong. He stopped by almost every week to say hi and see what they were working on, always offering to post flyers or do other odd jobs, just because. He had grown two inches at least, was going to school regularly, and had quit smoking.

Dani followed Detective Whitton through the house to the back-yard, where they found everyone talking at once. It wasn't until Quinn stepped to the side that Dani saw Ali Cross. Dani had talked to Mary Cross on the phone many times. Of course, Quinn visited the family on a regular basis, helping them in any way she could, but the last time Dani had seen Ali was not an image she wanted to remember.

Dani introduced herself and Ali chuckled. "I know who you are," Ali said. "I've been away at college; otherwise I would have come to see you and thank you for everything you did to help rescue me."

"Ethan and Quinn are the real heroes," Dani said, and she meant it. If not for Ethan's and Quinn's determination and perseverance, they never would have found Ali.

Dani and Ali stood under the warm sun, where smoke from the grill floated upward, and talked about school and how much Ali was enjoying UCSB. Her teeth had been fixed, but she had a scar on the left side of her mouth. Despite multiple surgeries on her ankle, she still walked with a slight limp. She talked about Dylan and the shocking moment she'd found out he was truly gone. Therapy helped with the guilt, but she missed him terribly. Dani was surprised when Ali brought up Carlin Reed. Ali was writing a book about her experience. She said she'd talked to a therapist about memory erasure but decided to write the book after she'd begun transferring her nightmares to paper. The process was difficult but also cathartic—an exorcism of sorts to help evict the monster from her memories.

According to Detective Whitton, if Carlin Reed hadn't gone into cardiac arrest and died in the hospital, he would have been serving two life sentences for the torture and kidnapping of Ali Cross and for the murders of his mother, Gretchen Myles, and Dylan Rushdan.

After Ali was pulled away, Dani's gaze gravitated to her daughter.

While listening to Ali talk about her time with Carlin Reed, Dani thought about how Tinsley rarely talked about her time with Hattie. From what Dani gathered, Tinsley had not been physically harmed, but she had been fed a constant string of lies and lived a lonely existence in what was not a loving environment. It pained Dani to imagine Tinsley being on her own for so long, but she would follow Tinsley's lead and move forward as best she could.

The smell of shish kebabs wafted through the screen door as Dani made her way inside the house to help Teresa in the kitchen. She was chopping carrots when Teresa stopped and pointed at the TV in the family room. Teresa set down her knife, wiping her hands on a kitchen towel as she walked into the living room and turned up the volume.

"Wasn't Quinn's mom driving an orange Volkswagen Bug when she went missing?"

"Why?" Dani asked as she stopped to listen to the news to see what had caught Teresa's attention.

A reporter was at the scene, broadcasting live as a car in the background was being pulled from the water. "Scuba divers found a rusty orange Volkswagen Bug in the murky water off Old River Road with skeletal remains still inside. The condition of the car pulled from the river suggests that it has been in the water for years. Much of the car was still intact after being winched to shore. Foul play is being ruled out after partial remains in the trunk pointed to signs of this being nothing more than a trip to a grocery store gone awry. Once the remains have been identified, authorities hope the divers' find can give one family closure."

Goose bumps traveled up Dani's arms, and her breath caught in her throat. Later, she would make a few calls to confirm what she already knew in her heart—that the driver was Jeannie Sullivan. Quinn's mom had never meant to leave her family. When Dani and Quinn were alone, she would tell her the tragic story of a mother who'd gone out to get groceries and never made it home.

Quinn stepped inside just as the story ended and a commercial came on. "The shish kebabs are ready! Who's hungry?"

Teresa went to the kitchen to get the salad and headed outside.

Dani shut off the TV and turned to look at Quinn. Smiling as she walked over to her, Dani slung an arm over Quinn's shoulders, and together they walked outside into the sunshine.

Acknowledgments

I am so grateful to those who have given their valuable time to this book. A giant thank-you to my wonderful editors, Liz Pearsons and Charlotte Herscher; my super-supportive and incredible agent, Amy Tannenbaum; the amazing Karen B. and all the fact-checkers and proofers who never get enough credit; Detective Brian McDougle, who is always ready to answer any and all questions; Joe Ragan for listening to my endless chatter as I try to work out one plot problem after another; Cathy Katz for always being ready to give a first read; Brittany and Morgan Ragan for their social media expertise; Joey and Jesse, just for being awesome; and a big shout-out to James Lee Whitton and all my faithful readers!

ABOUT THE AUTHOR

Photo © 2014 Morgan Ragan

T.R. Ragan is the *New York Times*, *Wall Street Journal*, and *USA Today* bestselling author of the Sawyer Brooks trilogy (*Don't Make a Sound, Out of Her Mind*, and *No Going Back*), the Faith McMann trilogy (*Furious, Outrage*, and *Wrath*), the Lizzy Gardner series (*Abducted, Dead Weight, A Dark Mind, Obsessed, Almost Dead*, and *Evil Never Dies*), and the Jessie Cole novels (*Her Last Day, Deadly Recall, Deranged*, and *Buried Deep*). In addition to thrillers, she writes medieval time-travel tales, contemporary romance, and romantic suspense as Theresa Ragan. She has sold more than three million books since her debut novel appeared in 2011. Theresa is an avid traveler, and her wanderings have led her to China, Thailand, and Nepal. She and her husband, Joe, have four children and live in Sacramento, California. To learn more, visit www.theresaragan.com.